ALSO BY MELISSA DE LA CRUZ

Witches of the East

Melissa de la Cruz

sphere

SPHERE

First published in the United States in 2011 by Hyperion
First published in Great Britain in 2011 by Sphere

Copyright © 2011 by Melissa de la Cruz

The moral right of the author has been asserted.

A CIP catalogue record for this book
is available from the British Library.

ISBN 978-0-7515-4725-2

Printed and bound in Great Britain by
Clays Ltd, St Ives plc

Sphere
An imprint of
Little, Brown Book Group
100 Victoria Embankment
London EC4Y 0DY

An Hachette UK Company
www.hachette.co.uk

www.littlebrownbooks.net

for my family

"*When shall we three meet again,*
In thunder, lightning, or in rain?
When the hurlyburly's done,
When the battle's lost and won. . . ."
—*Shakespeare*, Macbeth

"It is possible that some *Waelcyrgean* chose to abandon Valhalla and settle in various parts of the country, where they began a new existence as witches."

—from *Encyclopedia of Things That Never Were* by Michael Page and Robert Ingpen

The Town at
the Edge of Nowhere

❧

N orth Hampton did not exist on any map, which made locating the small, insular community on the very edge of the Atlantic coast something of a conundrum to outsiders, who were known to wander in by chance only to find it impossible to return; so that the place, with its remarkably empty silver-sand beaches, rolling green fields, and imposing, rambling farmhouses, became more of a half-remembered dream than a memory. Like Brigadoon, it was shrouded in fog and rarely came into view. Perpetually damp, even during its brilliant summers, its denizens were a tight-knit, clubby group of families who had been there for generations. In North Hampton, unlike the rest of Long Island, there were still potato farmers and deep-sea fishermen who made a living from their harvests.

Salty sea breezes blew sweetly over the rippling blue waters, the shoals were heavy with clam and scallop, and the rickety restaurants served up the local specialties of porgies, blowfish, and clam chowder made with tomatoes, never milk. The modern age had made almost no impression on the pleasant surroundings; there were no ugly strip malls or any indication of twenty-first-century corporate enterprise to ruin the picturesque landscape.

Across from the township was Gardiners Island, now abandoned and left to ruin. Longer than anyone could remember, the manor house, Fair Haven, had been empty and unoccupied, a relic in the gloaming. Owned by the same family for hundreds of years, no one had seen hide or hair of the Gardiners for decades. Rumors circulated that the once-illustrious clan could no longer afford its upkeep or that the line had withered and died with its last and final heir. Yet Fair Haven and its land remained untouched and had never been sold.

It was the house that time forgot, the eaves below its peaked roof filled with leaves, the paint chipped and the columns cracked as it sunk slowly toward dilapidation. The island's boat docks rotted and sagged. Ospreys made their homes on the unadulterated beaches. The forests around the house grew thick and dense.

Then one night in the early winter, there was a sickening crunch, a terrible noise, as if the world were ripping open; the wind howled and the ocean raged. Bill and Maura Thatcher, married caretakers from a neighboring estate, were walking their dogs along the North Hampton shore when they heard an awful sound from across the water.

"What was that?" Bill asked, trying to calm the dogs.

"It sounded like it came from there," Maura said, pointing to Gardiners Island. They stared at Fair Haven, where a light had appeared in the manor's northernmost window.

"Look at that, Mo," Bill said. "I didn't know the house had been rented."

"New owners, maybe?" Maura asked. Fair Haven looked the same as it always did: its windows like half-lidded eyes, its shabby doorway sagging like a frowning old man.

Maura took the dogs by the grass but Bill continued to stare, scratching his beard. Then quick as a blink, the light went out and the house was dark again. But now there was someone in the fog, and they were no longer alone. The dogs barked sharply at the steadily approaching figure, and the old groundskeeper realized his heart was pounding in his chest, while his wife looked terrified.

A woman appeared out of the mist. She was tall and intimidating, wearing a bright red bandanna over her hair and a tan raincoat belted tightly around her waist. Her eyes were gray as the dusk.

"Miss Joanna!" Bill said. "We didn't see you there."

Maura nodded. "Sorry to disturb you, ma'am."

"Best you run along now, both of you, there's nothing to see here," she said, her voice as cold as the deep waters of the Atlantic.

Bill felt a chill up his spine and Maura shivered. They had agreed there was something different about their neighbors, something otherworldly and hard to pin down, but until this evening they had never been afraid of the Beauchamps. They were afraid now. Bill whistled for the dogs and reached for Maura's hand, and they walked quickly in the opposite direction.

Across the shore, one by one, more lights were turned on in succession until Fair Haven was ablaze. It shone like a beacon, a signal in the darkness. Bill turned to look back one more time, but Joanna Beauchamp had already disappeared, leaving no sign of footprints in the sand or any indication that she had ever been there.

six months later

memorial day
hearts desire

chapter one

Cat Scratch Fever

ᴖ

Freya Beauchamp swirled the champagne in her glass so that the bubbles at the top of the lip burst one by one until there were none left. This was supposed to be the happiest day of her life—or at the very least, one of the happiest—but all she felt was agitated.

This was a problem, because whenever Freya became anxious things happened—like a waiter suddenly tripping on the Aubusson rug and plastering the front of Constance Bigelow's dress with hors d'oeuvres. Or the normally lugubrious dog's incessant barking and howling drowning out the violin quartet. Or the hundred-year-old Bordeaux unearthed from the Gardiner family cellar tasting like Three Buck Chuck—sour and cheap.

"What's the matter?" her older sister, Ingrid, asked, coming up by Freya's elbow. With her rigid modeling-school posture and prim, impeccable clothes, Ingrid did not rattle easily, but she looked uncharacteristically nervous that evening and picked at a lock of hair that had escaped her tight bun. She took a sip from her wineglass and grimaced. "This wine has a witch's curse all over it," she whispered, as she placed it on a nearby table.

"It's not me! I swear!" Freya protested. It was the truth, sort of. She couldn't help it if her magic was accidentally seeping out, but she had done nothing to encourage it. She knew the consequences and would never risk something so important. Freya could feel Ingrid attempting to probe through the under-layer, to peer into her future for an answer to her present distress, but it was a useless exercise. Freya knew how to keep her lifeline protected. The last thing she needed was an older sister who could predict the consequences of her impulsive actions.

"Are you sure you don't want to talk?" Ingrid asked gently. "I mean, everything's happened so fast, after all."

For a moment Freya considered spilling all, but decided against it. It was too difficult to explain. And even if dark portents were in the air—the dog's howling, the "accidents," the smell of burnt flowers inexplicably filling the room—nothing was going to happen. She loved Bran. She truly did. It wasn't a lie, not at all like one of those lies she told herself all the time, like *This is the last drink of the evening*, or *I'm not going to set the bitch's house on fire*. Her love for Bran was something she felt in the core of her bones; there was something about him that felt exactly like home, like sinking into a down comforter into sleep: safe and secure.

No. She couldn't tell Ingrid what was bothering her. Not this time. The two of them were close. They were not only sisters and occasional rivals but the best of friends. Yet Ingrid would not understand. Ingrid would be appalled, and Freya did not need her older sister's reproach right now. "Go away, Ingrid, you're scaring away my new friends," she said, as she accepted the insincere congratulations from another cadre of female well-wishers.

The women had come to celebrate the engagement, but mostly they were there to gawk, and to judge and to titter. All the eligible ladies of North Hampton, who not too long ago had harbored not-so-subtle dreams of becoming Mrs. Gardiner themselves. They had all come to the grand, refurbished mansion to pay grudging homage to the woman who had won the prize, the woman who had snatched it away before the game had even begun, before some of the contestants were aware that the starting pistol had been shot.

When had Bran Gardiner moved into town? Not so long ago and yet already everyone in North Hampton knew who he was; the handsome philanthropist was the subject of rumor and gossip at horse shows, preservation society gatherings, and weekend regattas that were the staples of country life. The history of the Gardiner family was all everyone talked about, how the family had disappeared many years ago, although no one was sure exactly when. No one knew where they had gone or what happened to them in the interim, only that they were back now, their fortune more impressive than ever.

Freya didn't need to be able to read minds to know what the North Hampton hens were thinking. *Of course the minute Bran Gardiner arrived in town he would choose to marry a teenage barmaid. He seemed different, but he's just like the whole lot of them. Men. Thinking with their little heads as usual. What on earth does he see in her other than the obvious? Bartender,* Freya wanted to correct them. *Barmaid* was a serving wench with heaving bosoms carrying tankards of beer to peasants seated at rickety wooden tables. She worked at the North Inn, and their gourmet brew came only in pints and had hints of prune, vanilla, and oak from the Spanish casks in which it was stored, thank you very much.

She was indeed all of nineteen (although the driver's license that allowed her to pour drinks said she was twenty-two). She was possessed of an arresting, effervescent beauty rare in a time when emaciated mannequins were the zenith of female pulchritude. Freya did not look like she was starving, or could use a good meal; on the contrary, Freya looked like she got everything in the world she ever wanted, and then some. She looked, for lack of a better word, *ripe.* Sex seemed to ooze from every pore, to slither from every inch of her glorious curves. Small and petite, she had unruly strawberry blond hair the exact shade of a golden peach, cheekbones that models would kill for, a tiny little nose, large, catlike green eyes that slanted just a little at the tip, the smallest waist made for wearing the tightest corsets, and, yes, breasts. No one would ever forget her breasts—in fact, they were all the male population looked at when they looked at Freya.

Her face might well be unrecognizable to them, but not so the twins, as Freya liked to call them—they were not too big, they did not display that heavy voluptuousness that droll ex-boyfriends called "fun bags," which sounded to Freya too much like "fat bags"; no, hers were exquisite: perfectly round with a natural lift and a creamy lusciousness. She never wore a bra either. Which, come to think of it, was what had gotten her into trouble in the first place.

She had met Bran at the Museum Benefit. The fund-raiser for the local art institution was a springtime tradition. Freya had made quite an entrance. When she arrived, there was a problem with a strap on her dress, it had snapped—*ping!*—just like that, and the sudden exposure had caused her to trip on her heels—and right into the arms of the nearest seersucker-wearing gentleman. Bran had gotten what amounted to a free show, and on their first meeting, had copped a feel—accidentally, of course, but still. It happened. She had fallen—literally—out of her dress and into his arms. On cue, he had fallen in love. What man could resist?

It was Bran's acute embarrassment that had endeared him to her immediately. He had turned as red as the chrysanthemum on his lapel. "Oh god, sorry. Are you all right . . . do you need a . . . ?" And then he was just silent and staring, and it was then that Freya realized the entire front part of her spaghetti-strap dress had fallen almost to her waist, and was in danger of slipping off entirely—which was another problem, as Freya also did not wear any underwear.

"Let me—" And then he tried to step away but still keep her covered, which is when the hand-on-boob happened, as he had tried to pull up the slippery fabric, but instead his warm hand rested on her pale skin. "Oh god . . ." he gasped. Jesus, Freya thought, you'd think he'd never even gotten to first base with the way he was acting! And quick as a wink—because really, this whole experience just seemed to torture the poor guy—Freya's dress was back in its rightful place, safety pin procured, cleavage appropriately covered (if barely—nudity seemed a natural progression given the deep cut of the neckline), and Freya said, in that natural, off-the-cuff way of hers, "I'm Freya. And you are . . . ?"

Branford Lyon Gardiner, of Fair Haven and Gardiners Island. A deep-pocketed and generous philanthropist, he had made the largest contribution to the museum that summer, and his name was prominently featured on the program. Freya had lived in North Hampton long enough to understand that the Gardiners were special even among the old and wealthy families in this very northern and easternmost part of Long Island, which wasn't Long Island at all (definitely not *Long-guy-land*, provenance of big hair and bigger malls and more New Jersey than New York), but a place of another dimension entirely.

This little hamlet teetering at the edge of the sea was not only the last bastion of the old guard, it was a throwback to a different time, a bygone era. It might have all the accoutrements of a classic East End enclave, with its immaculate golf clubs and boxy hedgerows, but it was more than a summer playground, as most of its townsfolk lived in town year-round. Its charming tree-lined streets were dotted with mom-and-pop grocery stores, its Fourth of July parade featured wagon-pulled firetrucks, and its neighbors were far from strangers, they were friends who came to visit and sip tea on the veranda. And if there was something just a bit odd about North Hampton—if, for instance, Route 27, which connected the moneyed villages along the coast, did not appear to have an exit into town, or if no one outside of the place had ever heard of it ("North Hampton? Surely you mean East Hampton, no?")—no one seemed to mind or notice very much. Residents were used to the back country roads, and the fewer tourists to clog the beaches the better.

That Bran Gardiner had been long absent from the social scene did not distract from his popularity. Any quirks displayed were quickly excused or forgotten. During the rebirth of his house, for instance, Fair Haven would be dark for days, but one bright morning the colonnade would appear completely restored, or else overnight the house would suddenly boast new windows or a new roof. It was all a mystery since no one could remember seeing a construction crew anywhere near the property. It was as if the house were coming alive on its own, shaking its eaves, shining with new paint, all by itself.

Now it was the Sunday of the Memorial Day holiday, and what better way to kick off another idyllic summer in the Hamptons than with a celebration at the newly restored manor house? The tennis courts gleamed in the distance, the view of the white-caps was unparalleled, the buffet tables heaved under the weight of the extravagant spread: chilled lobsters as big and heavy as bowling balls, platters of fresh, sweet corn, pounds and pounds of caviar served in individual tiny crystal bowls with mother-of-pearl spoons (no accoutrements, no blini, no crème fraîche to dilute the flavor). The unexpected rainstorm that morning had put a little damper on the plans and the party had been moved to the ballroom and out of the crisp white tents that stood empty and abandoned by the cliffside.

That Bran was thirty years old, smart, accomplished, unmarried, and rich beyond imagination made him the perfect catch, the biggest fish in the bridal pond. But what most people did not know, or care to know, was that most of all, he was kind. When Freya met him, she thought he was the kindest man she had ever met. She felt it—kindness seemed to emanate from him, like a glow around a firefly. The way he had been so concerned about her, his embarrassment, his stammer—and when he had recovered enough, he had brought her a drink and never quite left her side all evening, hovering protectively.

There he was now, tall and dark-haired, wearing an ill-fitting blazer, shuffling through the party and accepting the well wishes of his friends with his customary shy smile. Bran Gardiner was not at all charming or erudite or witty or worldly like the men from his background, who relished zooming about the unpaved streets in their latest Italian sports cars. In fact, for an heir, he was awkward and self-conscious and *Talented Mr. Ripley*-ish—as if he were an outsider to an elite circle and not the very center of the circle itself.

"There you are." He smiled as Freya reached to straighten his bow tie. She noticed the sleeves of his shirt were worn, and when he put an arm around her she smelled just the slightest hint of body odor. Poor boy, she knew he had been dreading this party a little. He wasn't good with crowds.

"I thought I'd lost you," he said. "Are you all right? Can I get you anything?"

"I'm perfect," she said, smiling at him and feeling the butterflies in her stomach begin to calm.

"Good." He kissed her forehead and his lips were soft and warm on her skin. "I'm going to miss you." He fiddled nervously with the monogram ring he wore on his right hand. It was one of his little tics, and Freya gave his hand a squeeze. Bran was traveling to Copenhagen tomorrow on behalf of the Gardiner Foundation, the family's nonprofit venture dedicated to promoting humanitarian charities around the globe. He would be gone almost the entire summer for the project. Maybe that was why she was feeling so jittery. She didn't want to be without him now that they had found each other.

The first night they met, he hadn't even asked her out, which annoyed Freya at first until she realized it was because he was simply too modest to think she would be interested in him. Instead he showed up the next night during her shift at the Inn, and the next night, and every night after that, just staring at her with those big brown eyes of his, with a kind of wistful yearning, until finally, she had to ask *him* out—she could see that if she left it up to him, they would never get anywhere. And that was that. They were engaged four weeks later, and this was the happiest day of her life.

Or was it?

There he was again. The problem. Not Bran, not the sweet man she had pledged to love forever—he had been stolen away by the crowd and was now in the middle of chatting up her mother. His dark head was bent over Joanna's white one, the two of them looking like the best of friends.

No. He was not the problem at all.

The problem was the boy staring at her from across the room and from all the way down the length of the great hall. Freya could feel his eyes on her, like a physical caress. Killian Gardiner. Bran's younger brother, twenty-four years old, and looking at her as if she were on sale to the highest bidder and he was more than willing to pay the price.

Killian was home after a long sojourn abroad. Bran had told

Freya he hadn't seen his brother in many years, as he moved around a lot and traveled the globe. She wasn't sure where he had just come from—Australia, was it? Or Alaska? The only thing that mattered was that when they were introduced, he had looked at her with those startling blue-green eyes of his, and she had felt her entire body tingle. He was, for lack of a better word, beautiful, with long dark lashes framing those piercing eyes, sharp-featured with an aquiline nose and a square jaw. He looked like he was always ready to be photographed: brooding, sucking on a cigarette, like a matinee idol in a French New Wave film.

He had been perfectly gracious, well-mannered, and had embraced her as a sister, and to her credit, Freya's face had betrayed none of the turmoil she felt. She had accepted his kiss on her cheek with a modest smile, had even been able to engage him in the usual cocktail conversation. The soggy weather, the proposed wedding date, how he found North Hampton (she couldn't remember, she might not have been listening: she had been too mesmerized by the sound of his voice—a low rumble like a late-night disk jockey). Then finally someone else had wanted his attention and she was free to be alone—and that was when all the small but awful things at the party began to happen.

Cat scratch fever. That was all it was, wasn't it? Like an itch you couldn't quite reach, couldn't placate, couldn't satisfy. Freya felt as if she were on fire—that at any moment she would spontaneously combust and there would be nothing left of her but ashes and diamonds. Stop looking at him, she told herself. This is insane, just another of your bad ideas. Even worse than the time you brought the gerbil back to life (she'd gotten an earful from her mother for that one, lest someone on the Council found out, not to mention that zombie pets were never a good idea). Go outside. Get some fresh air. Return to the party. She glided over to the vase of pink cabbage roses, trying to suffocate her whirling emotions by inhaling their scent. It didn't work. She could still feel him wanting her.

Goddamnit, did he have to be so good-looking? She thought she was immune to that kind of thing. Such a cliché: tall, dark, and handsome. She hated cocky, arrogant boys who thought women lived to service their voracious sexual appetites. He was the worst offender of the type—screeching up in his Harley, and that ridiculous hair of his—that messy, shaggy, bangs-in-your-eyes kind of thing, with that sexy, come-hither smolder: but there was something else. An intelligence. A knowingness in his eyes. It was as if, when he looked at her, he knew exactly what she was and what she was like. A witch. A goddess. Someone not of this earth but not apart from it either. A woman to be loved and feared and adored.

She looked up from the vase and found him still staring directly at her. It was as if he were waiting the whole time, for just this moment. He nodded his head, motioning to a nearby door. Truly? Right here? Right now? In the powder room? Was that not just another cliché that went with the motorcycle and the bad-boy attitude? Was she really going to go into the bathroom with another man—her fiancé's brother, for god's sake—at her engagement party?

She was. Freya walked, as if in a daze, toward the aforementioned rendezvous. She closed the door behind her and waited. The face that stared at her from the mirror was flushed and radiant. She was so happy she was delirious, so excited she didn't know what to do with herself. Where was he? Making her wait. Killian Gardiner knew what to do with wanton women, it seemed.

The doorknob turned, and he walked in, smooth as a knife,

locking the door behind him. His lips curled into a smile, a panther with his prey. He had won.

"Come here," she whispered. She had made her choice. She didn't want to wait a moment longer.

Outside the door, in the middle of the party, the cabbage roses burst into flame.

chapter two

Country Mouse

೨೨

Old Maid. Tight-ass. Spinster. Ingrid Beauchamp knew what people thought of her; she had seen the way they huddled and whispered behind cupped hands as she made her way across the library, putting away returned books to their proper shelves. In the decade that she had worked there, Ingrid had made few friends with her patrons, who found her strict and high-handed. Not only did she never forgive a fine, she had a tendency to lecture on the proper care and maintenance of the books under her jurisdiction. A book returned with a broken spine, a drenched cover or dog-eared pages was sure to garner a cool reprimand. It was bad enough that their operating budget barely covered their expenses; Ingrid did not need the patrons doing unnecessary damage to the books in her care.

Of course Hudson was supposed to do the grunt work, but even if Ingrid was the ranking archivist she enjoyed the physical aspects of the job and didn't like to sit behind a desk all day, steaming blueprints. She liked the feel and weight of the books—to stroke the pages softened with wear, or put a mismatched jacket to rights. Also, it gave her an opportunity to police the library, wake up any of the bums sneaking a nap in the carrels, and make sure there weren't any teenagers necking in the stacks.

Necking was such an odd word. Not that anyone "necked" anymore. Most of the teens had moved far beyond and below the neck. Ingrid liked the kids—the teenagers who visited the library and clamored for the latest dystopian post-apocalyptic releases made her smile. She did not care what they did in the comfort or discomfort of their own homes or untidy cars. Against popular belief, she knew what it was like to be young and in love and unafraid—she lived with Freya, after all. But a library was not a bedroom, or a motel room; it was a place to read, to study, to be quiet. While the kids did try to comply with the last rule, heavy breathing was sometimes the loudest noise of all.

In any event, necking wasn't limited to the kids alone. The other day Ingrid had had to cough quite a few times to make sure a middle-aged couple was successfully untangled by the time she walked through the aisles with her cart.

Located in a grassy quadrangle across from city hall and next to a community park and playground, the North Hampton Public Library was neat, organized, and as well-kept as its meager funding would allow. The city budget had shrunk along with the rest of the economy, but Ingrid did her best to keep it stocked with new books. She loved everything about the library, and if sometimes she wished she could wave her wand (not that she had one anymore, but *if she did*) and set everything to rights—spruce up those shabby couches in the reading corners, replace the antiquated computers that still flashed with black and green monitors, create a proper storytelling stage with a puppet theater for the little kids—she could still console herself with the inky smell of new books, the dusty musk of old ones, and the way the late-afternoon sunlight flowed through the glass windows. The library was on prime beachfront property; the reference room had a spectacular view of the ocean, and once in a while Ingrid would make a point of stopping by the small, cozy nook just to look at the waves crashing on the beachhead.

Unfortunately it was this same breathtaking view that threatened the library's very existence. Recently North Hampton's mayor had made not-so-unsubtle noises that selling off the prime beachfront property would be the easiest way to pay off the city's mounting debts. Ingrid was not opposed to the project per se, but she had heard that the mayor thought it might be a fine idea to do away with the library altogether, now that so much information was available online. The bureaucratic destruction of her precious library was too distressing to think about, and Ingrid tried not to feel too helpless that morning.

Thank goodness nothing terrible had happened at Freya's engagement party last Sunday. For a moment there Ingrid had been worried when one of the floral arrangements inexplicably caught on fire, but a quick-thinking waiter doused the flames with a pitcher of iced tea and no more harm was done. The fire was Freya's doing of course, her nerves causing havoc with her untamed magic. Understandable that Freya would be skittish about making a commitment of this magnitude, but she usually displayed better control, especially after centuries of living under the restriction. For now, Ingrid was just glad to be back at work and the routine of her daily life, finding comfort in the familiar. It had not been so long ago when her life had been quite different, when her work had been exciting and unusual. But that was the past, and it was best not to dwell on it too much.

The library was not merely the usual suburban outpost, at least. Upon its establishment, thanks to a generous bequest from a grande dame of the neighborhood, it also housed one of the foremost collections of architectural drawings in the country, as many famous designers had built homes in the area. As an archivist, Ingrid was responsible for preserving the work for posterity, which meant setting up a steam tent where the drawings were unrolled; and once they were moisturized, flattened, and dried, she tucked them away in drawers under linen. She had one under the plastic tent now, the paper soaking up all that moisture. Archiving was tedious and repetitive-injury making, so Ingrid liked to take a break by walking around, shelving books.

Tabitha Robinson, the middle-aged librarian for young adult books, a bright, cheerful woman with a passion for children's literature, stopped for a friendly chat when they chanced upon each other in the aisles. Ingrid was very fond of Tabitha, who was efficient and professional and took her job seriously. When Tabitha wasn't reading the latest coming-of-age novel, she had a weakness for what Ingrid dubbed "man-chesters," romance novels featuring shirtless hunks on the cover. Bodice rippers (heaving cleavage bursting out of corsets) were passé. These days it was all about the beefcake. To each her own, Ingrid thought. Her guilty pleasures involved historical sagas: anything concerning those quarreling Tudors got her vote. They exchanged the usual cozy pleasantries and town gossip shared by old friends and colleagues when Tabitha's cell phone vibrated. "Oh! It's the doctor's office," she beamed. "Sorry, I have to take this," she said as she walked away hurriedly, her long braid swinging down her back.

Ingrid picked up the next book to put away—*tsk tsk*, another doorstop-heavy tome from that local author who was something of a pest. He had thrown a hissy fit to find his books heaped in the cardboard boxes left in front of the library for patrons to take for free. But what could she do? They only kept books that were in regular circulation on the shelves. No one had read his last one, and it was clear this one would soon be consigned to the remainder bin as well.

Ingrid tried to give each author a fair shake by placing less-popular books by the front desk, suggesting little-known titles to those who asked, and borrowing each book at least once. But one could only do so much. The author, one J. J. Ramsey Baker (good lord, what was that, four names?—certainly two initials too much), author of *Moribund Symphony*, *The Darkness at the Center of the Essence*, and his latest, an obvious desperate grab for a book club pick, *The Cobbler's Daughter's Elephants*, would have just another month to tell his story of a blind cobbler in Lebanon in the nineteenth century and his daughter's pet elephants until out it went. Ingrid thought that not even a little magic could help move that product.

It was really too bad none of them were allowed to practice magic anymore. That was the deal they had made after the judgment had been handed down. No more flying. No more spells. No more charms and powders, potions or jinxes. They were to live like ordinary people without the use of their ferocious powers, their magnificent, otherworldly abilities. Over the years they had each learned to live with the restraint in their own way. Freya burned through her energy through her manic partying, while Ingrid had adopted a severe personality in order to better suppress the magic that threatened to well up from inside.

Since there was nothing she could do to change it, Ingrid found she could not quite resent their present reduced circumstances. Resenting and regretting only made things worse. Why hope for what could not be? For hundreds of years she had learned to live like a quiet mouse, tiny and insignificant, and had almost convinced herself that it was better that way.

Ingrid patted the bun at the back of her head and put the cart back against the wall. On the way to the back office, she saw Blake Aland perusing the new releases. Blake was a successful developer who had given the mayor the idea of selling the library in the first place, offering a handsome bid if the city ever decided to take it on the market. A month ago he had dropped off his firm's documents and Ingrid had had the delicate task of telling him their work was not aesthetically important enough to keep in their archive. Blake had taken it well, but he had not taken her rejection of his invitation to dinner quite as graciously. He had continued to persist until she had finally agreed to dine with him last week, on an evening that had gone disastrously, with hands fending off hands in the front seat of the car and hurt feelings all around. It was him she had to thank for giving her the odious nickname "Frigid Ingrid." How unfortunate that in addition to being despicable he was also clever.

She hurried away before he spotted her. She had no desire to wrestle with Octopus hands any time soon. Freya was so lucky to have found Bran, but then again, Ingrid had known for a long time that one day Freya would meet him. She'd seen it in her sister's lifeline centuries ago.

Ingrid had never felt that way about anyone. Besides, love wasn't a solution to everything, she thought, patting a cache of letters that she kept folded in her pocket.

In the back office, she checked on her blueprint: almost all the creases were out. Good. She would put it in its flat box and then put the next drawing under the steam. She made a note on an index card, writing down the architect's name and the project, an experimental museum that had never been built.

When she returned to her cubicle there was a sniffing noise from the next desk, and when Ingrid looked up, she noticed Tabitha was wiping her eyes and setting down her mobile phone. "What happened?" Ingrid asked, although she had a feeling she already knew. There was only one thing Tabitha wanted even more than getting Judy Blume to visit their library.

"I'm not pregnant."

"Oh, Tab," Ingrid said. She walked over and embraced her friend. "I'm so sorry." For the past several weeks Tabitha had been resolutely optimistic following yet another in-vitro procedure, expressing a manic certainty that it had worked mostly because it was their final attempt at parenthood. "Surely there's something else you can do?"

"No. This was our last shot. We can't afford it anymore. We're already in debt up to our ears for the last one. This was it. It's not going to happen."

"What happened to the adoption process?"

Tabitha wiped her eyes. "Because of Chad's disability, we got passed over again. Might as well be a dead end. And I'm sorry, I know it's selfish, but is it so wrong to want one of our own? Just one?"

Ingrid had been there since the beginning of Chad and Tabitha's journey: she knew all about the turkey basters (the IUI treatment), the hormone pills, the infertility cocktail (Clomid, Lupron); she had helped push syringes as big as horse needles into Tabitha's left hip at the designated hours. She knew how much they wanted a baby. Tabitha kept a photo on her desk of her and Chad at a luau during their honeymoon in Kona, goofy in Hawaiian shirts and leis. It was fifteen years old.

"Maybe I'm just not meant to be a mother," Tabitha cried.

"Don't say that! It's not true!"

"Why not? It's not as if there's anything anyone can do to help." Tabitha sighed. "I have to stop hoping."

Ingrid gave her friend another tight hug and walked out of the office, her cheeks burning and her heart thumping in her chest because she of all people knew that what Tabitha said wasn't true. There *was* someone who could help, someone who could change her life, someone much closer to Tab than she thought. *But my hands are tied*, Ingrid said to herself. *There's nothing I can do for her.*

Not without breaking the bonds of the restriction. Not without putting myself in danger as well.

She went back to her station behind the front desk, just another small-town librarian immersed in her daily task. Her sweater was still damp from her friend's tears. If Ingrid had never resented their situation before, had never chafed against the restriction that was placed upon them before, well. There was always a first time for everything.

chapter three

Home Fires

~ᴄ~

Old houses had a way of getting under your skin, Joanna Beauchamp knew; not just your skin but into your soul, as well as deep into your pocketbook, defying reason or logic in an ever-elusive quest for perfection. Over the years, the Beauchamp homestead, a stately colonial built in the late 1740s with pretty gables and a saltbox roof located right on the beach, in the older part of town, had been refashioned in many ways: walls torn down, kitchens moved, bedrooms redistributed. It was a house that had weathered many seasons and storms, and its crumbling walls echoed with memories—the massive brick fireplace had kept them warm for countless winters, the multitude of stains on the marble-topped kitchen counters recalled various cozy repasts. The living room floors had been stripped, redone, then stripped again. Now oak, then travertine, currently wood again—a gleaming red cherry. There was a reason old houses were called money pits, white elephants, folly.

Joanna enjoyed putting the house in order on her own. To her, a home renovation was constantly evolving and never quite finished. Plus, she preferred doing it herself; the other week she had personally retiled and grouted the guest bathroom. Today she was tackling the living room. She dipped her roller back into the aluminum tray of paint. The girls would laugh—they teased her for her habit of changing the wall colors several times a year on a whim. One month the living room walls were a dull burgundy, the next a serene blue. Joanna explained to her daughters that living in a static house, one that never changed, was stifling and suffocating, and that changing your environment was even more important than changing your clothes. It was summer, hence the walls should be yellow.

She was wearing her usual tromp-about-the-house attire: a plaid shirt and old jeans, plastic gloves, green Hunter boots, a red bandanna over her gray hair. Funny, that gray. No matter how often she dyed her hair, when she woke up in the morning it was always the same color, a brilliant silver shade. Joanna, like her daughters, was neither old nor young, and yet their physical appearances corresponded to their particular talents. Depending on the situation, Freya could be anywhere from sixteen to twenty-three years of age, the first blush of Love, while Ingrid, keeper of the Hearth, looked and acted anywhere from twenty-seven to thirty-five; and since Wisdom came from experience, even if in her heart she might feel like a schoolgirl, Joanna's features were those of an older woman in her early sixties.

It was good to be home and to have the girls with her. It had been too long and she had missed them more than she would admit. For many years after the restriction had first been imposed, the girls had wandered far and away, alone, aimless, and without purpose, and she could hardly blame them. They checked in only once in a while when they needed something: not just money, but reassurance, encouragement, compassion. Joanna bided her time; she knew the girls liked knowing that no matter where they went—Ingrid had lived in Paris and Rome for much of the last century, while Freya had spent a lot of time in Manhattan lately—their mother would always be at the kitchen counter, chopping onions for stock, and one day they would come home to her at last.

She finished with the far wall and assessed her work. She had chosen a pale daffodil yellow, a very Bouguereau shade: the color of a nymph's smile. Satisfied, she moved on to the other side. As she carefully painted around the window trim, she looked through the glass panels across the sea, to Gardiners Island and Fair Haven. The whirlwind around Freya's engagement had been exhausting, all that bowing and scraping to that Madame Grobadan, Bran's stepmother, who made it clear she thought her boy was too good for Freya. She was happy for her daughter, but apprehensive as well. Would her wild girl truly settle down this time? Joanna hoped Freya was right about Bran, that he was the one for her, the one she had been waiting for all these long years.

Not that anyone needed a husband. She should know. Been there, done that. And if some days she felt like a shriveled-up old hag whose insides were are dry as dust, whose skin had not touched that of a man for so long, those were the days when she was just feeling sorry for herself. It wasn't as if she had to be alone; there were many older gentlemen in town who had made it quite clear they would welcome the chance to make her nights less lonely. Yet she was not quite a widow, and she was not quite divorced, which meant she was not quite single or as free as she would like to be. She was separated. That was a good word. They lived separate lives now, and that was how she wanted it.

Her husband had been a good man, a good provider, her rock, when it all came down to it. But he had not been able to help them during the crisis and for that she would never forgive him. Of course it was not his fault, all that hysteria and bloodshed, but he had not been able to stop the Council from passing down their judgment either, when the dust finally settled and the evil had passed. Her poor girls: she could still see them, their lifeless bodies silhouetted in the dusk. She would never forget it, and even though they had come back relatively unscathed (if one considered being declawed, powerless, and domesticized un-scathed) she could not quite find it in her heart to make room for him in her life once again.

"Right, Gilly?" she asked, turning to her pet raven, Gillbereth, who was privy to her thoughts and was currently perched on top of the grandfather clock.

Gilly fluffed her wings and craned her long black neck toward the window, and Joanna followed her gaze. When she saw what the raven wanted her to see she dropped her roller, splashing a few drops of paint on the stone floor. She rubbed it with her boot and made it worse.

The raven cawed.

"Okay, okay, I'll go down and check it out," she said, leaving the house through the back door and walking straight down to the dunes. Sure enough, there they were: three dead birds. They had drowned—their feathers were mottled and wet, and the skin around their talons looked burned. Their bodies formed an ugly cross on the pristine stretch of sand.

Joanna looked down at the small, stiff bodies. What a pity. What a waste. They were beautiful birds. Large raptors with pure white breasts and ebony beaks. Ospreys. The birds were native to the area, and a large colony lived on Gardiners Island, where they built their nests right on the beach. The birds were dangerous creatures, natural predators, but vulnerable as all wild creatures were vulnerable to the march of progress and de-velopment.

Like her girls, Joanna struggled to conform to the bounds of the restriction. They had agreed to abide it in exchange for their immortal lives. The Council had taken their wands and most of their books, burned their broomsticks and confiscated their cauldrons. But more than that, the Council had taken away their understanding of themselves. They had decreed there was no place for their kind in this world with magic, and yet the reality was that there was no place for them without it either.

With her fingers, Joanna began to dig at the wet sand, and gently buried the dead birds. It would have taken only a few words, the right incantation, to bring them back to life, but if she even attempted to wield an ounce of her remarkable abilities, who knew what the Council would take away next.

When she returned to the house, she shook her head at the sight of the kitchen. There were dirty pots everywhere, and the girls had taken to using every piece of china and silverware they could get their hands on rather than run the dishwasher, so the sink and the counter were overflowing with a messy jumble of expensive antique porcelain plates. The china closet in the hall was almost empty. If this went on any longer, they would be eating from serving trays next. It would not do. One expected this of Freya, of course, who was used to chaos. Ingrid always looked impeccable and that library of hers was spotless, but the same could not be said for her housekeeping skills. Joanna had raised her girls to be lovely, interesting, as strong in character as in their former talent for witchcraft, and as a consequence they were completely useless in domestic matters.

Of course, as their mother she was not completely blameless in this field. After all, she could have spent the morning cleaning up rather than painting the living room again. But while she enjoyed refurbishing and renovating, she detested the daily household chores that kept life on an even keel. Or at least kept it sanitary. She saw Siegfried, Freya's black cat and familiar, slink in through the pet door.

"The girls have invited lots of little mice here for you, haven't they?" She smiled, picking him up and cuddling his soft fur. "Sorry to tell you it's not going to last, *liebchen*."

For want of a wand, a house was lost, Joanna thought. If she could use magic to clean her house, she would not need a dishwasher. The doorbell rang. She wiped her hands on her jeans and ran to answer it. She opened the door slowly and smiled. "Gracella Alvarez?"

"*Si,*" smiled a small, dark-haired woman standing at the doorway with a little boy.

"*Bueno!* Come in, come in," Joanna said, sweeping them into the half-painted living room. "Thank you for coming so early. As you can see we really need some help around here," she said, looking at the house as if for the first time. Dust bunnies sprouted in the corners, large sacks of laundry bloomed in the stairway, the mirrors were so cloudy it had become impossible to see one's reflection.

The agency had recommended the Alvarezes highly. Gracella kept house while her husband, Hector, took care of the grounds, which included the pool, the landscaping, the gardens, and the roof. Gracella explained that her husband was finishing a job out of town but would meet them that afternoon. The family was to stay in the cottage out back, and they had brought their things in the car.

Joanna nodded. "And who's this cherub?" she asked, leaning down to tickle the boy's belly. The boy jumped away and flapped his arms, giggling.

"This is Tyler."

At his mother's prompting the boy spoke. "I'm four," he said deliberately, rocking his heels up and down. "Four. Four. Four. Four Four."

"Wonderful." Joanna remembered her own boy, so long ago. She wondered if she would ever see him again.

Tyler's Mickey Mouse T-shirt was stained and his eyes were bright and merry. When Joanna moved to shake his hand he shied away from her but allowed her to pat his head. "Good to

31

meet you, Tyler Alvarez. I'm Joanna Beauchamp. Now, while your mother gets settled, would you like to take a walk down to the beach with me?"

TYLER SPENT THE AFTERNOON running around in circles. Joanna looked at him affectionately. Every once in a while he would look over his shoulder to make sure she was still there. He seemed to take to her immediately, which his mother remarked upon before letting him accompany her to the beach. When he got tired of running, they picked seashells together. Joanna found a perfectly formed cockleshell that the boy immediately brought up to his ear. He laughed at the sound and she smiled to see it. Still, she could not help but feel apprehensive, even in her delight at her new young friend. It throbbed right underneath the idyllic moment, just below the surface.

There was something not quite right about the three dead birds on the beach this morning, the ones she had buried a little ways away in the sand, but Joanna could not put her finger on it just then. Was it a threat? Or a warning? And for what? And from whom?

chapter four

Every Little Thing
She Does Is Magic

ೕಲ

Before acquiring a certain curly-haired bartender last fall, the North Inn bar was a sleepy little place, the kind of shabby pub that locals liked to congregate in to trade gossip and visit with one another without having to fight scores of inebriated preppies for a table. Memorial Day meant that summer had officially arrived, and even if the town was obscure and unknown, the seasonal swell of tourists to the East End brought a good number of visitors who found themselves within the city limits, and several new establishments had begun to cater to this crowd. But not the North Inn. The well drinks were strong and cheap, and other than a decent view of the water, that was pretty much all it had going for it.

How things had changed. It was still a local place but it was no longer quiet or hushed. The joint, as they said, was jumpin', and did it ever. There was a loud, throbbing jukebox that played only the good stuff, when rock 'n' roll was performed by real rock stars—yet another dying breed of the new era. Men in tight pants who sang lustily about women, drugs, and depravity had been consigned to celluloid parody or reality-TV rehabilitation. The old rock swagger was the exclusive province of rap music now, the only genre that still celebrated indulgence in all its forms. The boys with guitars had turned to writing moody little songs, safe little emotional ditties that no one could dance to.

Freya liked rap just fine, and was known to blast the latest gangster throw-downs now and then, but at the North Inn she preferred the classics. The Brits: The Sex Pistols. The Clash. The '70s rock-opera–stylists: Queen. Yes. Early Genesis (this was crucial—*Peter Gabriel*–led Genesis, not the earsore it became under Phil Collins). Metal: Led Zeppelin. Deep Purple. Metallica. Party Rock: AC/DC. Def Leppard. Mötley Crüe if she was feeling a tad ironic. Since she'd arrived to work at the North Inn, the place was always blasting with the screech of guitars and the fist-pumping dance-floor anthems that drove the crowd to its feet. But next to the drinks she poured, the music was almost irrelevant.

The redheaded bartender had a way of making the cocktails just right: the gin and tonics tart and bracing, the dark and stormies luscious with bite. It was a party every night, and every evening ended with patrons dancing on the bar, losing their inhibitions and occasionally their clothing. If you came into the North Inn alone and feeling blue, you left with either a new friend or a hangover, sometimes both.

However, a week after her engagement party, the bar, like Freya, was a bit subdued. While the music was still loud and strong, it had an underlying mournful echo. The Rolling Stones sang "Waiting on a Friend": *I'm not waiting on a lady, I'm just waiting on a friend* . . . , the cocktails were limp and sweet, the gin fizz didn't fizz, the champagne was flat, the beer turned lukewarm after only a few minutes. It was just like the engagement party, but worse. She was glad Ingrid wasn't around to notice; she didn't want her sister any more suspicious than she already was. What happened with Killian that evening had been an impulsive act, but it was over now and everything would be all right. There was no need to panic. So what if all she could dream about was Killian? So what if he had invaded her consciousness, had become the subject of her every waking thought? When she closed her eyes, she could still see his beautiful face, hovering above hers. She would make it go away. She would make *him* go away. If only it was Killian who was halfway around the world and not her love.

Bran called earlier: he had arrived safely in Denmark and was on his way to his meeting. She knew she had to get used to it; from the beginning he had explained that his life and his work entailed a great amount of travel and that he was rarely home, but he was planning to slow down after the wedding. Hearing his voice had cheered her up a little, but her dark mood continued to build as she leaned back on the bar, watching customers arrive. Dan Jerrods and his new girlfriend, Amanda Turner, walked in, and an image flashed in Freya's mind: Dan had Amanda up against a wall, the two of them gasping and clutching at each other, Amanda's blouse unbuttoned, Dan's jeans at his knees. That was just a few minutes before they'd set off for the bar. It was early in their relationship, and sex was still their way of saying hello. Freya certainly spoke that language.

Right behind the postcoital couple was Mayor Todd Hutchinson (fervent masturbation last night in front of a computer), with his friend, flashy developer Blake Aland (a tangle of some sort in his car the other week: it was blurry and the vision wouldn't focus, but Freya sensed some kind of sexual frustration here), then the good reverend and his wife (a flash of leather whips and masks over the holiday weekend). Sometimes Freya felt a bit dizzy from all the information. She should be used to it by now, her talent— she refused to call it a "gift"—but it still came as a surprise.

This was just another manifestation of her nature, the ability to see intense emotion—and it wasn't just sexual passion or romantic love that she was able to see. Freya could also read intense anger and hatred, the opposite of love as it were: murderous rage, overwhelming anxiety. Over the centuries, her talent had been very useful. Although there was very little of it, North Hampton was not immune from crime. When it did happen, it was usually scandalous and spectacular, like the chilling murder of a socialite who had been poisoned at her own dinner party, or sad and unusual, like what had happened to Bill and Maura Thatcher. Their bodies had been found on the beach just last winter, both of them bleeding from the head. Bill died from his injuries but Maura was still in intensive care, comatose at the hospital.

Freya had been instrumental in bringing the socialite's murderer to justice. An aggrieved housekeeper who was an occasional patron was behind the heiress's death. Freya saw exactly how she did it, putting a thimbleful of poison into the champagne, expertly popping back the cork. She had pointed the police in the right direction so that they were able to build their case. The detectives had found a bottle of the toxic substance among the housekeeper's possessions, which led to the conviction, a thrilling conclusion all around.

She was glad to be helpful, to be able to use her natural talents in a discreet way that was technically still within the restriction placed upon her. She wasn't practicing any witchcraft, after all. She couldn't help it if she could see motive, intent, and guilt, and since almost everyone in town walked into the North Inn, Freya kept the pulse of the community in hand. She always knew who had stolen from the cash register, or broken into the guest house, or vandalized the public school. If the policemen had once been skeptical of her they were no longer, except for that one detective who kept badgering her for explanations of her hunches. So it was odd that she still had no idea what had happened to the Thatchers, who had both been well-liked. Perhaps the police were right, it was a random act of a vagrant, a stranger, but it frustrated Freya not to know.

She served Dan and Amanda their drinks. She smiled at the honeymooning couple—the first two weeks of any relationship was a honeymoon as far as Freya was concerned. Couples waited so long to marry these days, or had been living together for years before, that most honeymoons had very little mooning or honey. The sex, if there was any, was usually of the garden variety, missionary style. Most couples were much more excited about their plush hotel rooms than about seeing each other naked. The days of trembling virginal brides slipping in between cold sheets were long past. Which was why Freya looked on new couples with affection. These were her people, worshippers at her temple. She blessed them with her smile and copious free drinks.

The reverend and his wife ordered a decent bottle of wine, and Blake wanted a beer. She set the orders on the bar and turned to her final customer. "What can I get you, sir?" she asked the mayor.

"Whiskey, straight, thanks Freya."

"Sure thing, Mayor," she said. Todd Hutchinson was young, slick, and ambitious. He had big plans for North Hampton and had swept into office on the campaign donations of people like Blake Aland. The young mayor was popular around town, although Freya knew her sister, Ingrid, was not a fan ever since she'd gotten wind of his proposal to sell the library. Poor Ingrid, there was nothing she would be able to do if the proposal was approved.

Unlike Ingrid, Freya had nothing against Todd, who was polite and tipped well. He was married to a local news anchor rumored to be in line for a national spot on the network. Maybe that was the reason he'd had to resort to online porn. Two huge careers meant couples rarely had time for each other. It was too bad. Freya handed him his whiskey and turned back to the bar.

"What's up tonight? So quiet for a Friday," said her boss, Sal McLaughlin, who'd inherited the North Inn and its bar from his brother, who'd retired. Sal was a cheerful man of seventy, with wiggly eyebrows and a belly laugh. He had hired Freya on the spot and acted as her honorary grandfather. Sal coughed noisily into his handkerchief and wheezed.

"You all right? That sounded pretty gross," she teased as Sal blew his nose again with a big honk.

"Allergies." He shrugged. "Must be the change of weather." He wiped his nose and sighed, his eyes tearing. "Always hits right about June." It had been an unusually abrupt change from a rainy spring to a humid summer; the air was thick and heavy, even more so than usual. And the heat was not usually quite this stifling or oppressive so early in the season.

"It's like a funeral in here. Who died?" Sal joked, as he cranked up the AC.

Freya shrugged. She knew it was her energy that was causing the gloom, but she couldn't help it. So it was an off day. She couldn't be expected to keep the party going forever, could she? A hand waved and she walked over to the opposite counter of the U-shaped bar where Becky Bauman was downing dirty martinis like candy. "Another one?" Freya asked.

"Oh, why not." Becky sighed as she stared at her husband, flirting with his date, across the bar. Becky and Ross had recently separated. They had not been married long, but they were the parents of a six-month-old; and Freya saw that a darkness had clouded the love that had once held them together, as exhaustion and sleep deprivation led to nonstop arguments and quarreling that left both of them even more unhappy and unsatisfied, until Ross had finally had enough and moved out.

Ross was currently deep in conversation with Natasha Mayles, a former model who was one of the town's too-too-toos: too rich, too pretty, too picky. Too good for any man to come near when it came down to it. The Natasha Mayleses of the world certainly thought too much of themselves to settle down with just anyone. It was a wonder what she was doing with Ross Bauman, who was not even divorced yet.

"What happened to us?" Becky asked, as she watched Freya assemble her cocktail. "I hate him. I really do. I don't know what I'm going to do."

Freya caught a flash of an image: another argument, this one vivid and gut-wrenching, culminating in a violence that had not been there before—arms flailing, the baby crying, a push down the stairs. . . . She turned away and hesitated. Regardless of what her mother or sister believed, truly she did not do very much to the drinks except make them taste better, a by-product of the fact that she made them. Everything Freya made or cooked tasted delicious, a consequence of her magical heritage.

But the ugly scene she had just witnessed—and she did not know who exactly was in peril, Becky, Ross, or their baby; the image did not reveal that much—made her think. Maybe if there hadn't been a shred of love between them Freya would never have considered doing what she was about to do. But there *was*. She saw the two of them sneaking glances at each other when they thought the other was not looking. Besides, Natasha Mayles was all wrong for Ross. She swanned into the North Inn with her haughty accent and bored, quasi-European attitude.

Truly, it was a ridiculous rule anyway, why *couldn't* they use magic? Why not? Just because of a few silly girls who told a few lies? So a couple of lying bitches were allowed to ruin their lives forever? Freya would never forget the way those awful girls had spun their artful story, their crazed histrionics in the courtroom, the growing list of suspects, the carriages that took the condemned down to Gallows Hill. How stubborn and blind she had been! She had assumed no one would believe their accusers, that no one in their right mind would think that she and Ingrid were capable of such evil. To add insult to injury, her own kind, their own Council, took away their powers after everything they had been through—hard punishment indeed. Well. She had had enough. She was tired of feeling afraid. Tired of feeling useless. Tired of trying to pretend she was something she wasn't. Tired of hiding her light in a corner. Under a lampshade, behind a curtain, in a dark room. *Tired.*

Freya Beauchamp was *made* of magic. Without magic she was just someone who poured drinks. She had been so good for so long, all of them had, and for what? What was the point of it all, really? It was a waste of their talents; were they really supposed to just live in the shadows and fade away? Act as if they were ordinary for the rest of their immortal lives?

Freya thought of everything they had given up: flying, for one; she still remembered how it felt, zooming through the skies, the wind in her hair. She missed the midnight capers in the woods as well, the powerful rituals that were taboo now that *pagan* was a bad word. The world had moved on, of course, that was to be expected; maybe it would have happened even without the restriction, but now they would never know. Like the rest of her family, she was stuck on this side of the bridge, with no way to return home.

She made up her mind. She touched Ross's beer glass and added just a smidge of gingerroot and lemon zest. Then she stirred it with the red straw from Becky's cocktail. The pint of beer turned a bright shade of pink for a split second. Now, this was *definitely* against the rules, this little concoction she had made, this little love potion. Sure, she had practiced a little magic before, here and there—that boy back in New York, that vampire's familiar she had healed, for instance. But that was in the East Village, where she had been fairly certain what little, insignificant, inconsequential magic she had performed had been artfully concealed and absorbed by the city's own kinetic energy.

This was something quite different, different even from the little nudges she gave the police to help solve crimes. This was the first real love potion she had created in . . . well, when the number of years was so big, who was counting? Besides, it was a shame to let such a good couple go to waste, and she shuddered at the thought of what might be if she did not: that terrible argument, a child growing up without parents, one dead, the other in jail. Freya increased the potency of the drinks she was about to serve. It didn't have to happen. All they needed was a little help to get over the bump. They just needed a little reminder of why they had been together in the first place. She set the martini in front of Becky and the beer in front of Ross. "Cheers!" she told them, holding up her own glass.

"To our health," Becky mumbled. She was probably embarrassed to have revealed so much to Freya earlier.

"Bottoms up," Ross called to Becky from across the bar. He took a huge pull from his glass; and for a moment his face turned gray and it looked as if he were going to be sick, or throw up. Freya felt a fluttering of nerves—what if she had forgotten to mix it just right? What if she had poisoned him somehow—what if she had forgotten the correct amount to put in the elixir? She rushed to his side, hoping there was still time to serve him an antidote, when the color returned to his cheeks and he took a deep breath. "What's *in* that?" he asked Freya.

"Why? Is there something wrong with it?" she asked, trying not to feel too alarmed.

"There's nothing wrong with it! It's awesome!" he declared, and downed the whole thing in one huge gulp. When he was done, his eyes seemed to light up, and he looked across the bar at his wife with a face full of wonder, falling in love with her all over again. Becky returned the smile tentatively, and in a few minutes the two of them were giggling, then howling with laughter, while Natasha looked confused and surly. Then Ross excused himself from his date, walked over to his wife, and gave her a back-dipping "Times Square–World War Two has ended" victory kiss. Natasha stomped off in a huff.

Freya sighed in relief. A few minutes later, she was smiling like a Cheshire cat. Her potion had *worked*. She still knew exactly how to make them. In an instant, the music on the jukebox suddenly pumped to life: Axl Rose screeching a love song: "Sweet Child o' Mine." *She's got a smile that it seems to me, Reminds me of childhood memories* . . . The music began to fill up the night, lecherous and passionate, making girls grab their boys' hands to lead them to the ad hoc dance floor in front of the jukebox. Dan and Amanda began to dirty-dance, and even the reverend and his wife took a spin. In the corner, the Baumans were making out so heavily— was that Ross's hand up Becky's shirt?—they should really think of leaving; it was getting a tad too heated. Even the mayor sat at the counter with a dreamy look on his face.

Freya drummed her fingers on the counter, swaying to the music. Sal had been right. It had felt like winter in there for a moment. But the frost had melted now. Of course, she still felt terrible about what happened with Killian. But a little magic went a long way.

chapter five

Sister Talk

~~~

Y ou didn't!" Ingrid said, looking up from her bowl of cereal
and quickly putting the letter she had been reading back
into her pocket.

"I did!" Freya said gleefully, too gleefully, Ingrid thought,
feeling a twinge of jealousy at her sister's exuberance as she
picked off a few grapes from the bowl to feed her pet griffin, a
part-eagle, part-lion hybrid, the one magical concession from
their past that the Council had allowed, only because there was
no way to separate a witch from her familiar without destroying
either one. Truly Oscar was getting too big for the nonentity
spell she'd placed on him centuries ago; he was almost the size of
a Labrador, but he had the soul of a pussycat.

"And nothing happened?" Ingrid asked doubtfully. "Oh, Siegfried, I hear you, too. But you don't like grapes," she reminded the
black cat.

"Not a thing!" Freya crowed, rooting around the cupboard
for flour. She had just returned from her graveyard shift at the
bar. It had been a long, busy night, one of their best in recent
memory. "I feel like pancakes, do you want some?"

"I guess. So what are you going to do?"

"What do you think? I'm going to do it again! It felt *good*, Ingrid. I felt . . . like I was me again . . . you know?" She began

cracking eggs in the bowl, looking around and admiring the newly clean kitchen. Things were so much nicer in the house now that the Alvarezes were taking care of it. Joanna had really taken to the little boy, too. It was cute. They all found him adorable. Tyler was an interesting kid, wise beyond his years. He could beat any of them at chess and could already add and subtract large numbers in his head. One day he had told them with a solemn face that it took fifty-seven steps to get to the beach from their house. Most of his diet consisted of dessert, which made him perfect for Joanna, who had yet to discover a cake she did not like. Ingrid brought him chess books from the library and Freya chased him around the garden. The house was happier with the Alvarez family inside it.

She noticed Ingrid surreptitiously reading her letter again. Her sister had begun receiving letters over the summer. They always arrived in a plain white envelope with no return address. Whoever sent them, Ingrid did not say, and Freya did not ask. Since moving back home, the sisters kept an easy peace. Freya did not ask Ingrid why she had spent her last several years as a humble library clerk, and Ingrid did not ask why Freya had dropped out of NYU and sold her bar in New York. If they felt like telling each other, they would. They shared confidences like clothes, but respected each other's privacy.

It was funny how at home they fell back on their old habits, taking their usual places at the familial tree. Ingrid worked days, Freya took the late shifts, and they usually met for breakfast, at the beginning of Ingrid's day and the end of Freya's.

After a few seconds she flipped the pancakes. She didn't need magic to know they would taste fantastic: light and buttery with a nutty sweetness. She stacked two plates and brought them to the table. She drizzled her pancakes with maple syrup, while Ingrid ate hers with fruit.

"Did Mother tell you about the dead birds on our beach the other day?" Ingrid asked.

Freya nodded, forking her pancake. "Yeah. What's the big deal?"

"She's not sure. She thinks it's an omen."

"Uh-huh. Remember when she thought my old English teacher was a warlock who was out to get us after he accused me of plagiarism in eighth grade?"

Ingrid snickered. "Poor Mr. Sweeney, it's a good thing she's not allowed to or Mom would've hexed him!" she said, enjoying the sisterly solidarity. One of the greatest pleasures of their lives was talking about their formidable mother. That subject could never be exhausted.

"What Mom needs is a date," Freya said, feeding Siegfried from her plate. "She's got to get over Dad at some point." They hadn't seen their father since the restriction had been handed down, which was one of those subjects they never talked about. Bringing up their father only made their mother angry all over again. It was a shame what had happened between their parents, but there was nothing they could do about it. Dad was gone, Mom didn't want to talk about it, end of story. Freya tried not to hold it against her mother, or her father, since he dropped out of their lives and never even tried to contact them afterward.

It was easier that way, just like it was easier to pretend there had only always been two children in the family. It was too difficult and sad to think about her missing twin brother, and aside from lighting a candle every year on his Feast Day in February, they never mentioned him. As for Dad, there was no candle and no remembrance, only a void, an empty seat at the table. "So what do you think? Mom and Sal? I could make it happen." Freya smiled naughtily. "He's got a crush."

"No. Don't do that to Sal. Mom would eat him for breakfast.

You've got to stop thinking everyone's problems can be solved by falling in love," Ingrid said, looking uncomfortable and pushing away her plate.

"Huh," Freya sighed, getting up from the table and beginning to stack dishes.

"You should be careful. You might have gotten away with making a potion this once, but who knows what will happen next time?" Ingrid warned. "You're going to get in trouble if you keep doing it."

"Maybe." Freya nodded. "But I don't care. I just don't care anymore. And until they actually come down here to tell me to stop, I'm going to keep on doing it," she announced. "I'm sick of living with my hands tied behind my back!" She paused, letting the hot water run over the dirty dishes. Somehow the pristine kitchen and the presence of the Alvarezes inspired her to clean, something she had never done before. "But whatever you do, don't tell Mother."

"Don't tell Mother what?" Joanna asked cheerfully, breezing into the kitchen and smiling at her beautiful daughters, Gilly flying by her shoulder.

"Nothing," the two of them mumbled. For a moment they were kids again and had just finished burying Freya's wretched zombie gerbil in the backyard. The ground had kept shaking for an endless amount of time, it seemed. Ingrid had found one of Joanna's old books, the ones they weren't supposed to touch, which their mother had hidden away when the restriction was passed, and had finally hit upon the right incantation to stop Freya's wayward spell.

"Hmmm . . ." Joanna said, looking from one to the other with skepticism. "Why do I have a feeling no one ever tells me anything around here?"

chapter six

A Knot in Her Belly

❧

Ingrid was thinking of her sister's newfound zeal when she arrived at work that morning. She realized that she had never seen Freya so happy, not in a long time. Not just happy, there was something else. Freya looked more vibrant somehow, she was more *present*. Living without magic had caused them to fade a little; without even noticing, they had become as drab and gray as the mundane world around them. Ingrid latched her bicycle by the front gate and let herself into the dark library. Passing by Tabitha's empty desk, she felt another prick of frustration. For years Ingrid had kept silent, had let science and medicine do their work, but now she felt a reckless courage stirring in her soul. She couldn't stand to see her friend in so much pain anymore. So much unnecessary pain.

Ingrid looked around fearfully. What was she thinking? She wasn't her sister, daring and courageous. Ingrid remembered all too well how she had been left to starve in that cell, the jeers from the mob, how terribly frightened she had been, alone and hated. If she did this, she would be breaking the agreement that allowed her to remain in this world.

But what did Freya say that morning? *I'm sick of living with my hands tied behind my back.* Well, so was Ingrid. She had had it with being useless and insignificant.

When Tabitha arrived for work Ingrid took her aside. "Tab? Can I have a sec?" She led Tabitha to the back office, where they stored the archival material. "You have to trust me, okay?" she said, as she switched off the lights. The room was bathed in a greenish darkness that came from the window film.

"What's going on?" Tabitha asked a bit nervously. "What's gotten into you, Ingrid? You're like . . . possessed."

"Just stand there," Ingrid instructed. She knelt on the floor and began to draw a pentagram around the perimeter of Tabitha's feet. The white chalk outline glowed in the dark room.

"Is that a—?"

"Shush!" Ingrid ordered, removing a white candle from her pocket and placing it in the center of the five-pointed shape she had made. She lit the candle and mumbled a few words. Turning to Tabitha, she said, "You trust me, don't you? I'm trying to help you." They were colleagues but friends as well, and Ingrid hoped Tabitha would trust their friendship enough to allow her to do this. She continued to work in a serene and thoughtful manner, but her heart was leaping in her chest. She was doing it—she was practicing witchcraft again. Magic. Freya was right, it was as if something that had been deeply buried in her soul was coming alive again, as if she just discovered she could breathe underwater all along. Ingrid felt dizzy and giddy. She hadn't done anything like this in . . . longer than she could remember. She waited for a thunderbolt to strike. But there was nothing.

With the witch sight from the pentagram she took a good long look at her friend, until the junior librarian squirmed under the penetrating gaze. The pentagram revealed what Ingrid had always suspected. There was something blocking Tabitha's energy, a darkness in the core, a silver-colored mass, tight and constricted, knotted, like a fist or a tumor. No wonder she couldn't get pregnant. Ingrid had seen them before, but nothing quite this deadly. She placed a hand on Tabitha's belly and yanked it out, almost falling backward in her attempt. But she got it out, all right. The malignancy dissipated as soon as it had been removed from a physical host.

Tabitha just stared at her as if Ingrid had gone insane. She hadn't felt a thing; it looked as if Ingrid was just waving her hands about and babbling. "Are we done now?"

"Not quite," Ingrid said. Removing it was only the first step. She flicked the lights back on and blew out the candle. "You also need to do something about your hair," she said.

"My hair! What do you mean?" Tabitha looked skeptical.

Ingrid realized, in all the time she'd known her, she'd never seen Tabitha wear her hair down. Tabitha's hair was brushed back from her forehead so tightly it looked painful, and then it was knotted and woven so that it was almost as thick as rope. Ingrid noticed other things, too: Tabitha's clunky oxfords were tightly laced. Her sweater (it was chilly indoors with the air-conditioning) was tied with ribbons instead of buttons. The woman had more knots on her person than a sailing ship. If she kept it up, there was a possibility that the silver evil could form again. The darkness fed on constriction; it was attracted to it, like moths to flame.

She whispered fiercely, "Try it for once. Wear your hair down. And get rid of those shoes. And that sweater. Wear slip-on shoes. One of those cardigans that open in the front. No zippers. No buttons. Nothing but free-floating fabric. Free. And no knots."

"What does that have to do with anything?"

"Just try it for a couple months. I read somewhere that it might work, it's like a karma thing." These days New Age wisdom was an easy enough explanation for a little bit of white magic. Tabitha told her she would consider it, but she left the storage room shaking her head.

Ingrid brushed off signs of the pentagram and went back to

work, her mind still racing. Of course, wearing flowy fabrics didn't cut it on its own. She had to fight fire with fire, or knots with a knot of her own. When Tabitha wasn't looking, Ingrid took some of Tabitha's hair that had shed on her office chair. Now all she needed was one of Chad's. . . . Then she thought, Tabitha kept an afghan in their car. . . . Chad had dark hair, so it would be easy enough to find one of his since Tab was blond. During her break, Ingrid let herself into Tabitha's Camry and found what she was looking for. Back at her office, she threaded the two strands together, making a tiny, insect-size knot, while she hurriedly chanted the right words for the charm.

Her heart thrummed within her chest, and goose bumps prickled her arms as her fingers worked quickly, twisting and turning. This wasn't magic, she kept telling herself. It was just a few words. A tiny little knot. No one would ever have to know. This was even more fun than removing that blockage; instead of merely cutting out the garbage, here she was *creating* something. Ingrid felt the magic bubbling inside, the thrilling rush that came from harnessing and directing a wild and unimaginable power to her bidding, and she felt her cheeks turn red with excitement. She had missed this more than she could admit.

"What are you making?"

The sound of the voice shook her and the spell broke. Ingrid quickly put the knot away in her pocket. "Matthew Noble! You surprised me." She didn't answer his question.

"It's Matt, I keep telling you." Matthew Noble smiled. He was a senior detective with the police department and even at thirty still looked like the college athlete he had once been, tall, with light brown hair, a pleasant Irish face, pale skin, sunburned nose, clear blue eyes, wearing his uniform of rumpled sports jacket and tan slacks. She could sense something in the way he looked at her—too frankly and too, well, appreciatively. He was certainly good-looking, but she wasn't interested—not at all—and it was becoming something of a nuisance, his crush on her. It made her uncomfortable. Especially since he never did anything about it. If only he would ask her out so she could crush his crush. Yet he seemed satisfied with merely looking at her and needling her for books. She doubted he ever read them. He didn't seem the bookish type.

"Sorry to bother you, but there was no one at the front desk. And I thought you might have a book to recommend." When he smiled his teeth actually shone.

"I sure do," Ingrid replied, thinking quickly. "Here," she said, pressing J. J. Ramsey Baker's latest into his hands. Ha. See what he thought of that! Serves Matthew Noble (did they live in *Our Town*? Could his name be even more corny?) right. At least she had found a way to put his attraction to her to good use. "If you like the book I'd love it if you could recommend it to a lot more people." Maybe that way she could keep it on the shelves and the sensitive author wouldn't have a temper tantrum when he found it kicked to the curb, she thought, as she stamped his library card and logged the transaction in the computer.

"Sure will." Matt nodded, putting the book away without even glancing at its cover. He looked as if he were going to say something more, then decided against it. Ingrid watched him leave, noting his broad shoulders and easy glide, then went back to her weaving. Before the end of the day, she slipped the little knot of hair in Tabitha's purse.

No magic here. Just a lucky knot to help a friend, that was all it was, Ingrid kept telling herself. No one would ever know or find out.

chapter seven

A New Boy

~

Motherhood had robbed Joanna of her figure, of that she was sure. No matter how much she dieted (and she had tried them all: the Atkins and the Zone, the low-cal and the low-carb, the cabbage and the cookie, the Jenny and the Watchers, the South Beach and the Sugar Busters, the tea and juice cleanses, the endless hours spent exercising—first the running and then the spinning—the step classes and the yoga and the Pilates), she never could get rid of those dreaded last ten pounds, that tire around her belly. Her daughters chided her on her obsession, telling her she looked good *for her age*. And what age would that be exactly? Six thousand years?

It was understood that women of a certain age no longer cared about their looks, but it was a lie. Vanity did not die of old age, especially in beautiful women, and oh, she had been beautiful once—so beautiful that she had wed the most fearsome god of all. But it was too late to think of what had been. Her husband had abandoned her, along with her good looks, a long time ago. Oh, in the right light she was attractive, she supposed, she was still "handsome," but who wanted to be called handsome when one was once beautiful?

The problem, as she saw it, was that right when she would finally get her figure back, *bam*, she would find herself pregnant again, and the whole cycle of gaining and losing would start up once more. The children had to be reborn whenever they got themselves into trouble and had to leave the world, or else had been pushed out of it by accident (a car crash, maybe; Freya had once perished in a hotel fire) or malice (like the crisis that had claimed their lives in the seventeenth century), and Joanna would begin to feel the symptoms. It usually happened after she hadn't heard from her girls in a century or two. First, her gray hair would turn blond again. She would marvel at her changed appearance, the loss of wrinkles, the fat in her cheeks, strong hands that did not ache from arthritis. Then it would happen: the vomiting, the nausea, the exhaustion. And she would realize: goddamnit, she was pregnant!

Nine months later she would have a fat, crying baby to care for and love. This time the girls were reborn just a few years apart, so that in the current lifetime they had grown up like proper sisters again, squabbling over toys, annoying each other on long car rides. Life had been a happy tedium of preschool and swimming and gymnastics and endless birthday parties along with the occasional accidental magical outburst: Ingrid's griffin causing havoc with the flower beds; and having to keep Freya from hexing mean girls she did not like.

It was easy enough to fool the neighbors; the restriction did not prohibit Joanna from using her considerable power to keep their immortality hidden. It wouldn't do to have people wonder why the "widow" Beauchamp suddenly looked half her age and was pregnant to boot. Magic was useful in that matter at least.

No matter what, though, no matter how long it had been, with every hopeful pregnancy she never got her boy back. Never. Of course she understood it was useless to hope that she would. That had been made clear to her during the sentencing after the bridge between the worlds had collapsed. Joanna knew he was still alive, but no witchcraft could help him now. He was out of her reach.

One would think after so many lifetimes the pain would dull a little, but it never did. If anything, every passing year just made it ache that much more. She missed him more than ever and thought about him every day. That was the problem with motherhood: not only did it make you fat and put anxiety lines in your forehead, but the love you felt—that intense, all-consuming love for one's child—was like owning the sharpest and most exquisite knife. It stabbed her right in the heart. Her boy was alive somewhere but he might as well be dead to her, since she would never get him back. They had taken that away from her. It was the worst kind of sentence a mother could endure, which was why it had been given.

Her beautiful boy, her happiest child: his smile was the sun, his light lit up the whole entire world. It was true what they said about mothers and sons: it was a special bond, a mutual admiration society. It was also true what they said: one loved one's children the same amount, but sometimes you *liked* one child more than another. She had been mourning his loss for so long, and the girls were a great comfort. Still, it had never been the same. But now she had this wonderful new boy: this Tyler Alvarez, of the quirky flapping hands and the mischievous smile, who would not embrace her yet would head-butt her if he wanted a kiss on the top of his head. He did not heal the hole in her heart, but he did fill a gap that had been empty for a very long time. Joanna took to the boy immediately. He called her Abuela, or "Lala" for short, and she called him Checkers. She wasn't sure where that came from, something with his cheeks maybe. She was constantly pinching them. She loved her daughters, but they did not need her anymore. They were grown-ups with their own problems. Tyler was another story.

Right now they were making a pie. Motherhood might have robbed her of her figure, but to be honest Joanna had been something of an accomplice in that matter. Aside from constantly renovating the house, her other weakness was baking. The kitchen always smelled like melted butter, enveloping the air with its rich, creamy, caramel fragrance. Joanna was teaching Tyler how to make a nectarine and blackberry pie. The fruit had been picked from the family orchard, the nectarines bursting with sweetness and the blackberries tart and tangy.

Tyler held the measuring spoon. "How much sugar?" he asked, his fingers hovering above the bag of sugar on the counter. She had given him the task of sweetening the syrup.

"More, darling, more," Joanna urged as she pounded and rolled the dough that would form the crust.

After Tyler had added what looked like two cups of sugar into the mix, she cut into a long black vanilla bean and scraped the contents, adding it to the filling. Once the pie was assembled, Tyler helped her place it into the oven, an old Aga stove that she had purchased during a previous renovation.

"Now what?" he asked, his face smeared with fruit stains and his hair white with flour.

"Now we wait," Joanna smiled.

Yesterday they had made brownies, the day before cupcakes, the day before that a moist and chewy nut roll. It was an orgy of baking, more so than usual, and Ingrid and Freya had begged the sugary tidal wave to stop. They might be immortal but their bodies were not immune to the havoc wreaked by a steady diet of baked goods.

Joanna had told them they would just have to deal with it the way everyone else did, with discipline and restraint. Just because she made these delicious treats did not mean they had to eat them. She wasn't shoving brownies and cake into their mouths, now, was she? Besides, Tyler loved baking, and she was enjoying herself too much to stop. She was finding it was great fun acting like someone's mother without the burden of responsibility. All she had to do was nurture and feed while someone else would do the disciplining and the time-outs.

"We'll need ice cream to eat with the pie," Joanna said, removing a carton from the freezer. "Extra scoops?"

Tyler nodded vigorously and she ruffled his hair. There was something about little boys. Boys in general adored their mothers. Girls were tricky. She knew the girls loved her, but she also understood that deep down, they blamed her for their father's absence. They didn't understand her, and sometimes she didn't understand how to talk to them. Everything she said was taken as criticism, as judgment. Over the years she had learned she should never comment on anything.

So did she say anything when Ingrid moved back home and, instead of taking that position at the university, chose to work as a clerk at the local library? No! Did she ever mention her disappointment that her brilliant daughter with the doctorate had steamed paper for the last several years? Not a word! Did she say anything when Freya opened that bar in New York without a proper liquor license? Nope! Did she ever suggest that Freya might want to dress a little less provocatively? Never! Or that perhaps she was rushing into marriage? Of course, Freya and Bran were meant to be together; just one look at their happy faces told her everything a mother needed to know. But even if she did not approve, Joanna knew better than to get into it with her daughters. Because just one "Perhaps we have had enough cookies?" (After all, the girls had eaten three each already!) and there was *that face*. The one that said *Mother knows least*.

Or else she would be shut out as she had been that morning. Did they think she did not notice? She was jealous sometimes, of the bond the sisters had between them, just as she had been jealous a long time ago of the easy relationship they had had with their father. Daughters. They could cut you with a look.

She knew Tyler would never look at her that way. Tyler adored her and the feeling was mutual. Joanna now paid for him to attend a fancy children's year-round preschool, and while his parents shared the morning drop-off it was Joanna who picked him up every afternoon with a snack or a treat in hand. After school they would go to the beach, where Tyler would spend the rest of the afternoon chasing birds and collecting seashells while Joanna watched him.

There hadn't been anything odd since the three dead birds a week ago, and Joanna was starting to relax. Maybe that nagging worry in the back of her mind was just a by-product of their history. Perhaps she was just seeing signs where there weren't any. Life in North Hampton never changed; she herself had seen to that when she first moved into town.

Oh dear, the pie had burned. She had forgotten to set the timer and now it was black and smoking. If she had been Freya, this would never have happened, but her magic was of a different sort. Tyler's face crumpled, threatening an avalanche of tears. Lala had *promised* that there would be pie and ice cream.

"I'm so sorry, darling," Joanna sighed.

"Pie," Tyler said stubbornly. "Pie."

"We'll just have to make another one . . ."

"Pie."

Joanna put her hands on her hips. She had overheard her daughters talking that morning. Something about how Freya had made a love potion—of the three of them, Freya had always been the bravest due to her natural impulsiveness and daring. But if nothing had happened to Freya, then . . . well . . . wouldn't it stand to reason that she could do the same? It would just be a simple flick of the wrist, one little incantation and all would be right with Tyler's world. It wouldn't use up that much energy, after all, and truly, the oracle had been silent for many years; who knew if the restriction even applied to something so *small*? . . . Joanna's hands began to shake. She wanted to do this. She *would* do this. It was just a pie, after all, she told herself. It was just part of the baking process. Bake pie. Burn pie. Restore pie.

"Don't tell anyone," she whispered. Recovery and renewal was her brand of witchcraft. She covered the burned pie with a dish towel, whispered a few words, and when she removed it, the crust was golden brown and perfect.

Tyler's eyes widened and he began to bounce on his heels. "You're a witch!" he said with glee.

"Shhh!" Joanna's eyes danced but she looked around in fear. No one had called her that for centuries. It brought back too many memories, not all of them good.

"Are you? Are you a witch?"

Joanna laughed. "What if I am?"

For a moment the little boy looked frightened and shirked away from her, probably thinking of witches in fairy tales, ugly hags who shoved children into ovens and baked them into pies.

Joanna wrapped him in her arms and for once he let her hold him, let her soothe him with a kiss on the nape of his neck. The little boy smelled like baby lotion and sugar. "No, my darling. Never. You have nothing to fear from me."

chapter eight

Gift Horse

ھو

E xcuse me, Ingrid? There's someone here for you," Hudson Rafferty whispered, coming into the back office. The junior librarian raised an eyebrow so that Ingrid would understand this wasn't a usual patron with a question about toddler story-time hours or whether their library fines could be waived (the answer was always "no," so why they even continued to ask, Ingrid could never understand).

"Who is it?" Ingrid asked, taking off the spectacles she used to read the fine print in the design elevations.

"I don't know but he is *quite* fetching," Hudson said in his usual understated way. He favored argyle vests, engraved cuff links, and bow ties, and was in his seventh year of getting his doctorate in Romance languages at Harvard. Hudson's family practically owned the eastern shore, and truly he did not need a summer internship shelving books. The other librarians joked that he was the world's oldest (he'd just turned thirty) and best-dressed intern; his suits alone cost more than their entire ward-robes. He was exacting in his work and moved very deliberately. One could not imagine Hudson running, for instance, or hurry-ing for any reason, or perspiring. He was a natural dilettante, with a breadth of knowledge on many subjects concerning the humanities and the arts, as well as a seasoned world traveler.

Hudson was the one to ask if you needed to know, say, the price of a Ruscha lithograph, where to find the best tapas in Madrid, and whom to call if your hotel in Cairo suddenly "lost" your prepaid reservation. He had "fixers" and a network of acquaintances around the globe and happened to be one of Ingrid's best friends, as they shared a love for theater, opera, and classical music.

"Do excuse me, allergies are bad this year," Hudson said, wiping his nose and coughing. "Well, don't keep the gentleman caller waiting. Someone else might snatch him up."

For a moment Ingrid thought Hudson was talking about Matt Noble, and she felt irritated that the detective had come back so soon. Surely he couldn't be done with that thousand-page book yet? But when she walked to the front desk the man waiting for her was not Matt.

Killian Gardiner was leaning against the main desk. His gray T-shirt was pocky with holes and his jeans were slung low on his hips. Even in the heat, he was wearing a black motorcycle jacket. He looked like a movie star, with the gold-trimmed aviator shades and the five o'clock shadow. No, not a movie star. Like an icon. He had the kind of face that should be plastered on posters in every teen girl's bedroom. When he saw her he took off his sunglasses and pecked her on the cheek.

"Hi, Killian," she said, trying to inject some warmth into her voice. Something about the younger Gardiner brother put her on edge. It wasn't just that he was spectacularly good-looking; as a rule, Ingrid was skeptical and hostile toward pretty men—she found them vain and self-assured and selfish. Blake Aland had pretty much confirmed the fact on their first and only date. She preferred homely guys; not that Matt Noble was homely—far from it—which was probably why she felt annoyed with him, since she liked him despite his looks. Handsome men took female adoration as their due, and Ingrid did not take to people who assumed too much.

Killian Gardiner was a vain peacock, and it was clear he knew exactly how good he looked, with that dark hair that fell over his eyes just so, and that lean, ripped body underneath the worn T-shirt and battered jeans. She could see the carved V shape of his hip muscles jutting above his waistband. When they had met at the party she had asked him what he did, and he'd been purposefully vague. Later she found out it was because he didn't seem to do much of anything. She heard that Killian was a fly-by-night, that he moved with the seasons, he'd run a scuba-diving boat off the coast of Australia, worked as a galley chef on an Alaskan freighter. There were other rumors: that he'd gotten a girl pregnant, that he'd been in jail, that he was a drug addict. Whether they were true or not, Ingrid knew that a man that beautiful was definitely Bad News and she didn't expect to hear anything that proved otherwise.

"I thought you had left town already," she said. Hadn't Killian seemed bored and preoccupied at the party? "How can I help you?"

"Actually I'm helping you," he said, picking up an extra-large L.L. Bean tote bag and setting it on the table. In the bag were several rolled-up blueprints. "I overheard you asking Bran for them at the engagement party, and I thought I'd drop them off this morning."

"Oh—that's so nice! I didn't expect to get them so quickly! Bran said he had to get back to me—he wasn't sure where they were or if they even existed. How wonderful!" She took the bag, handling it reverently. The library was setting up an exhibition of drawings from the collection that would showcase the design plans of all the important houses in town. As the oldest and most prominent house in the area, Fair Haven was crucial to their catalog. Many architecturally important homes had blueprints lying around somewhere; the former owners kept them pristine for the new owners as part of a tradition of handing down a precious object of art.

Ingrid clasped her hands and beamed at Killian, whom she regarded much more fondly this time. What he did with his time was no business of hers, after all. He was free to waste his life on indolence and apathy. "This is going to be so great!"

"Glad to help," Killian said. "I can't wait to hear what you think. It's a really interesting old house, there's a lot of history there. If you need anything else, don't hesitate to call." He glanced at the wooden postbox Ingrid kept by the main desk for "Library Donations." "What's this?"

She explained the situation: the city's deficit, the library's precarious fate at the hands of the city council.

Killian frowned. "You're not going to raise money by keeping a box by the door. You know what you should do, Ingrid, is get them to pay for something only you can provide."

"I'm not really sure I know what you're talking about," Ingrid said, slightly confused. "But thanks for the plans." He really was so charming, she thought, getting the benefit of his megawatt smile. So thoughtful, too—to drop off the plans without being asked, and asking about the library as if he truly cared about its future.

"My pleasure," he said, waving a hand. "See you at the hoedown on Saturday?" A hospital charity was throwing a "barnraiser" that weekend, complete with haystacks and square-dancing, the usual North Hampton summer theme party.

Ingrid shook her head. Freya threw herself into the social scene, but Ingrid liked to stay home to knit, read books, and listen to old songs on her turntable. If she ventured outside the home it was usually with Hudson, two hens off to see a Truffaut revival. "I'm not going but I think Freya is."

At the mention of Freya's name Killian perked up. "Is she, now?"

Ingrid nodded. "So you're staying then? For the summer?"

"I think so." Killian nodded. "See what kind of action I can get going around here." He winked. "Don't worry, I'll be good."

"Guess we'll be seeing you around, then." Ingrid nodded.

Killian bade a cheerful good-bye and roared off on his motorcycle, making a huge noise that rattled the windowpanes.

WHEN SHE RETURNED to the back room, Hudson was waiting for her with his arms crossed. "Well?"

"Well what?"

"Did the handsome young man invite you out? Or did the two of you just exchange phone numbers"—at this juncture Hudson made air quotes with his fingers—"for a future 'booty call'?" His lips twitched with a smirk. Sometimes Hudson was thirty going on eighty with the way he faux-adopted the language of "the youth," as he called it.

"No!" Ingrid wrinkled her nose. "Course not! He was just dropping off blueprints of Fair Haven. You know, for the show," she said, holding up the bag. "And anyway, he's much too young."

"Oh." Hudson looked disappointed. "*Quel dommage.* You looked so ecstatic for a moment I believed you had a date." He went back to the card catalog. He had the thankless task of typing in all the archaic information into the computer. After resisting for many years, the library system was finally going digital. He began to type, hunting and pecking with one delicate finger.

Ingrid shook her head. She checked on the drawing under the steam tent. Once she was done with it she would begin steaming the Gardiner blueprints. The exhibit was scheduled for the end of August, as part of the library gala that usually closed the summer season. The fund-raiser would be the library's last hurrah, and all the proceeds would help offset the costs of moving, if it came down to that.

Caitlin Parker, who had a desk next to Hudson's, pretended not to hear their conversation. Unlike the others, Caitlin did not have a particular affinity for books or design and had fallen into the job almost by accident. She was pleasant and amiable enough, and never gossiped about anybody. Pretty and sweet, like a kindergarten teacher. Ingrid wanted to like Caitlin, there was nothing *not* to like, but she found her dull and insipid. Honestly, the girl was almost too nice; she always let patrons take out the rare books that were not allowed out of the reserve room and she never, ever collected late fees. It drove Ingrid crazy.

The three librarians worked in silence for a while, until Hudson piped up. "So, have you seen her yet?"

"Who?" Ingrid asked.

"Stevie Nicks."

"What do you mean?"

Right at that moment, Tabitha walked in. Her hair was long and loose. She was wearing a long T-shirt, a skirt that swept the floor, and some kind of drapey caftan-like cardigan. The entire effect was not unlike a seventies hippie chick at the beach.

Hudson began humming "Landslide" under his breath.

"What's so funny?" Caitlin asked, looking up from her computer as Hudson stifled a giggle and Ingrid smiled broadly. "I don't get it."

"I feel weird," Tabitha admitted, looking self-conscious as she took her seat by the doorway.

"No, you look great. Really," Ingrid told her. She didn't need a pentagram to see that there were no more traces of the silvery menace anywhere around Tabitha; her friend projected health and happiness. Unloosening the knots had done the trick. Already she could see the magic working its way through Tabitha's body, weaving an invisible glow around her, opening her chakras, letting in the air, freeing the spirit, preparing her body and soul to create new life and bring it to the world. She would conceive by midweek.

chapter nine

Love the One You're With

ᘓᘒ

Bran was back from his trip abroad and would arrive in North Hampton by ten o'clock that evening. Freya asked Kristy Hannagan, a bartender Sal had hired over the summer to pick up the slack, to cover her shift; otherwise she would have to work until last call as usual. Kristy's family had worked the shore for generations, her father and brothers on the lobster trawlers, while her boyfriend fished for bigeye tuna they sold at auction to Japanese food vendors. She was a flint-eyed dame, with a sharp tongue and an easy smile, and had fast become one of Freya's closest friends in town.

"You don't mind, do you, Kris?" Freya asked.

Kristy shook her head and gave her a broad smile. "Not at all. If I had a guy like that I'd take off for the night, too. Go on, now." Kristy was twice divorced and had four kids under the age of five. She likened her work at the bar to wrangling a bunch of toddlers. "I'll man the ship."

"I owe you one," Freya promised, bumping Kristy's hip affectionately on the way to the ladies' room so she could freshen up. Bran was going to walk into the bar at any minute. Freya splashed water on her face, to try to rub the guilt out of it. She was dreading seeing him but couldn't put it off any longer. This was the first time they would see each other since celebrating their engagement. (And, boy, did she ever celebrate, she thought, thinking of Killian and kicking herself again.)

He was waiting for her when she returned to the bar, sitting at his usual barstool, a newspaper spread in front of him, looking crisp and manly in his dark suit and red tie. "There you are," he said, pulling her close and squeezing her waist. "Remind me never to leave you ever again," he said as he ducked his head under her chin.

She laughed and squeezed back. "I'm sorry you had to wait, but Sal's not feeling well and I had to wait until Kristy's babysitter arrived." She was glad to find that upon seeing Bran, she felt exactly the same way: that same warm, solid love that had drawn her to him in the first place. It was still there. He was the one she'd been waiting for, all these long years. She nuzzled his head and pressed her body closer to his, liking the immediate jump in his heartbeat that resulted. It had been a very long time since she'd felt this way.

"Is it serious? Poor Sal," Bran asked, concerned, tapping his gold ring with the family crest.

"He'll be all right," she said. "He's stubborn and won't take his allergy medicine."

"Ha!" Bran nodded. Even if Bran had only recently arrived in town, Freya took it as a good sign that Sal had given him his seal of approval when they announced their engagement. Not only because Bran was the only one who professed to like Sal's homemade moonshine, although it never hurt. "He's a quiet one, your boy," Sal had once told her. "One of those people that take a while to get to know. I like that. Not like all these garrulous meatheads who talk your head off and say nothing."

"How was the meeting? Is all the money gone yet?" she teased. His aim, he had told Freya, was to give away his inheritance to those who needed it more.

"Almost." He laughed. "Working on it."

"I guess we're not Elizabeth and Mr. Darcy—carriages and Pemberley will not be a part of my future." She sighed dramatically, as his hand around her waist inched a little below her jeans, rubbing the skin underneath, marking his territory, letting the world know she was his. Not so shy anymore, was he.

"I hope it's not too disappointing," Bran said with a grin, as he already knew the answer. "What's this?" he asked, picking up one of the new laminated cocktail menus.

"Oh, it's nothing," she said, shrugging, even though she was proud of it. After her success with the Baumans, she had been emboldened to expand her reach. Her new cocktail menu at the North Inn bar was an immediate hit, and it was not difficult to see why. *Love Potions*, it announced in big pink letters, *seventeen dollars ea*. Sal's only comment about the new menu was that if she was going to use top-notch liquor and fresh ingredients, she should charge for them.

Infatuation: A blend of hibiscus rosewater and English gin. Turn heads for the evening and inspire a burning affection.

Irresistible: Vodka, pureed cherries, powdered cattail, and lime juice. Not for the shy. Prepare to lose your inhibitions.

Unrequited: St. Germain liqueur, honeyed lavender, and Prosecco. Stop yearning and start loving. Guaranteed to fulfill your heart's desire.

Forever: Two glasses of the best French champagne, fortified with crushed daisy petals. For those hoping to rekindle their passion for each other.

"It's just something I put together for Sal," she said, hoping he wouldn't ask her too many questions.

"Good stuff," he said, sliding it away. "Everything you touch turns into gold." Only Bran could say things like that without it sounding corny. "By the way, I hope that party didn't scare you away too much." His forehead crinkled. "Did you have fun?"

68

"It was beautiful," Freya said. "I don't scare easy, so don't worry." She felt a slight shiver of anxiety and wished he hadn't brought it up, as an image of Killian, the two of them locked in a tight embrace, suddenly sprung to mind. She turned away from Bran for a moment, her golden hair hiding her suddenly red face.

"So what did you think of that no-good brother of mine?" he asked, his smile fading slightly.

"He's all right," Freya said, hoping to change the subject. Luckily Bran didn't seem to notice anything askew. They left the bar and walked to his car, holding hands, both of them quietly happy to be together.

They took the bridge over to Gardiners Island, and Freya marveled again at how well Fair Haven and its surrounding grounds looked. She knew Bran had overseen the design changes and had kept much of the island's natural growth intact, without disturbing the wildlife or the flora. He parked the car in the garage and turned to her as he cut the engine. "Listen, I know everything's happened so fast. . . . If you need to change anything, if you change your mind . . . I'll understand. I can wait for you. I just want you to be happy." Then he looked at her with those kind brown eyes of his and she fell in love with him even more. Close up, he was starting to have fine lines around his eyes, but it only made him look more distinguished. "I want you to be sure of me."

"Sweetheart." She sighed. "I'm not sure of anything *but* you." She pulled him in for a kiss, and she understood then why she had agreed to marry him after knowing him for less than a month. Of all the guys she had ever met in her immortal life, he was the only one who made her feel this safe. She who distributed love only felt loved herself with his strong arms around her.

———

Fair haven was dark and shrouded, but Bran elected not to turn on any of the overhead lights. "Shhh . . ." he said. "Let's not wake Madame Grobadan."

"Let's not!" Freya agreed. Madame might have been the boys' stepmother, but she had basically raised them and remained a formidable presence in Bran's life. Freya was half-afraid of her, and had let her run the engagement party and make all the decisions, meekly acquiescing to her stringent demands. Madame loved the boys like her own, and with her intimidating posture and dismissive attitude, she was in some ways even more frightening than a real mother-in-law.

If possible, the house looked more impressive than it had at the party, with its vast open spaces empty of people. The grand piano gleamed in the moonlight, and Bran opened the French doors so they could hear the sound of the ocean. The house was so large, the main hall could hold an army, and the residential wing might as well have been in a whole other zip code. Freya walked over to the bar cart and made Bran a martini, extra dry. The bottled olives looked a little puny, but with a tap of her finger they turned juicy and plump. She fed him the olives one by one and he downed the drink in one gulp.

Bran set the glass aside then slouched in one of the roomy club chairs by the fireplace and loosened his tie, which was his way of telling her he wanted her to sit on his lap. He had been so unsure and hesitant in the beginning, as if not quite daring to believe that she would oblige him. His masculine gentleness was so appealing, and she quickly straddled him, so that her long, thick, curly hair brushed his face. He pulled her down to him hungrily, and soon his hands were slipping her dress above her head and she was unbuckling his belt and helping him kick off his pants.

"But what about . . . ?" she asked. "Should we move to your room?"

"They're miles away and asleep. . . . We'll be quiet," he whispered.

In the moonlight her body looked as perfect as a statue; when she sank herself on him her breath caught at the rush of feeling, of being broken and taken, as they moved gently together, so that with each thrust she felt as if she were opened anew. He groaned, his face tense with desire as he picked her up, the two of them still joined; then they were on the floor and he was turning her over, so that she was kneeling with her back in front of him, her head in her hands, thrilling at the way he held her by the waist, the way he pushed himself into her, his hands strong as he moved her every which way, now on her back, now on her stomach, now on top, mastering his strength and keeping her gasping. He was always in control, and she had never met anyone who made her feel quite as . . .

Well no, that wasn't *quite* true, now, was it . . . ?

There *was* someone else who . . .

She pushed the image from her head . . . but there it was. . . .

Killian, with his strong hands under her skirt, as she unzipped his jeans. . . .

It didn't belong there . . . especially not *now*. . . . Why was she even thinking of him? She didn't want this. She didn't want to think of him at all, and certainly not at this particular moment, but she couldn't help but remember . . . how she'd been on her knees, how she'd taken him in her mouth, had tasted him, and Killian had pushed himself against her and she thought she might explode from desire. . . .

No . . . stop . . . please. . . . She had to stop thinking about it . . . had to stop dreaming about it . . . had to stop thinking about him. . . .

Then she was straddling Bran again, his hands on her breasts, and her hands on his, kneading and pinching. They clenched fists and she ground her hips on his lap, keeping the frantic, rhythmic pace . . . and she willed Killian's image away . . . trying to focus instead on Bran's handsome face, on his body and his lust. . . .

But against her will, the other face came back to her mind. . . .

She couldn't help it, the wrongness of it, of what she had done the other night at her own engagement party—the two of them against the small bathroom wall, her legs around Killian's waist as he pushed himself deeper into her—combined with what she was doing now . . . and she moaned and lost herself in the wicked sensation of being with one man while thinking of another. . . . She bit her lip and lost control as her body shook with spasms. . . .

At the same time, below her, Bran let out a magnificent roar (so much for being quiet!) and slammed his body against her again and again and again until he shuddered and was still and they collapsed into each other, her body feeling the ache of longing as he pulled out from her so slowly.

Bran kissed her on the cheek in a sweet gesture of gratitude, as if unable to believe the extent of his extraordinary luck. Freya smiled to feel his lips on her skin, her whole body trembling, and when she opened her eyes, she saw a figure move in the shadow of the hallway.

They were not alone, after all.

Someone had been watching them—someone with the dark hair and glittering, aquamarine eyes of the man who had ravished her only in her mind.

But when she looked again, Killian was gone.

chapter ten

Witch Business

~~

J ust as Ingrid had predicted, Tabitha was soon pregnant. It took only a week for the news to spread around town, and only a few days before certain women decided that they, too, wanted to see if their local librarian could help them with their problems. On a bright Monday morning in June, the glowing mother-to-be regaled yet another group of women gathered around the main counter with her story. It was one they had heard already, but it didn't keep Tabitha from telling it, and her audience was happy enough to hear it once more while awaiting their turn to see Ingrid.

"The doctors said it was a medical miracle! Because our tests came back, you know, and they were *bad*. They said it was virtually impossible for me to get pregnant, but it happened! All thanks to Ingrid! Did you hear what she did for Stephanie Curran? Cured her of that rash that never went away! I swear, the woman is a miracle worker! Well, not a miracle worker but some kind of witch, maybe!"

"Witch!" Mona Boyard repeated, a bit shocked.

"Witch, *please*," Hudson interrupted, with a hand on his hip. "This is North Hampton. We prefer 'special caregiver.' You know, like a reader or a psychic," he said brightly.

No one knew exactly how Ingrid helped people, only that it

worked without any obvious medical or scientific explanation. So it had to be some kind of . . . magic? But who believed in magic in this day and age? The women of North Hampton didn't care what it was called, only that they wanted it for themselves if it worked.

At first Ingrid had not wanted to take the credit for Tabitha's pregnancy, or to dispense any more help or advice, but she soon found it difficult to refuse. Since no lightning bolt came flying out of the sky after she'd given Tabitha the fertility charm, it seemed only fair to help everyone who asked. Maybe Freya was right, maybe it had been so long that the Council had forgotten about them, maybe nothing would come of it this time. Ingrid was willing to take that chance. She couldn't deny it either: practicing magic again was not only enjoyable but gave her a sense of purpose. There was meaning in her life again. She had wasted so much time and effort in denying her innate talents, burying herself in endless small tasks and taking a job at a library: one she enjoyed, of course—but still. *This* was what she was put on earth to do. To hell with that restriction, surely after so many years they had earned a pass? Maybe the Council wouldn't even notice. Besides, the citizens of North Hampton were enlightened, neither fearful nor superstitious. They were curious and skeptical, but willing to try something new.

She was surprised to find an unusual run of bad luck in each supplicant's tale. Some problems, while minor, had been impossible to fix in the ordinary sense: strange aches and pains that no amount of medicine could cure; temporary blindness, bizarre headaches, frequent nightmares. There were several women, much younger than Tabitha, who had also been having trouble conceiving, their spirits blocked by the same silvery mass she had first seen in her coworker. Ingrid worked hard, creating pentagrams, lighting tapered candles, giving out a few little knots, a charm or

74

a spell or two. She accepted clients, as Hudson called them, only during her lunch hour. After all, she had an exhibit to plan and documents to steam. As recompense, Ingrid asked that they donate what they could afford to the library fund, raising money by charging people for something they wanted and that she could give them. Maybe she could close the gap in that budget yet, and their ambitious mayor would drop the idea of selling off the library.

Her last visitor was Emily Foster, an attractive woman in her late thirties. Emily was a well-regarded artist around town, known for her giant abstract murals of seascapes and horses. She lived with her husband, Lionel Horning, who was also an artist, on a farm at the city's edge, where they raised animals. They kept the Beauchamps stocked with fresh eggs and milk and never asked for payment since Joanna regularly dropped off vegetables from her garden. "How can I help you?" Ingrid asked.

"It's such an odd thing," Emily said, blowing her nose. "But I need something to . . . I don't know . . . it's so stupid. . . ."

"There are no judgments here, Em," Ingrid promised.

"I just . . . I can't seem to focus lately. I've never had this problem before . . . being blocked, you know? But it's like I can't even paint or anything. . . . It's so strange. I mean, of course once in a while you get stuck . . . but it's been two weeks now and I can't seem to concentrate on it. It's like my mind is just . . . blank . . . like I can't see anything, no shapes or anything . . . just grayness." She barked a laugh. "Can you cure artist's block?"

"I can try," Ingrid said.

"Thank you." Emily's eyes watered. "I've got an exhibit in a few months. I'd really appreciate it."

She placed Emily in a pentagram, lit the candle, and assessed her spirit. Yes, there it was, that same silvery mass, right in the middle of her torso, and by now Ingrid was quite adept at yanking it out. Ingrid realized it did not just block the creation of life, but it blocked the process of creation itself. Ingrid thought she might have to mention it to Joanna at some point. There were just too many instances lately to be random. There was something odd going on here.

LATER THAT AFTERNOON, Ingrid resumed her real work and began the task of preparing the Gardiner blueprints for the show. She stood at the conference table and slowly unrolled the heavy set of drawings. The sheets were large, almost as big as the table, and the paper was yellowed and fragile. Ingrid expertly thumbed through the pages until she found the site plan. She always started there. A set of design plans was like a novel in a way, a text prepared for the builder, a story written by the architect on how the house should be built. The site plan was like an introduction to the novel.

The site plan showed wavy concentric lines circling a single point at the center, a blocky shape drawn in dark pencil, which represented Fair Haven. She leaned in closely to examine the heavy pencil lines. Each set of drawings contained its own language of keys: symbols and marks that led to specific drawings for each part of the house. A design set blossomed from the outside in, from the site plan to the main floor plan to specific elevations and details.

As she moved through the drawing set, an image of the house began to form in her mind. She glanced from the key on the main floor plan to an elevation of the main ballroom, and turned back to make sure she had read it correctly. That was odd. The elevation key was different from the one that resided on the site plan. Most architecture keys were made up of numbers and letters such as "A 2.1 /1" inside a small circle, but this number tag was elaborately decorated with twisting patterns.

Ingrid pulled a chair out so she could sit down and look more closely at the tiny cartouche. There was something intriguing about the dense pattern of shapes. The swirling lines appeared floral in nature, suggestive of the arabesques of art nouveau, and as she continued to stare at them, the shapes began to resemble letters; but if they were letters they were from a language she could not understand, had never seen before. They weren't Egyptian hieroglyphs or any dead language that she had a passing familiarity with in all her time on earth.

She went through more of the drawings and found several similarly decorated tags, not just room tags and wall tags, but tags for fixtures and finishes, each emblazoned with the elaborate script, and each one unlike the other. She had never seen anything like it in any drawing set before. Ingrid was familiar with the standard architectural keys, and was certain that whatever was written around the keys was not meant for any builder or contractor. Drawing keys were meant to carry the reader from one drawing to another, but these keys had some other function hidden within them, one that had nothing to do with the architecture or construction of the house.

Ingrid pulled her phone from her pocket, zoomed in on one of the strange tags, and snapped a picture. She dropped it into an e-mail. While she couldn't read the language, she knew someone who might, thinking of the letters she always kept in her pocket.

chapter eleven

The Sunshine of Her Life

❧

So this is what it felt like to be a grandmother. Joanna had never been privy to that particular experience. Not with those bachelor girls of hers, who chose to live alone for centuries. Maybe it was a blessing in disguise: look at what creating all those half-deities did for the Greeks. Messy. Perhaps Freya would change her mind when she and Bran were wed, but Ingrid was probably a lost cause.

There was no doubting it, little Tyler Alvarez had captured her heart. After the incident with the blackberry pie, Joanna, like her daughters, had become more and more daring with practicing her magic. She delighted in surprising him. She made his toy soldiers come to life, and they spent hours sending their troops into battle. With Joanna in the playroom, the teddy bears talked and the puppets danced without strings. She was a nanny and a conjurer, the best kind of playmate. She even showed him Ingrid's pet griffin. "This is Oscar," she told him. "No one outside of the family is allowed to see him. But I want you to meet him."

Oscar nuzzled Tyler's hand and swished his lion's tail proudly as Tyler fed him his favorite snack, Cheetos.

"It's our secret," she said.

True to his word, the four-year-old never said anything to his parents about what Joanna was capable of doing. Besides, for

Joanna, making a few inanimate objects approximate life was easy. It didn't take much to entertain a toddler.

That afternoon she was tackling the garden. She always kept a tidy little bed behind the house. Something small, although of course with her talents for keeping things growing she had the largest, juiciest vegetables in the Hamptons. She grew corn and zucchini, cucumbers and cabbage, beefsteak tomatoes as large as basketballs. She was weeding the little plot when her cell phone rang. She glanced at the number, and her heart began to race when she saw it was the Sunshine Preschool. The school did not make it a habit of calling during the day, which could only mean one thing: something had happened to Tyler. Her hands began to shake as she answered the phone.

"Joanna?" asked the calm voice of the director. Marie May had founded the school thirty years ago, and in a small town like North Hampton where everyone knew one another the two women often made small talk when they bumped into each other at the grocery store, the gas station, or the fruit stand.

"Marie, what's wrong?" she asked. If something had happened to Tyler the director would not sound so pleasant, she told herself. If he had hit his head or hurt himself badly Marie would sound a bit more panicked, wouldn't she? Joanna wished she had Ingrid's talent for seeing into the future. What was going on? Why was the school calling her now? Gracella had dropped the boy off at nine and Joanna was meant to pick him up at two. She was going to show him how to make indestructible soap bubbles today with the help of a fortifying spell.

"Darling, I don't want you to panic, but there's something wrong with Tyler. He hasn't fallen or hurt himself, but he won't stop crying. We've tried everything to calm him down, and I've tried both his parents but they're not picking up. You were listed as another emergency contact. Would you mind . . . ?"

"Oh my goodness! Of course! Hector and Gracella are in New Jersey helping his brother move. I'm responsible for the child. I'll be there right away."

Joanna's heart was beating so rapidly and her legs were trembling so hard that it was a moment before she realized she was flying. Somehow she had conjured a broomstick from her rake and had taken off to the skies, still wearing her bucket hat and her gardening clogs. She zoomed high above the tall trees and the gabled houses, taking care to shield herself under a canopy of clouds from any eyes below. Now, this was definitely against the rules, but she did not much care; it had been as natural as breathing. Once she had allowed magic back into her life it was as if it had always been part of it. Why wouldn't Tyler stop crying? What was wrong? Marie had been kind enough to try to mask her concern, but Joanna read a note of real fear in her voice.

Tyler never cried. He was the most cheerful kid Joanna had ever met, merry in an old-fashioned way, with his twinkling eyes and adorable munchkin face. Of course he was far from perfect; like many four-year-olds he threw the occasional massive tantrum, especially if one tried to feed him something outside of his four favorite food groups. He ate only apples, tunafish, goldfish crackers, and dessert. He sniffed the bread his mother made for his sandwiches to make sure it was the proper kind, as he wouldn't eat it otherwise. Joanna could already feel her heart clench at the thought of anything happening to the boy.

The Sunshine Preschool was located in two low-slung beach cottages surrounded by a metal gate. Whenever Joanna picked Tyler up, he was always holding some kind of art project that he'd made—macaroni stuck to a paper plate or a new toilet-roll creation—and there was a cheerful weekly newsletter with surplus attachments: photographs or videos of the children in the sandbox. It was a clean, safe, and happy school, and Tyler enjoyed going there. She forgot the code to the security door and waved a hand so that it swung open quickly. There was no time; she wanted to see the boy *now*. Joanna told herself not to panic even as her mind began to race with apocalyptic scares. There were so many diseases that could affect children nowadays, a whole host of incurable flus and mysterious ailments that could attack a developing immune system. As she ran she began to imagine the worst: swine flu, meningitis, staph infection. Marie was in her office and stood up as soon as she saw Joanna. "He's all right— still crying. I hate to alarm you but I thought it was best if we called . . ." she said.

At that moment one of the teachers, a large, sweet Jamaican woman who was Tyler's favorite, walked in with the wailing boy in her arms. His whole face was red and he was sobbing, big fat tears falling down his chubby cheeks. He pointed to his right ear and howled.

"I'm so sorry, we've tried everything," the teacher apologized. "A couple of kids have come down with a nasty virus that's kept them out of school the past couple of days. Tyler probably caught it."

"It's probably an ear infection; they're very painful," Marie said knowledgeably. "We thought it a bit premature to call an ambulance, as he was not vomiting or running a fever, but perhaps it's best to take him to his pediatrician."

"Of course, of course," Joanna agreed, taking the weeping boy in her arms and kissing his wet cheeks. "Tylerino," she said gently, "it will be all right, baby." She bid a hasty good-bye and thank-you and was out the door, her clogs clippety-clopping down the pebbled path.

The doctor's office was just a few blocks away, which was a good thing since in her haste Joanna had forgotten she did not have a vehicle. The nurse shepherded them to an examination room as soon as they arrived. Tyler was still crying, softly now, exhausted wheezes and sniffs. His shirt was drenched in sweat. Joanna held his hand tightly and hoped against hope that Marie was right. That this was a mere cold, a virus that had run awry. The doctor, who had cared for both of the girls in their youth, examined Tyler and gave his verdict. Of course, the girls had never been sick, not once in their entire lives. As immortals, they were immune to disease.

"Looks like a bad case of otitis. It's been going around," he said, as he put away the tongue depressor.

"What's that?" Joanna asked, hugging the boy close.

"Ear infection." He wrote a prescription on his pad for a regimen of antibiotics. "Make sure he takes all of them. Are you his legal guardian? I'll need a signature of consent for the medicine."

Joanna felt a rush of relief flood her. "No, I'm not but I'll get it to you as soon as possible. They should be back in town by tonight." Tyler finally stopped crying and was now sniffing and blinking. The nurse gave him a sticker, as well as a teaspoon of Children's Tylenol for the pain.

"Ice cream?" Joanna suggested, kissing him on the cheek.

The little boy nodded, too tired to speak. Joanna hugged him close. Tyler was going to be okay. She had never felt so grateful for mundane medicine.

chapter twelve

Library Fines

❧

When Ingrid arrived at work the next day, there was a message in her e-mail in-box. She stared at the computer screen. She had sent the photo of the design key only yesterday afternoon and already he had replied. She had expected it, but it still surprised her to hear from him so soon.

<<good to hear from you. interesting thing you've got there. will get back to you with analysis. been a long time. i assume this means you received my letters?>>

Yes, she got his letters. She was almost tired of reading them, really, although she wondered how she would feel if they stopped coming. If a week went by and no letter arrived, would she be happier or sadder? She massaged her temples. She shouldn't have responded to him. Her mother and sister would never approve. But this wasn't about her or them or even him. There was something in those ornately decorated design keys. Something important, she could feel it, something that she had forgotten, and he was the only one who knew how to decipher it. The only one who could help her unlock the mystery of the code. She wrote him back.

<<got yr letters. not sure this is the right time to get together. but am hoping you can still help me with this?>>

The reply was instantaneous.

<<of course. you know you don't need to ask.>>

She sighed and did not send a response. It was time for her "witching hour," as Hudson called it. The line in front of the main desk was out the door. Some of the women had been there since before the library opened. They had been waiting patiently all morning, some perusing the shelves, some reading books, most content to merely stand and wait. The impressive results from Ingrid's work kept pouring in: the nightmares that stopped, the strange aches and pains that were cured, the rash of positive pregnancy tests.

Becky Bauman, who had recently reconciled with her husband, was one of her first clients. Becky took a seat across from Ingrid's desk.

"How can I help?" Ingrid asked.

"I don't know if this is the right place to ask or if you can help. I just . . . I feel like our place is haunted. I get the weirdest feeling at night, like there's someone there. Ross said I should come here even though he's never felt it. But I'm quite sure there's another presence in the house. The lights go on and off. The television turns on at odd times. Do you believe in ghosts?"

"No," Ingrid replied slowly. Ghosts did not exist, but she also knew that what humans referred to as ghosts—phantom specters and wraiths seen in shadowy light as well as other supernatural phenomena—was usually due to proximity to the edge of a seam, where the physical world and the world of the glom came so very close that those on the other side would be able to sense the presence of another world just beyond their sight. The edges of the seam were supposed to be held by a powerful binding spell Joanna had set long ago when they moved to North Hampton. It seemed only natural, Ingrid supposed, that spells would lessen and weaken with age, although it had never happened before. She fashioned Becky a talisman that would help keep the boundaries tight and get rid of the pesky paranormal inconvenience—no more blaring televisions at three in the morning, in any case.

Ingrid attended to the usual mix of unexplainable grievances until an unexpected visitor arrived in her office.

"Hey, there." Matt Noble entered the office. He was so tall he looked funny sitting on the little stool across from her desk. "So I hear that you can help people."

"I do. What brings you here, Matt?" Ingrid asked, smoothing her skirt and not quite able to look him in the eye. She was irritated with herself for acting like a flustered old maid around him.

Matt leaned forward on the desk and she forced herself to look into those clear blue eyes of his. "I have a problem . . ." he said huskily.

"Which is?"

"I like this girl, see. I really like her. She's smart and pretty and sweet and she really seems to care about people. But she doesn't seem to like me in return."

Ingrid tensed. "I see."

"So I guess. . . . How do I get her to say yes when I ask her out?" His eyes sparkled and there was a hint of a smile forming on his face.

She frowned. Ingrid did not like when people made fun of her; she had a sense of humor but she didn't like a joke when she was the punch line. It was so obvious he was talking about her, and if this was his way of asking her out on a date, he should really know better. Let him down gently, Ingrid told herself. The poor guy was obviously in love with her, and she would not want to hurt his feelings. She wasn't completely heartless.

"Listen, Matt, you're a great guy but I . . ."

"Man! You really think Caitlin won't go out with me?" he interrupted.

It took Ingrid a second to recover, but the moment flashed by without the detective noticing. He was talking about *Caitlin*. Her coworker. The one who didn't even read books. Ingrid thought back to when they had hired the girl. It was right about the time that the handsome lawman began his regular visits to the library. So in all that time he was interested in Caitlin, not Ingrid. She'd been so mistaken it was embarrassing. So why had her heart dipped a little when he had spoken her coworker's name? It's not like she cared whom he liked. Really, she was incredibly relieved. She gave him a tight smile. "Actually that sort of thing isn't my arena. Romance, that is. You're better off seeing my sister at the North Inn. Ask her to make you a drink from her fancy new cocktail menu. Tell her the same thing you told me and maybe she'll help you."

"Is that right?" he asked.

She nodded, and briskly ushered him out of her office. She looked at her watch. She had meant to work for only an hour but it was almost two thirty and she hadn't eaten lunch yet. Freya had made her a tuna salad sandwich on wheat bread. Like everything Freya made it was usually delicious, but for some reason today it tasted like sand.

Oh, well. So I was wrong. He likes Caitlin. Who doesn't like Caitlin? Everyone in town liked Caitlin, who didn't take books seriously and didn't give lectures on missed library fines and proper care of manuscripts and bore people with talk about old houses and design. Caitlin didn't engender mean nicknames like "Frigid Ingrid," nor did people think she was aloof or strange for having a line of people clamoring for charms and spells. She was just a nice, normal girl, pretty if rather boring, the kind of girl whom Ingrid could never be, had never once been.

After her tasteless meal Ingrid went back to her documents, determined to give Matt Noble no more thought.

chapter thirteen

Aftershocks

❧

"Come back here, woman," Bran growled, pulling Freya back into bed.

"I'm late for work already, stop." She laughed, trying to put her shoes on as he nuzzled her neck. His warm hands encircled her waist and she gave up, kicking off her sneakers and letting him pull her back under the covers.

She had refrained from his touch since that night by the fireplace, too shamed by her thoughts of Killian. She had faked headaches, begged off due to exhaustion. But she knew he would not be denied today. Bran was leaving again that afternoon. The separation would be brief—only a few days in Stockholm this time, for which Freya was glad. She didn't think she had it in her to be a foundation widow, and although she understood the good work he was promoting around the globe, she missed him.

He pulled off her T-shirt and kissed the valley between her breasts, and she ran her fingers through his soft brown hair. "Don't go," she whispered, almost to herself.

Bran looked up at her worriedly. "I don't want to, believe me. I'd rather be here with you."

"I know. Don't mind me." She shook her head and looked away, toward the open window. Bran's room faced north, and she could just glimpse the dock where the boats were anchored below.

Bran sighed and leaned down to lick a pink nipple. She dutifully whimpered and clutched his hair, pulling him closer, and with her other hand she reached for him, finding him hard and ready, and guided him inside. He entered her then, and she clung to him fiercely; and as they bucked and panted together, he covered her face with kisses and she sucked on his tongue as hard as he pounded into her. But for once Freya's heart wasn't in it. Maybe it was because she was despondent that he was leaving again, or because she was trying very hard to make sure her mind did not wander off somewhere it should not, but she couldn't enjoy herself; she was just going through the motions. Killian had spoiled everything, but it wasn't Bran's fault, it was hers.

They dressed and left the house. As they were walking out the door, he stopped, almost tripping on the hallway rug. "I forgot something," he said, running back up the stairs.

"Your passport?" Freya called. She found it resting on a side table. "It's down here."

"And my ring." Bran nodded as he came back, holding up his gold crest ring and slipping it on his finger. He accepted his passport with a kiss.

"What's up with you and that ring, anyway?" she teased.

"It was Father's," he said. "It means a lot to me. It's the only thing I have left from him." Freya nodded, abashed. She knew Bran and Killian had been orphaned in their youth.

He dropped her off at work, and she was bursting with excuses and apologies when she arrived at the North Inn, knowing the Saturday-night crowd would be keeping everyone on their toes. But instead of the usual mayhem she was surprised to find the music silent and everyone crowded in front of the tiny television.

"What happened?" she asked Sal, as she stowed her purse

underneath the counter. She squinted up at the screen, which showed a helicopter view of the Atlantic coast. There had been some kind of explosion, deep beneath the sea, not too far from the shore. An earthquake maybe, experts weren't sure yet, the local anchorwoman was saying. But now there were all these dead fish floating around, and some kind of silvery-gray gunk was seeping out into the water. Experts had ruled out an oil leak, as they were miles away from the nearest pipeline.

"Look at that," someone said, as the camera pulled away to show a dense mass growing in the blue-gray waters of the Atlantic. "That can't be good."

Now a scientist being interviewed on the local news was saying it was some kind of natural disaster, most likely an underground volcanic explosion that had released an oil-like toxin into the sea. He warned that the gray, tarry substance would not only threaten the surrounding wildlife and their habitat, but that it wasn't safe to fish or to eat fish or seafood of any kind that came from the North Hampton waters. Also, until further notice, no one should swim in any of the local beaches until the toxin was examined.

"Yikes," Freya said, to no one in particular, while the crowd in the bar began to murmur nervously among themselves.

"What I'm wondering is . . ." She heard a clear voice next to her, and was surprised to find Killian Gardiner sitting on a bar stool, watching the television and sipping his beer. He didn't seem to notice her either, as he only had eyes for the screen.

"You didn't finish your sentence," she prodded. It was the first time the two of them had spoken since the night of her engagement party, and she tried to keep her voice normal. She blushed to remember the other night—if he had truly seen her with Bran. And if he still thought about what had happened between them on Memorial Day.

"I'm wondering . . . how long has it been in the water?" He barely glanced at Freya as he gulped down the rest of his pint and left the bar without another word.

ALL WEEKEND the disaster was all everyone in town talked about, and on Monday morning even Ingrid and her staff at the library were feeling jumpy about it. While North Hampton had its share of hurricanes, it was a lucky kind of place: no brushfires in the summer like in Malibu, no flash floods; it wasn't on a fault line. The underground earthquake and the resulting gray muck felt like an unlucky break, a jinx, a pox upon their little oasis. The library had one old television set in the back office, which they kept tuned to the news stations. They showed the grayish mass growing in the water, nearing the North Hampton shores. Whether the earthquake had kept clients away, Ingrid wasn't sure, but for once she was able to take her lunch hour outside the library. A familiar face was waiting for her when she returned.

"We were just watching you on television!" Ingrid said, unlocking the door to the back office.

Corky Hutchinson gave her a wry smile. "I'm on a break. I don't have to be back at the station until the four o'clock news this afternoon." The mayor's wife was a glamour girl, and her features were heavily made up and exaggerated for the camera. She looked out of place in the drab surroundings.

"Are you here for a consultation?" Ingrid asked. "I'm sorry but I have to ask you to return tomorrow, as I only do those between noon and one."

"I know, your girl told me." Corky sniffed. "But I'm hoping you could make an exception."

Ingrid frowned. She knew this was going to happen eventually. There would always be people like Corky Hutchinson who thought they were too good to wait in line. She also didn't like how Corky called Tabitha her "girl"; Tab wasn't a secretary. But Ingrid knew that women like Corky Hutchinson, with their Black-Berrys and their overstuffed schedules, did not like taking "no" for an answer. "Just this once, I suppose. Come on in," Ingrid said. "So do they know what that thing is yet?"

"They're still not sure. It's been sent to a couple of labs. There was a similar case out in the Pacific a few months ago, near the Sydney harbor. And the same thing happened in Greenland, apparently. The same symptoms: dead fish, some kind of poison in the water—decimated most of the local whale population. Underwater volcanic activity, but they weren't sure."

"Curious," Ingrid said. She dimly recalled reading about it as well but had not paid much attention. "Anyway, I know you didn't come in here to talk about that. How can I help you?" She knew a little about Corky. She and the mayor made quite the power couple. Their wedding had been the social event of the year, and when he was elected there was a five-page spread in a glossy magazine about their romance.

Corky hesitated then blurted, "I think Todd's cheating on me."

Ingrid wasn't surprised. The sisters sometimes gossiped about the secrets they discovered about the people they knew, and Freya had told her that the mayor had been a lot more intimate with his computer than his wife lately. It didn't make Ingrid feel any better to know salacious facts about her enemy, and in the past few weeks she had thought of Todd Hutchinson as nothing less than her greatest nemesis. The proposal to sell the library property to raise public funds would be voted on by the city council by the end of the summer. It was on the table, and as far as Blake Aland was concerned, it was already a done deal. He had come by with his assistants the other day, measuring exactly where the wrecking ball would hit.

Ingrid tried to appear neutral. No matter who Corky Hutchinson's husband was, the woman was entitled to the same service from Ingrid as anyone else. "Why would you think that?" she asked.

"All the usual stuff. He works late. He comes home and smells like perfume. He doesn't answer his cell phone when I call, and when I ask him about it he has all these excuses. He changed the passwords on all his e-mail accounts. His voice mail, too. I checked," she said bitterly. "I was on camera all weekend because of this disaster and didn't hear from him once."

"What would you like me to do about it?" Ingrid asked.

"I don't care about the affairs. I don't want to confront him. I don't really want to get into it. I just want—I just want him back. I want him home with me. I know I've been working a lot, not just this week, but all year. But still, I don't deserve this. I love my husband. And I think he still loves me. I brought this." She thrust a paper bag in Ingrid's direction. "I heard you have to bring . . . hair . . . for the . . . whatever you do. The knots." The mayor's wife exhaled. "I mean, it's probably just some kind of voodoo and I should really just deal with it myself but, whatever."

Ingrid accepted the bag. For a moment she wanted to tell her to go away, that she couldn't do anything to help her. She found it odd that a woman like Corky Hutchinson—glamorous, confident, aggressive—would decide to solve her husband's infidelity by consulting a witch. Corky wasn't the type. She was the type to throw her knowledge of her husband's infidelity right in his face and have a screaming match. Followed by passionate makeup sex if they were lucky. Freya would know more about that.

She wasn't sure helping her was the right thing to do, especially since Corky Hutchinson had used the *v* word—*voodoo*—which meant she thought very little of Ingrid's talents. But she also knew that a go-getter like Corky would not leave Ingrid's office until she got what she came for. What could it hurt? Maybe if the mayor's home life was happy he would stop trying to sell the library from under her. Ingrid opened the bag and went to work, creating a little knot from Todd's hair, weaving it together with a thread from his wife's blouse that Ingrid had surreptitiously taken when she'd shaken her hand. She put the knot in a tiny velvet pouch and handed the little talisman to the mayor's wife. "Put this under your mattress. It will keep him from straying, and you will have him all to yourself from now on. It will keep him home, like you want. But you've got to put in the time as well. If you're not at home enough, the power of the knot will fade."

Corky nodded. "How much?" she asked as she opened her pocketbook.

"I only ask for a donation to the library fund," Ingrid said. "Whatever you think you can spare, we would very much appreciate."

"Is that all?" Corky laughed as she wrote the check. "You don't really know much about people, do you?"

Ingrid felt an instant dislike for the arrogant news anchor. She probably should not have helped her with the knot. Well, it would keep the mayor from straying but it wouldn't keep him there for long if his wife did not do anything to help him stay. She thought of that lavish six-page spread on Todd and Corky Hutchinson's fabulous new life in the local glossy. They had been bursting with happiness and love. People who were so shiny that Ingrid could not help but feel just a tiny bit jealous, the way the magazine wanted you to feel—that there were people in your midst who were living more glamorous and important lives than you could ever imagine. How funny that the truth was never quite that perfect. You never knew about people, she mused. Marriage was like the surface of an ocean, seemingly placid and serene above; yet if you weren't careful, seething and raging with underground earthquakes below.

chapter fourteen

Friends with Benefits

～～

T his being North Hampton, the only appropriate response to a disaster was through prodigious fund-raising. "Fishing for a Cause," as it was nicknamed, brought the community out in force. The party was held on the grounds in front of city hall, with Todd Hutchinson shaking hands and promising vigorous lobbying for federal and state funding to get the waters clean again. Yet there was still no official explanation as to what the mysterious oceanic substance was made of. None of the scientists could figure it out.

The Gardiners were the primary sponsors of the event. Bran was supposed to make an opening speech, but his flight was delayed, so Killian had played host instead.

"Thank you all for coming here today," he said, waving to the assembled crowd. The younger Gardiner looked handsome and earnest under the spotlights. He cleared his throat. "North Hampton is a very special place, and we want to keep it that way. It means a lot to my family. I know we haven't been back here in a long time, but even if I've been here only briefly, I consider this place my home." He was very articulate and moving as he continued to speak about his family's close historical connection to the area and how much they were putting into the rehabilitation of the coastal waters and helping those whose livelihoods depended on it.

Freya attended the event with her mother and sister. A disaster of this magnitude forced Ingrid out of her antisocial stance, and Joanna had pledged to help in any way she could. Freya knew her mother was itching to use her talents to restore the delicate ecological balance in the area, but the restriction kept her from doing so. She was impressed with Killian's words, although she tried not to be. "What a pompous idiot," she whispered to her sister.

Ingrid looked taken aback at her vehemence. "Jeez . . . I thought he gave a nice speech. What do you have against the guy? Every time his name comes up you look like this." She made a sour face, imitating Freya's grimace.

"Nothing," Freya muttered. "Forget I said anything." She didn't really want to talk about Killian. Instead she took a lap around the room and chatted with the mayor, who looked a bit worse for wear, with dark circles under his eyes. "This thing keeping you up nights?" she asked him.

"Yeah. I'm having a hard time sleeping for some reason. My doctor prescribed some sleeping pills, but they don't kick in."

Freya regarded him keenly. She could see the traces of the spell, recognized it as a working of Ingrid's. It was an infidelity charm, which kept his sexual history obscured, as each sister's magic canceled out the other's. Freya hoped his wife knew what she was doing. Those fidelity knots of her sister's were no joke.

Freya continued to flit about the party, concerned with avoiding Killian at all costs. She really did not have anything to say to him, and she didn't want to make their relationship any more awkward than it had to be. She hadn't bumped into him since that day at the bar when the news broke out about the explosion. So when she found him standing next to her in the buffet line, she smiled politely, picked up a fruit skewer, and put it on her plate. Unfortunately, Killian had other plans. It turned out he had a lot to say to her this time. "I saw you," he whispered in her ear. He was so close his breath made the hair on her skin prickle a little. "The other night. In front of the fireplace."

So she was right. He *had* seen her. Freya felt her cheeks get hot.

"You were *amazing*."

"Stop it," Freya hissed. "Stop it."

"I know you were thinking of me. I could feel it. That's what brought me downstairs," he said. "Tell me, were you thinking of me when you—"

"Killian. Please. Not here."

"Where, then?" he asked quickly.

"Nowhere." She shook her head and looked around to make sure no one had noticed the two of them together, talking like this. Ingrid was looking mournfully across the room at that handsome detective, Matt Noble, the only one who had questioned Freya's ability to work at the North Inn bar, citing her high school graduation not too long ago (the trick on her driver's license had not worked on him for some reason). He was talking to one of the young librarians who worked with Ingrid, an arm around her shoulders. Meanwhile Joanna was eating profiteroles at a nearby table, her face a mask of bliss. "I told you, like I told you that night. I can't see you again," Freya whispered.

"But you want to," Killian insisted.

"No. No, I don't."

Yes, they had made love the night of her engagement party . . . no, they had *fucked*. The minute he had locked the door behind him she had practically thrown herself at him, had ripped his clothes off to be able to touch his body. It had taken every ounce of her willpower not to scream the moment his hand slipped between her legs. When he'd pinned her against the sink and had his way, she was open and hungry and afterward . . . afterward . . . she had looked into his beautiful face and wanted to cry. In response, he had kissed her again, and they had made love for the second time, slowly this time, savoring every moment, which made it even hotter than the first. . . .

But that was enough. After that she had regained her senses. She had told him under no circumstances could they ever do that again, as she had made a terrible mistake. She had fled the party and had not looked back, not once.

Freya was aware she wasn't perfect, and she never claimed to be. But she would never do anything to hurt someone she loved so dearly. It was a slip, an accident, bridal jitters, her own commitment issues. After all, it had been a *very* long time since she'd had a husband . . . but now she was set and determined. She loved Bran and one moment (or two, really, if one was counting) of weakness with Killian did not change that. It did not change anything.

"Killian, I should have called you to talk about it. I'm sorry I didn't. I meant what I said to you that night, I don't know what I was doing, I was out of my mind, it was a horrid lapse of judgment."

He placed a strawberry on her plate, ripe and luscious. "Call it what you want . . . but you know where to find me." He slipped a key into her pocket. "This will get you into the *Dragon*, it's docked on the far side of Gardiners Island. Don't worry, Bran never goes there. I'll be waiting for you every night this week. If you don't come see me by Sunday night, I won't bother you anymore."

Before she could reply he stepped away suddenly and disappeared into the crowd.

"Sorry! What did I miss?" Bran asked, finally appearing by her side, looking tired and drained from his travels. "Has the silent auction started?" he asked, picking up the fruit skewer from her plate and taking a bite. "I'm starved! Is there any food left?"

"Let's go see," Freya said. She kissed her beloved on the cheek, the key heavy and hot in her pocket, an iron poker.

chapter fifteen

A Certain Wild Magic

❧

Her dress pinched at the waist and Joanna squirmed in her old-fashioned girdle. It was why she did not go to very many fancy parties these days, as she despised wearing tight clothing. Was it her imagination or was her dress so much smaller than she remembered? Her feet hurt, too; why did she let Freya talk her into wearing heels? It was a nice event, and good to see the community pulling together after a disaster. There was a lot of unease and uncertainty in the air. No one was quite sure how it would affect the local economy, but certainly not only the fishing industry but many of the local restaurants that specialized in seafood from the coastal waters were in danger. It was such a shame, and one that no one mentioned since it was much too painful, but the consequences were already being felt; instead of the usual northeastern summer spread, the dinner entrée was some sort of chicken à la boring.

Joanna bade her good-byes to her daughters: Freya was huddled somewhere with Bran, while Ingrid sat at a table with a few of her cohorts from the library. She left the party and began to walk home. The city square was a few blocks away from the beachfront, and her house was just a mile down the shore. It was a pleasant summer evening, and the grassy dunes made this stretch of beach seem more private than the rest of the shore.

She could scarcely hear the last sounds of the party behind her as she stepped onto the warm sand. She removed her shoes and carried them by their straps, and stepped onto the warm crystals. The heat of the day was still radiating from the ground and it felt good on her feet, like the heated marble floors they had in high-end hotel room bathrooms.

The tall dunes formed a private corridor, a place where she could be alone with the roar of the ocean and the chirping of the gulls. It was quieter tonight than usual. The waves were calm and the gulls absent. Perhaps it was that gray mass out there in the ocean that had silenced the birds. She looked at the sea and it seemed darker than normal, as if whatever was happening out there had pulled all of the shimmer from the water. The ocean looked dead and empty, blacker than the sky above.

She wished she'd worn her trenchcoat, as the first cool breezes rolled off the water toward her. She could not make out the sounds of the party anymore, only the rushing, rolling waves. Joanna stopped to look at a circle of yellow police tape held aloft on metal posts just to her left. The tape was tattered and blowing in the wind; it had been there since January, when an early-morning jogger had found Bill and Maura on the ground. She wasn't close to either of them, but like the couple had shared an affinity for this place. In the evenings she'd often catch the two of them walking in the high dunes, sometimes perched on the tallest bluff, staring out at the ocean or upward at the bright stars. Joanna made a wide arc around the police line, glancing only sideways at the ragged yellow tape.

The sand by the water's edge was cold and wet, so Joanna decided to walk up the sandy dune instead. She climbed up, feeling the thick grass and withered stems scrape at her legs, until she was on top of it. The wind was colder up here, but the view was better. She could see all the way across to Gardiners Island and

Fair Haven, to the lighthouse that Bran had restored. Joanna decided to sit and rest for a minute, and idly grasped a stalk of the long, dead grass that covered the mound. She hated to see dead things, and the brittle gray stem began to loosen and expand in her grip, its ashen color changing from silver to a brilliant green as life poured back into the plant. Hold on, what was happening? She had not done anything to bring it back to life, she was quite sure. Joanna watched in fascination as the green spread like a wave across the dune, bringing all the plants to life. She threw the stalk away and gazed in wonderment at the thick green grass. It felt lush and soft to the touch, and had grown waist-high.

She almost laughed, but there was a sudden tickle at the back of her neck and she spun around. All around her the grass had multiplied and was winding upward around her on all sides. The verdant green now seemed a darker color, as if covered by a shadow. The stalks whipped violently around her. This was not cute anymore, nor part of her magic, if it had ever been. She turned to leave, but before she could act, Joanna felt a powerful tug and she was thrown to the ground. The stars faded as a wash of darkness flowed over her body and the grass wrapped and twisted around her throat and chest. The texture of the grass was no longer soft but coarse, its stems harder and denser. Joanna struggled, but as the grass wound tighter it formed a kind of natural straightjacket, binding her limbs and flattening her chest. She felt a mass push down on her as if to force the air from lungs. Joanna screamed and heard her voice echo against the lonely beach. The party was distant, its loud sounds inaudible.

Joanna pulled at the stalk nearest her head and squeezed, shouting an incantation she had not used in a very long time. But the words worked, and the tangle around her face dispersed. She could see the stars again, and the stalks began to weaken and slide away, thinning like an old man's hair right before her eyes.

Whatever had brought the plants to life was gone, and all around the grass was gray and withered as before. She wasn't sure if the plants had reacted to her presence, or if her magic had accidentally disturbed them. Certainly North Hampton was a place where things like this could happen, being so close to the seam and all. Ingrid had mentioned something in passing the other morning, about how she had noticed a gray darkness in the spirits of the people in town. Joanna had meant to look into it but had been busy with home renovations and with Tyler. The boy had recovered from that nasty ear infection and was back to his old habits: lining up his trains, running around in circles, refusing to eat anything but tunafish sandwiches.

Joanna chided herself for allowing herself to be distracted; constant vigilance was key to keeping North Hampton protected. She stood and scurried down the bluff, tearing at the dead grass as she cut through it on her way back to the beach. First the three dead birds, now this. There was something new and strange in town; something wicked this way had come.

chapter sixteen

Friend or Fraud

ce

S hall I send in the rabid hordes?" Hudson asked, leaning on
the office door, his hand on the doorknob. Ingrid knew he
found the whole enterprise on the droll side—he insisted on calling her the White Witch of the Library, and had threatened to
market T-shirts, or worse, start a Web site.

"Don't make fun." Ingrid frowned as she put away her files
and cleared her desk in anticipation. She liked the office to look
generic when her clients entered and not messy and stacked with
blueprints and archival material.

Hudson looked hurt. "I'm not. I find it all sweet, really."

"Do you believe what they say about me?" she asked. They
had never really talked about what she was doing; everything
had happened so quickly that they hadn't had a second to themselves to chat. They used to spend lunch hours together, but Ingrid
had little time for office camaraderie lately.

"The magic thing?" Hudson asked. "The spells and charms?"
He put a finger against his cheek. "Not sure I believe in anything,
really. I think you just tell them what they want to hear. Isn't that
how so-called 'psychics' work? Like that bearded quack on the
cable network who speaks to the dead?"

"Hudson! You think I'm a fraud!" Ingrid barked a laugh, trying not to feel too offended. She had expected to hear that he

was skeptical or doubtful, but not that he assumed she was merely playing parlor tricks.

"You're not?" Hudson asked, a face of innocence. "I thought it was all a ruse to get people to come to the library and read books, and donate to the cause. Very clever, really. You're always trying to figure out how to make the library more popular—I assumed you'd finally figured out how."

When he put it that way, it sounded so reasonable, but Ingrid itched to show him just how much she could do. She gave him a look.

"Wait a minute, so you're not just making it up?" Hudson asked.

"Try me," Ingrid said. "Surely there's something you want that you can't get otherwise."

"You can't help me." Hudson shrugged. He fished in his back pocket and showed her a worn brochure. Ingrid unfolded it slowly and read the headline. GAY? YOU DON'T HAVE TO BE! HETEROSEXUALITY IS JUST 12 STEPS AWAY!

"Mother is insisting I consult this . . . 'therapist.' One of those people who can, you know, cure me of my *disease*."

"Oh, dear." Ingrid put a hand on her mouth.

"I suppose it is amusing." Hudson sighed, rolling his eyes in agreement.

"Of course not. It's just . . . Hudson, this is ridiculous." She returned the brochure to him and held his hand for a beat longer than necessary. "Hudson?"

"Yes, ma'am?"

"Come to the back with me, let me read your lifeline."

"No thanks. I don't like knowing the future. I don't even know where I'll be tomorrow."

"You'll be here. Working at the library until the wrecking ball hits. Come on. I insist," Ingrid said, leading him to the storage room. She placed him in the middle of the room and drew a pentagram around his feet.

Hudson tried not to giggle. "Spooky!" he said.

"Shush!" Ingrid said, trying to peer into his lifeline. With the witch sight from the pentagram, it should have been clear, but there was something blocking her view—a hazy gray darkness, a blankness right where the vision should be. She lit another candle and murmured a few words, and the gray haze dissipated somewhat and she was able to see a little more clearly.

She switched on the lights and faced her friend. "For what it's worth, your mother will come around one day," she told him. She had seen it in his lifeline, the slow thawing of his mother's stubborn heart, the ingrained homophobia (it was all right for her hairdresser, her interior decorator, her personal chef to be gay—*just not her son!*) battling with the fierce love she felt for her handsome boy. Missing him during every lonely Christmas. The slow, tentative steps toward reconciliation and forgiveness. A mother, son, and son-in-law trip to Paris. "She loves you, Hudson. Don't give up on her."

"Hmm" was all Hudson would say, but she knew he was moved. Later he left a bouquet of her favorite flowers on her desk.

OVER THE NEXT HOUR Ingrid helped a variety of women with their concerns: more headaches, more bizarre skin infections, a pet or two who had died suddenly. Ingrid was not sure what they thought she could do about their dead animals, but she made a note of it, thinking of the dead birds her mother had seen earlier that summer. Emily Foster, the artist who had been blocked in her work, walked in at the end of the hour.

"I'm sorry to bother you," she told Ingrid, looking pale and wan in an Indian tunic and silk pants stained with paint.

"It's not a bother, Em. Blocked again?"

"No, no, the work is going well. It's Lionel," Emily said, her voice cracking. "I don't know if you heard, but he's in bad shape."

"I hadn't heard, what happened?"

"He was out in the water the day of the accident—you know, that big explosion off the coast. He always takes his sunfish out in the mornings. The waves knocked him out cold and he swallowed a lot of water." Emily wiped the corners of her eyes with her fluttering hands and took a deep breath. "He would have died—he would have drowned—but luckily a couple of surfers found him and brought him to shore."

"Oh my god."

"I know." Emily nodded. "They knew CPR, so they got his heart to start beating again and they took him to a hospital."

Ingrid looked relieved. "So he's alive?"

"Barely. He's on a respirator. The doctors say he's brain dead." Emily began to weep openly.

"I'm so so sorry," Ingrid said, taking Emily's hand across the table and squeezing it in sympathy. Lionel was a good friend to their family; he was the one to whom the Beauchamps turned to replace hard-to-reach lightbulbs or perform small carpentry and handyman tasks around the house.

"I just can't believe it. I mean, he was fine that morning and now . . . he's brain-dead?" Emily began to cry. "And on top of that, his mother hates me. She's kicking me out."

"Pardon?"

"See, technically, it's Lionel's house. We never got married," Emily said. "We didn't plan on having kids so we didn't see the point. God, I wish I hadn't been so stubborn back then! Me and my idealistic bohemian ideals! Now they want the house back. They're giving me until the end of the month to pack my things. They're moving in so they can be closer to Lionel, and good riddance to me. They never liked me anyway, thought I was never good enough for their family.

"We've lived in that house since we first met. It's my house.

My studio is there. I don't know where I'll go. If only he would wake up. The doctors said there's no hope. That he's a vegetable."

"What do you want from me?" Ingrid asked.

Emily looked up from her wet handkerchief and balled up tissues. "I know he's in there. He can't leave me. He's got to wake up. He's got to. Could you wake him up, Ingrid? Please?"

"I wish I could, I really do," Ingrid said, shaking her head. "But my magic—I mean, what I can do, it doesn't work that way."

The grieving woman nodded. "I understand. I just thought I'd ask." She began to gather her things, and seeing her friend looking lost and defeated stirred something in Ingrid's heart. It was the same impulse that led her to help Tabitha get pregnant and throw off the bounds of their restriction.

"Hold on. I can't help him," Ingrid said, getting up from her chair. "But I know someone who can."

chapter seventeen

Midsummer
Night's Dream

～

For an agonizing week Freya kept the key to Killian's boat in her pocket, and on Sunday night found herself standing in the shadows away from the dock. The dreams of Killian were getting more vivid each day; she could not walk a step or breathe a mile without thinking of him. His kisses had branded her, and at night she could feel his desire press upon hers.

The boat was a midsize sport fish, popular in the community for its twenty-foot outriggers. Her father had once owned a boat like it. She knew Killian was inside; she could sense his presence nearby, could feel him waiting in the quiet. If she closed her eyes and concentrated she could even see what he was thinking—the swoon of his body against hers, what they would do once she let herself inside. That was all she had to do. Step off the harbor and climb aboard. Put the key in the lock. Open the door. And fall off a cliff. Freya removed the key from her pocket. It felt as if it were vibrating, but it was only because she was trembling so much.

There was movement on the deck and Killian appeared from the cabin below, gazing out into the dark night. "Freya . . . ?" she heard him whisper. "Are you out there? Come on in."

That was enough to steel her willpower. With a heroic toss, she threw the rotten key into the ocean and ran back to her car.

She could feel it begin to form in her, a darkness, a recklessness that she would not be able to stop, would not be able to contain. She had to get away from him.

Later that same evening, Freya had a dream. It began when she realized she was not alone in bed, and a body lay heavy on hers. It was a familiar weight, and she struggled against it. She couldn't speak, couldn't open her eyes, and finally she stopped fighting as a quiet peace washed over her. When she blinked her eyes open she was walking in the woods, holding hands with Killian.

He smiled at her. "Don't be afraid."

"I'm not," she told him. She knew where she was. They were walking to the middle of the forest behind her house, to a secret spring that only she knew, right into the heart of the wilderness, the only virgin maidenswood that remained in their keep, by the banks of a clear blue pond, a natural swimming hole.

"How did you know about this place?" she asked Killian, whose blue-green eyes were alight with mischief.

"You were the one who brought me here," he said.

Freya wondered about that. She did not know if she was dreaming or if this was real. It certainly *felt* real, but there was a strange quality to it. How did she get here? She could not remember.

She walked to the banks of the pond and, with one fluid gesture, pulled off her dress to show she was naked underneath. She let him look at her, his eyes grazing over breasts, over the curve of her waist, her taut stomach, and toned legs. It was as deep as a physical caress.

"Follow me!" she yelled, diving into the water.

And soon he was kicking off his shoes, unbuttoning his shirt, and throwing his belt to the ground along with his pants. "Nothing you haven't seen before," he said with a wicked grin, following her lead and diving into the lake, his body a straight arrow falling gracefully into the water. He splashed up in a wave of water, sending a huge spray that drenched her to the bone.

The air was warm as a blanket on her skin as she dove back into the water. She swam as deep as she could until she couldn't hold her breath any longer. She kicked to the surface and Killian splashed her. They swam and played, ducking away from each other, teasing and laughing, taking turns dunking each other underneath the water.

Freya felt the water move with her, her happiness filling the air like the cry of the Valkyries. She remembered their old traditions: dancing naked by the bonfire, covered with tar and paint; the masks, the chanting, the ecstatic communion with nature and everything that had made the earth. Once upon a time humanity had shared in that ecclesiastic connection, but no more. But here, with Killian, she was herself again, dancing and laughing and celebrating the beauty of being young and alive forever.

The water swelled and rose, erupting in a playful fountain that shone with dazzling light, her magic expanding as her joy grew, Killian laughing and smiling in wonderment. The very earth seemed to bless them, the grass wet and dewy, the sound of the wind whistling a complementary melody through the trees. She dove into the water and swam to the deepest part of the pond, and when she came up again Killian put his arms around her waist and pulled her toward him. She kissed him back and felt the deep passion of his kisses. Her heart beat faster and faster, as his hands traced circles around her body, over her breasts, between her legs. He brought her up on the riverbank and lay on top of her.

She closed her eyes and began to consecrate the circle, calling up the earth and water elementals to bear witness to their union. She began to chant and sing under her breath. The woods were alive with magic; every living thing, from the blade of grass to the graceful canopy of oak trees above, thrummed with a celebration of their love.

"I give . . ." *I give myself to you*, she would have said, except she was not able to finish the sentence, as the skies broke with a crash of thunder and lightning, and Killian was pulled away from her body; the hot electricity between them instantly cooled. The magic ended. The elementals vanished. Killian was gone.

Freya opened her eyes. She was back in her bedroom and her phone was ringing. She picked it up. "Darling?" a concerned voice asked.

"Bran!" Her relief was overwhelming. She fell back against her pillows and heaved a sigh. She was saved—saved from herself again, and from Killian.

"I missed you—I have a few minutes before my connection to Oslo so I thought I'd call," he said. "I'm sorry to wake you."

"I'm so glad you did," Freya said, shaking. What just happened? What had she done? She had almost gone and married Killian for god's sake. If she had been able to say the words, it was over—*what the gods have wrought no one could tear asunder*—that was the rule, that was how it worked, how it always had been. . . . She would have been his and only his always and forever. It would have been the end of everything.

She clung to the phone and Bran's voice, willing the last vestiges of the dream away, until her heart stopped pounding and she fell asleep once again to the sound of the ocean waves lapping against the shore.

chapter eighteen

The Patron Saint of
Lost Causes

≈

W hy her daughter had promised this miracle Joanna did
   not know. She knew, of course, that Ingrid had set up
something of a clinic in the library, doling out her brand of practi-
cal charms and domestic talismans while Freya was now offering her custom concoctions in a brand-new cocktail menu at the
North Inn Bar. Both endeavors were clearly against the restriction, and yet Joanna could not find it in her heart to scold her
daughters for their actions or demand that they stop. As she had
overheard the girls say to each other the other day, it wasn't as if
she were completely innocent of the matter either. Already someone had reported a UFO sighting in the area after she had taken
off to the skies the other day—Joanna hadn't been as careful
with the cloud cover as she had thought. UFOs indeed! She had
not gained *that* much weight, had she?

At first she had told Ingrid there was no way she was going to
do it; it was simply out of the question. She was still unnerved by
her experience after the benefit; at night she could feel the vines
begin to slide around her legs and suffocate her mouth. Joanna
had performed a check of the seam, which she discovered had
frayed in certain places. She refrained from mentioning anything
to her daughters, since she did not want to worry them until she
knew what it was.

Also, it was one thing to make toy soldiers run around and fix a burned pie; it was quite another to perform the Lazarus-like undertaking her eldest was asking her to do. This was resurrection they were talking about here, and yes, she had been put on Earth precisely for this task. But those days were over: the restriction had seen to that—and there was also the Covenant of the Dead to consider. One did not tiptoe around Helda's territory lightly. Render to Caesar what was Caesar's and all that. Okay, so maybe Lionel was technically still alive, but according to the doctors he was a vegetable. Joanna shuddered at the term and wished people would stop using it. To think of a man as nothing more than a plant was too . . . demeaning somehow. Of course, that was the point—to ease the sorrow so that the family could let go, since their loved one wasn't truly there anymore.

But Ingrid had asked, and it really was an awful story: Emily, who painted those gorgeous seascapes and brought them beautiful brown eggs from her chickens and fresh milk from her cows, was getting booted out of her home just because of some nasty in-laws. Joanna definitely knew all about that. No one was ever good enough for anybody's precious sons. No one ever called daughters precious, and why was that? Things had not changed very much. In the end women like Emily and Ingrid and Freya and Joanna only had one another to lean on. The men were wonderful when they were around, but their fires burned too bright, they lived too close to the sun—look what happened to her boy, and to her man. Gone. Women only had one another in the end. So she agreed to do what she could for Lionel, for Emily's sake.

Privately, Joanna had started to wonder if provoking the Council might be a good idea, anyway. Freya's upcoming nuptials had put her in an optimistic mood. If the fickle goddess of Love was tying the knot on the night of the harvest moon (the

Labor Day weekend fell right on their traditional holiday—not that they were allowed to celebrate it anymore, of course), perhaps there was still hope that things would finally change around here.

But if she was actually going to do this she was going to need the right ammunition. It might be a good idea to have it anyway, after what happened the other night. They would need protection from whatever was out there. Joanna climbed up the attic steps and rooted around the cramped space until she found the false wall where she had hidden their greatest treasures. She had been very careful to make sure the Council did not take everything back then. *Ah.* There was the black steamer trunk, right where she had left it hidden under a piano sheet so many years ago. She pulled off the dusty sheet, unlocked the lid, and looked inside. The box was empty save for a simple wooden case, and from inside the wooden case Joanna removed three ivory wands, as pristine and beautiful as the day they were made.

"Mother? What are you doing up there?" she heard Ingrid call from below. "We need to leave for the hospital now, before visiting hours are over."

"Coming, dear," she replied. When she climbed back down she was holding the three wands tightly in her left hand. She handed two of them to Ingrid. "Make sure you give Freya hers when she gets home. But remember to be careful with them. Only use when absolutely necessary."

"Are you sure about this, Mother?" Ingrid asked, holding the wands reverently. They were made from dragon bone, from the skeleton of the old gods, older than the universe itself, the very bones that created the earth, the same ones that once supported the bridge. Translucent, white to the eye, they shone with an iridescent light.

"Not really. But something tells me it's time we took them out of storage," Joanna said. She stuck her wand in her coat pocket. "Now, come on, let's go see if we can wake up Lionel."

THEY ARRIVED AT THE HOSPITAL in the late afternoon, managing to make it right before the patients' rooms were closed to visitors. "So how long has he been out?" Joanna asked, rolling up her sleeves as they made their way to the correct floor.

"About a week or so."

"And there's no brain activity at all?"

"Some, but not enough to guarantee he would ever recover consciousness."

Joanna nodded. "Good. This shouldn't be too hard, then." If there was still some brain activity it meant Lionel was only barely submerged in the first level of the underlayer, and it would be easy enough to pull him to the surface.

"That's what I thought." They arrived at the right room, but before Ingrid opened the door, she turned to Joanna. "Thanks, Mother."

Joanna patted her daughter's arm. She would never have agreed to it unless Ingrid had asked, and since Ingrid never asked for anything, as her mother she couldn't refuse. Besides, Emily Foster's story piqued Joanna's sense of injustice. Marriages weren't held together by paperwork, and it angered her to think that a woman could be thrown out of her home simply due to bad luck and horrid in-laws.

Ingrid pushed open the door to find Emily Foster weeping by Lionel's bedside. His body was covered by a sheet, and Ingrid exchanged a startled look with her mother before approaching.

"They pulled the plug while I went home to change my clothes and check on our animals. When I came back the nurse told me his mother signed the consent forms. She knew I wouldn't agree so they did it behind my back. He's gone. He's gone, Ingrid. You're too late," Emily sobbed.

Joanna pulled off the sheet slowly and took the dead man's wrist in her hand. His skin was gray, and his fingernails were white and bloodless, but there was still a hint of color on his forearms. "The body's still warm. They did this when . . . just a few minutes ago?" she asked.

"Just before you arrived," Emily said.

"Emily, this is my mother. She's going to help Lionel."

"I remember," Emily said, blowing her nose. "Hi, Mrs. Beauchamp."

"Close the door," Joanna instructed. "Draw the curtains and take her out of here."

Ingrid did as told and guided Emily out of the room. "What's going to happen? I mean, he's dead, right?" Emily asked, looking at the two witches fearfully.

Ingrid and Joanna exchanged another glance. "Not quite. Even without a machine, the heart keeps beating, it's just undetectable as it's a very, very low pulse," Joanna said, hoping the newly bereaved woman would believe her tiny white lie. But it would be too difficult to tell her the truth: that she was going to bring Lionel back from the dead. He had been gone for only a few minutes, not even an hour, which was well within the allotted time.

When she was alone in the room, Joanna took Lionel's cold hand in hers. She closed her eyes and stepped into the glom, the twilight world of disembodied souls. In the glom was a path, a trail in the sand. Using her wand to light the way, Joanna saw that Lionel had made it only to the second level; he was climbing the mountain toward the gate, and once he crossed the gate it would be much harder to bring him back. For beyond the Kingdom of the Dead lay Hell's frontier.

There was something different about the glom, a sense of malice and despair that she had never felt before. "Lionel! Lionel!" she called. She wanted to get out of there as soon as possible.

Lionel Horning turned around. He was bald and severe-looking, dressed in his usual attire of paint-splattered clothing. When he saw her he smiled. "Mrs. Beauchamp, what are you doing here?"

Joanna climbed up next to him so that they were both looking over the view. "Taking you home."

"I'm dead, aren't I?" he asked.

"Only in human terms. Your heart has stopped beating," Joanna said.

"Did I drown? I seem to remember being all wet."

"You did."

"Emily always said that ocean would get the better of me one day."

Joanna analyzed his spirit. There were traces of a silver spiderweb around his soul; she had never seen that before and it worried her. "Would you prefer to stay here?" she asked Lionel.

He looked around. "Not really. What is this place?"

"Think of it as the halfway station. See that gate up there? Once you reach it, it'll be harder to get you to the surface."

"How's Emily?"

"Not good. She's about to get thrown out of your house."

"My parents!" he groaned. "I know I should have forced her to marry me. She's stubborn, you know." He sighed. "I can't leave her."

"Then don't."

He stared at the glimmering path, at the mountain trail that reached toward the silver gate. She knew how hard this decision was. He had been in the underlayer, in the glom, for a week now. He had forgotten about hardship and fear; he was beginning to transition to the spirit world. Perhaps this wasn't such a great idea. Perhaps she should never have agreed to do this.

He looked at the faraway gate, shining in the distance. "Right. Let's go, then."

Joanna took his hand and led him back down the way he had come. He started to walk back but suddenly stopped. "I can't move," he grunted. "My feet are stuck."

"Try harder," she ordered. She felt the hard tugging on the other side; that would be her sister, Helda, holding on to his spirit.

"Do not test me, sister!" Joanna called, waving her wand in the air so that it flashed with a hot white light. "Remember you agreed to keep to the Covenant! It is not his time yet!" She kept her hand on Lionel's arm and pulled. The wind howled, the oceans crashed, lightning flashed. The Kingdom of the Dead did not give up its souls that easily.

But Joanna's magic was stronger; this was the power that was rooted in her, older than the earth, older than the Dead, and her ferocious will held on to Lionel and pulled him up and out of the trail. . . . There was a mighty flash. . . .

Joanna was sitting by Lionel's bedside, holding his hand in a tight grip. The dead man blinked his eyes. He coughed and looked around. "Where's Emily?"

LIONEL'S PARENTS WERE THRILLED to have their son back, if a bit sore about losing the house, although they tried not to show it. Joanna and Ingrid bade their good-byes.

"How can I ever thank you? I don't know what you did, or how you did it, but thank you." Emily wept. "What can I give you? . . . anything. Take the house," she laughed. "Lionel's putting me on the deed."

Joanna embraced her and kissed her on both cheeks. "Take

care of each other," she said. "And keep an eye on him. He might be feeling a bit off for the next day or two. If anything changes with his condition, let us know immediately."

Ingrid led them down the hallway. "So, about this whole restriction . . . I'd say bringing a man back to life kind of breaks each and every one of those rules, doesn't it?" she teased.

Joanna smiled. The whole adventure had felt fantastic, like the good old days again. She stuck her wand into the bun of her hair. "To hell with it. We might as well admit it. We're witches. Just let them try to stop us this time."

the fourth of july

danger
brewing

chapter nineteen

Rhinemaiden

∽

"M att, hi. Caitlin's just finishing up processing a few new books; she'll be out soon," Ingrid said with what she hoped was a friendly smile.

The handsome detective nodded and took his usual seat at the bench across from the main desk. Ingrid felt as if she had blinked and when she opened her eyes, Matt and Caitlin were a couple. It happened so fast that she suspected Freya had slipped one of her now famous love potions in the lawman's coffee. Her sister swore up and down that Matt had not been to the bar in a while; nor had she recently served Caitlin, who was one of those girls who got drunk after one glass of wine and was hardly a North Inn regular.

Ingrid tried to concentrate on the files in front of her, but knowing Matt was sitting right across from her made it difficult. If he had been something of a regular before, there was no escaping him now. Every afternoon he would appear at the library around five o'clock right on schedule. Sure, today was Thursday and the beginning of a holiday weekend, but still. Didn't he have something better to do? How did he have so much time to spend lolling about waiting? Weren't there crimes to solve? It had been more than six months since Bill Thatcher had been found dead on the beach, and the police had no leads. His wife, Maura, was still in a coma, which was too bad as she was the only witness to whatever had happened to them.

The detective's constant presence was annoying, but not half as irritating as watching Caitlin get ready for her dates. The girl was in the back room, furiously slapping on blush and lipstick, telling everyone in earshot everything about her new relationship. Even Tabitha and Hudson had been pulled into the drama—Tabitha because she adored romance in all forms, and Hudson because he soaked up drama like a sponge. Ingrid had attempted to escape all the girly commotion only to find the lawman idling by the main desk.

She tried to pretend he wasn't there, or that she was immune to his presence, which was difficult, as something about seeing him made her throat tighten and her body freeze so that she could actually see the goose bumps forming on her arm. Ingrid pulled her cardigan firmly together and tried not to shiver. She would not let him affect her this way. Ingrid was concentrating so hard on appearing indifferent that she did not register that someone was standing in front of the main desk until Emily Foster poked her in the shoulder. "Ingrid? Earth to Ingrid?"

"Emily! Sorry. I was . . ."

"Daydreaming." Emily smiled and handed her a few books. "Don't worry, I'm used to it. Lionel's always gazing off into the distance."

"How's he doing?" Ingrid asked, glad for the distraction. From the corner of her eye she saw Matt tapping on his BlackBerry.

"Good. He's good," Emily said. "A little more absentminded than usual, but that's probably because he's busy working on a new series of paintings. They're beautiful and haunted-looking, trails that lead nowhere, some kind of mountain with a silver gate. He hasn't shown in New York in a long time and his gallery is very excited."

"Good to hear; please tell him we say hello," Ingrid said, handing Emily her stack of novels.

So far, after Lionel's resurrection there had been nothing from the Council. No messages from the oracle, no indication that they had even noticed or cared. It was a bit unsettling, and Ingrid wondered if they had followed the rules too closely. If the Council didn't care if the rules were broken, perhaps they should have used their magic a long time ago.

There were a few more patrons in line stocking up on books for the long weekend, which kept Ingrid busy. See, she wanted to shout to their pompous mayor, people still *use* the library—it was still relevant to daily life. There wasn't much hope, however. She had heard that they planned to move the architectural archive to a warehouse with a tiny office, but that was only because the bequest could afford it; as for the library itself, its future was grim.

At last the line dwindled and it was just Ingrid and Matt again. The silence between them was going to drive her mad, so she decided to take action.

"Let's see what's keeping her," she told him, as she finished tidying up the main desk. She walked briskly to the back office, where Caitlin was sitting at her desk, pursing her lips and surveying her reflection in her compact mirror.

"You know Matt is here, don't you?" Ingrid asked.

"I know, I'm so late." Caitlin sighed, snapping the compact shut. "He doesn't mind, of course, but I hate to make him wait. You know he's a stickler for time! Always so prompt; he makes me look so bad. I guess it's just part of his personality. Did you know his father was captain of the force before he retired? And his grandfather, too. Runs in the family—isn't that sweet?" It was as if the girl had developed a personality overnight. Suddenly she was a chatterbox; you couldn't shut her up. The staff was well-informed of her dear Matthew's eating habits (he took most of his meals at the diner by the highway), political views (like Ingrid, he didn't vote for the current mayor), and ex-girlfriends (not many). Ingrid was finding it increasingly difficult to refrain from hexing her. All it would take was thirteen black candles and a pentagram and that silly girl wouldn't know why she was breaking out in boils.

Ingrid would prefer not to know so much about Matt Noble. Especially since the picture Caitlin painted was of a simple, honest, hardworking guy, someone she couldn't help but respect and admire, if only from afar.

"Do you think this looks right, Hudson?" Caitlin asked, fretting about her outfit, a white linen dress that showed a hint of her tanned cleavage.

Hudson arched an eyebrow. "Considering I helped you pick it out, I think it's fabulous."

"You look great," Tabitha agreed, looking on enviously. She wasn't showing yet, except for a slight puffiness in her cheeks and the requisite bout of morning sickness. "Where is he taking you, again?"

"To the outdoor opera, you know, by the beach? I can't remember which one."

"It's Wagner, the Ring cycle," Ingrid said icily. She had made plans to see it as well. The North Hampton orchestra performed an abridged instrumental version every year over the Fourth of July holiday, with a fireworks show at the end. Ingrid had been planning to attend with her family, but Freya had canceled on her at the last minute, and Joanna had begged off the yearly tradition, saying she really didn't feel up to all the *Sturm und Drang* this summer. Ingrid had decided to skip it, as she didn't feel like attending the opera alone.

"Hold on," Hudson said and tightened the belt around Caitlin's waist to further exaggerate the dress's hourglass silhouette.

"That's better." He nodded approvingly. The traitor was Caitlin's new best friend, Ingrid lamented. Hudson had the soul of a thirteen-year-old girl. He couldn't help but swoon at a new love affair. It certainly beat recapping last night's reality shows.

Caitlin blushed and giggled, and Ingrid tried not to listen, telling herself that she was not jealous, she was not jealous! If only there was something she could do to stop feeling the way she did. She could help other women with their problems and yet she couldn't seem to fix her own. Freya would tell her to take one of her love potions and steal him away. But Ingrid didn't want that. She didn't want him to like her due to some magic trickery. Not that she liked him, anyway. Right? It was getting harder and harder to fool herself into indifference. She liked Matt Noble, and it wasn't just because he was now out of reach. Ingrid did not suffer from the affliction of loving men she could not have. To be honest, she had never loved any man, not one in her long life. She preferred her own company. So this infatuation with Matt came at just the wrong time. She thought he liked her, and so it had piqued her interest. She had been wrong about his attraction, but now she could not seem to do anything about her feelings.

Hudson whispered something in Caitlin's ear that made the girl blush furiously, making her look even prettier than she already was. "Well, if you really want to know," she said, and Ingrid could not help but overhear, "tonight's his lucky night!"

"Lucky night for what?" Tabitha asked. "Oh! Oh!" she said, as she realized what Hudson and Caitlin were talking about and giggled naughtily.

"We've been seeing each other for two weeks now and I think it's time," Caitlin said primly.

"Is that some sort of rule I'm not aware of?" Hudson asked. "The two-week shag?" He turned to Ingrid and Tabitha expectantly.

"Not for me," Tabitha chortled. "Chad was a one-night stand."

"Tab, you slut," Hudson teased. "A one-night stand that lasted fifteen years, huh?"

"I guess so." She smiled.

"What about you, Ingrid?"

Ingrid crossed her arms. Some days she really did feel like the world's oldest virgin. "A lady never tells." She shook her head at her colleagues and excused herself to the restroom. Caitlin followed her.

At the washbasins, Caitlin suddenly blurted, "I swear, it's so weird—the whole time I was sure he was always here to see you." She ran the tap and washed her hands. "He asked about you constantly."

Ingrid looked up with a start. "Really?"

"Yeah. What kind of books you liked to read. What kind of work you did with those drawings. I thought he had a crush on you . . ." Caitlin pressed her lips together tightly to blot her lipstick. "But it turns out he kept talking about you because he was so nervous because he was talking to *me*! Isn't that funny?"

Hilarious. Ingrid slammed the bathroom door and went back out to the main desk. The detective, the subject of all the gossip in the backroom, looked up from the book he was reading. He placed the book on the table. J. J. Ramsey Baker's opus, the thousand-page doorstop that Ingrid could not get anyone to borrow and read.

"Did you like it?" she asked sweetly.

Matt Noble thought for a moment. "It was . . . interesting but not really my sort of thing."

"What kind of books do you like, then?" Ingrid asked a bit defensively.

"I don't know . . ." He shrugged. She was right, she thought, pleased. He wasn't much of a reader, just a library lurker. He was probably one of those weirdos who liked to nap in the carrels.

"Well, what's your favorite book?" she asked, feeling confident that he would not be able to name one, or if he did, it would be something like . . .

"*To Kill a Mockingbird.*"

"Really?" Ingrid asked, taken off guard. "That's my favorite book, too." But was he just saying that? Or was it something Caitlin had told him? But when did she ever discuss *Mockingbird* with Caitlin? Caitlin didn't like to read. She spent her free time updating her online profile's status.

"Really." Matt smiled, and for a moment he looked a little like Atticus Finch, or maybe Gregory Peck playing Atticus Finch, if Gregory Peck had light brown hair and freckles and blue eyes. He held her gaze for a moment, and it looked as if he were going to say something more when Caitlin finally appeared, looking radiant in her white dress. "Matthew!"

He turned away from Ingrid and kissed Caitlin on the cheek while the two of them embraced. It was only then that Ingrid saw he was holding a picnic basket, a bottle of wine and a baguette poking out of the side.

Tabitha and Hudson followed behind. "All clear, boss lady," Tabitha said, meaning the library was empty. Ingrid turned off the main lights and set the alarm, and the group walked out of the building together. It was warm but breezy, and the night glowed; it would be light until late. A perfect summer evening for listening to music. Ingrid felt a pang.

"Hey, you want a ride to the concert?" Caitlin asked as Ingrid made her way to her bicycle. "Ingrid goes every year with her family," she explained to her date.

"No, it's okay—they can't make it this year. I think I should just go home," Ingrid said, as Tabitha waved good-bye.

"Oh, well, come with us then!" Caitlin offered.

"I couldn't . . . I don't want to crash . . ." Ingrid said, her cheeks beginning to burn again; if this kept up she would get a tan. If there was one thing she did not want to do, it was become a third wheel on a romantic date.

But for some reason Caitlin would not take no for an answer. "Not at all. Matt won't mind. Right, Matt?" He shook his head and smiled at Ingrid. "Not at all. Join us, please. I packed enough cheese to feed a cow."

Hudson unlocked his bike and began to wheel it away when Caitlin pounced on him as well. "We could make it a foursome! Hudson, come to the opera with me and Matt and Ingrid—she needs a date!" There seemed to be no dissuading Caitlin, and Ingrid felt helpless to resist.

Hudson looked at Ingrid questioningly. He had offered to take her that morning when she mentioned that her family had bailed, but she had declined, and Ingrid hoped her friend would not mention it. Thankfully, Hudson rose to the occasion. "Wagner's so dreary. I prefer Puccini. But sure."

THE ORCHESTRA HAD SET UP on a small stage in a grassy field a few miles from the beach. There was already a huge crowd waiting. They found an empty spot between two groups of opera devotees who were toasting the evening with wine in plastic glasses, balloons bobbing in the air as signposts to pinpoint their location for stragglers or lest anyone get lost on the way back from the restrooms. The sun began to set over the horizon, bathing the scene in a warm, orange light, and then the music began to play. It made for a very pretty scene, but Ingrid could not find any beauty in it.

Caitlin snuggled next to Matt the entire evening, and when

the two of them weren't nuzzling they were kissing. Ingrid thought she might burn all her Wagner records by the end of the night; she felt sick to her stomach. Her wonderful library was going to be razed to make room for condominiums, and the guy she liked had ended up with someone else. She promised herself she would get over Matt Noble somehow. Even if she had to take one of Freya's bitter-tasting antidotes to do so.

chapter twenty

Darkness Visible

∿

The Alvarezes had invited Joanna to celebrate the Fourth of July with them. On Friday night, after attending their festive barbecue, she walked along the shore back to the main house. Regardless of what happened the last time she had taken a long walk, Joanna still kept to the habit. She took a brisk turn around the neighborhood, to refresh the spirit and ruminate on the vagaries of the day, not to mention to try to walk off those extra calories brought on by that second slice of Gracella's red velvet cake. It had been a nice party, and Joanna had been glad for the company and the chance to catch up with her friends and neighbors. Several of them had heard about the miracle she had performed for Lionel Horning, and had asked if she would look into their ailing relatives. Joanna had promised to do so as soon as she could, though she cautioned that Lionel was a very special case.

The three Beauchamp women were getting quite a reputation in town lately for their abilities to do what others could not. Joanna wondered what the Council would make of that. So far, there had been no word from the powers-that-be; either they were choosing to ignore the Beauchamps' actions or they were still contemplating a response. In either event, the bravado she had displayed the other week was starting to thin. She was not frightened of the Council exactly, but she was anxious to see what they would do. There was no way to predict how they would react. She wished the oracle would come down and deal with them already and get it over with—punishment, reprimand, whatever. It was too hard to live with the uncertainty.

She was glad to find that after a few blocks Gilly had caught up with her, the raven flapping her wings silently. The two of them, witch and familiar, meandered through a well-worn path, down to the shoreline, past the great houses that overlooked the sea. Joanna was about to turn back toward home when the raven began to fly toward the footbridge that led to Gardiners Island.

"You want to go there? Why?"

Gilly regarded her keenly. *You need to see this.*

"Tonight?"

Come. You've put it off too long already.

"You're right, you're right as usual. I guess now is as good a time as any."

STRANGE THINGS WERE HAPPENING in town; she couldn't deny it anymore. Joanna's thoughts drifted to the dead birds, the silvery toxin that had polluted their ocean, as well as the grassy menace that had tried to strangle her the other evening. Ever since she had raised Lionel Horning from the dead Joanna had been especially worried. What was that silver spiderweb that had surrounded his soul? She had never seen anything like it before. Had she made a mistake in bringing him back from the Dead's Kingdom? But she had resurrected souls before and it was not such an unusual occurrence. Sometimes resurrection happened naturally. Humans called them "near-death experiences" when they came back to report that they had seen themselves floating over their bodies, or caught a glimpse of the white light at the end of the tunnel. Death was just the beginning of a journey that everyone took at some point.

Souls that had been taken by Death were not shrouded in a silver mist, they shone with a rainbow of colors. Joanna had chalked it up to the fact that she had not visited the world of the Dead in a very long time. Perhaps they had redecorated? She was being facetious and Gilly chided her for it, nipping her cheek and cawing. Joanna followed the bird's lead on the bridge. Fair Haven shone brightly in the darkness, lighting their way. By the end of the summer her daughter would be mistress to the house and the island, just as planned. But even if everything seemed to be going along well, the wedding date looming (Freya had even agreed to wear white), Joanna still felt a twinge of unease, which she couldn't explain, since everything was happening just as Ingrid had predicted.

"Let's be quiet now, won't we, Gilly? Make sure no one sees us?" she asked as they picked their way stealthily down the bridge toward the deserted beach. There were odd-looking piles of driftwood all around, but when Joanna came closer she saw they were not ocean detritus. The beach was littered with the bodies of dead ospreys. Hundreds of them, a thick, viscous sludge over their feathers, their beaks burned. They looked exactly like the birds she had seen dead on her beach earlier that summer. So. She was right, then. The birds had been a premonition, an omen, a warning. She wanted to tell her daughters I told you so, even though being right was shallow consolation. Her heart broke to see so much death all around. She could bring their souls back, but it was futile since their bodies were beyond repair.

Why had no one said anything? She looked over at Fair Haven, at the house that held the foundation of the seam that protected the town from the twilight world of the glom. Joanna had been there when it was first built; it was always meant to be empty. She was surprised when the Gardiners arrived. Perhaps there was more to their appearance than she'd imagined?

Joanna noticed the immense sand dunes that surrounded the house. She could not recall seeing such large ridges on Gardiners Island before. As she passed by them, she had the distinct feeling of being watched. The dunes were like little mountains of men, hillocks with eyes and strange noses; when she brushed against one it felt more like granite than sand. She squinted into the far horizon. Then she saw it. The silvery spot in the ocean had moved. It lapped about the shores of Gardiners Island, surrounding it in a dark perimeter.

She reached into her pocket and put on her gloves, a pair of nice, thick leather gloves that kept her hands warm in the winter, and knelt by the lapping waves. She had to see what was in the water.

The raven croaked a warning and Joanna soothed her pet. "Don't worry, these gloves are made from serpent-skin—nothing will penetrate." The gray-haired witch knelt down on the slippery rocks and dipped her finger in the black water.

Joanna rubbed her fingers and brought them to the light. The scientists still had no explanation for the explosion, nor had they managed to identify the toxic material that had seeped into the ocean waters. The townspeople had been advised to continue to refrain from fishing, swimming, and eating any local seafood. Worse, no one could tell the residents how they planned to clean the ocean or what could be done about it. No one was sure what it *was*.

She wiped her fingers together, assessing the liquid between them. It looked and felt slippery, but when she pressed a little further, she discovered there was something more to it. It was grainy and brittle, a hard, transparent crystal. Joanna felt a deep queasiness inside her soul. This was very bad. Whatever it was, she understood now why she had avoided dealing with it for as long as she could—had tried not to dwell on the broken seam boundaries, the gray darkness, the feeling of despair and anxiety that had settled into town. She remembered what Ingrid had told her: that the women of North Hampton were finding themselves barren, and a number of animals had died suddenly with no apparent cause.

Joanna lifted her wand. The containment spell would not hold for long. It would stop the poison from spreading but only for a short period of time. She could not meet this unknown danger alone; this was beyond her powers or understanding, and she knew immediately she would have to get help. Reinforcements. She and her daughters could not meet this threat alone. She removed her gloves and threw them in the water. Already there was a small hole right on the fingertip where she had held the dark crystal.

chapter twenty-one

The Only Way to Avoid
Temptation . . .

ع

The Friday night of the Fourth of July weekend, with the waters still off-limits, tourists had practically disappeared from the town, but the locals were still going to celebrate. At the North Inn Bar, Bon Jovi was blasting, and even if it was nowhere near midnight there were already a bunch of girls dancing on tables, camisole straps falling from their shoulders, their jeans loose and low on their waists.

As usual, Bran was out of town, and this would be their longest separation yet, as he was traveling through Southeast Asia this time with a large group of donors. She thought she would be used to it by now, and chided herself for being so weak.

To make herself feel better, Freya turned up the volume even louder, just as Killian Gardiner walked into the bar. She tried not to tense up, but felt her skin blush just at the sight of him and the flash of his sexual history, seeing a vision of herself in his arms as he kissed her down the entire length of her naked body. Yet it was firmly in the past, and as long as she kept her distance that was how it would remain. No matter how many dreams she had about him. He could fantasize about her all he wanted, he could replay that bathroom scene over and over again until the world ended, but nothing would ever happen between them again, she would see to that.

"Hey," he said, sliding over and taking a seat right in front. How did that happen? She was sure every seat had been taken, but at his appearance the crowd had parted like the rivers of the Nile.

"Killian," she said curtly. "I told you to leave me alone."

"I wanted to see you. Besides, Bran's away now. The coast is clear." Killian smiled. He picked up the laminated menu with the list of magical cocktails. "Love the hearts—very cute."

It had been Sal's corny idea to add the hearts. Freya wished she hadn't allowed him to talk her into it, but she hadn't wanted to hurt her boss's feelings.

She watched Killian read the menu, a sardonic smile on his face, wishing he was anywhere else but here tonight. She just did not need the aggravation. The North Inn crowd wasn't Bran's group of horsey socialites, but it was still a small town and tongues would wag if they appeared too friendly or intimate.

"Excuse me? Miss?"

"Hold on," Freya told him. She turned to her customer, a little brown wren of a girl who was studying the list of cocktails as if she were memorizing it for a final. "What can I get you?" she asked.

"Umm . . . I don't know . . ." Molly Lancaster was a jumpy little thing, a summer intern at city hall, a recent college graduate. Freya caught hints of a failed love affair, the usual teenage sexting of digital courtship. "I'd like *Irresistible*, please," Molly finally whispered.

"Make me one, too," Killian teased, flicking the menu back on the table.

Freya ignored him and began to mix Molly's drink. She kept the flowering cattails bunched in a glass jar, on a lower shelf; she removed them and began to crush the spikes with a pestle.

"Here, let me help you with that," Killian said, walking behind the counter so he could stand next to her and leaning forward so that she could feel his hot breath on her neck.

"Killian, please. Get back to the other side. Go on, now."

"But you're shorthanded," Killian said, nodding to a guy waving a twenty-dollar bill. He quickly served up the asked-for pint, made change, and slammed the cash register with a bang. "C'mon, let me."

It did seem like a good idea; the bar was five deep and everyone was waiting. Sal wouldn't mind, and Kristy had called in sick. Freya sighed. She could use the extra hand.

"So what else are you putting in there?" Killian asked, watching her measure the cattail powder into the cocktail shaker.

"Nothing. Just a jigger of lime juice, cherries, and a whole lot of vodka."

"Seems rather harmless; hard to believe something like that could turn that little mouse back there into Marilyn Monroe."

"I don't put all my ingredients on the menu," she said, reaching for another one of the secret black jars she kept in the under-the-counter refrigerator, and began to add a few drops of each into the cocktail: aster, maidenhair, vetiver root. She liked having Killian's eyes on her, his intent attention as he watched her work, and began to show off a little. She pulled out a small amber bottle containing grains of paradise, minuscule seeds full of potent magic, and shook a sprinkling of them into the mixture. The potion turned a deep vermillion with a flash. The air fizzed with smoke, carrying the heady scent of vanilla and honey.

"That smells almost as delicious as you do," Killian murmured, nuzzling her neck, his hand sneaking around her waist.

"Hey!" she protested, twisting away from him, but not quite making such a huge effort. "Hands to yourself! And you have customers—you're here to help me, remember?" she said, as she poured out the cocktail into a martini glass. Had she already put in the vetiver root? She couldn't remember and added just a little more just to make sure.

She handed the martini glass full of frothy purple liquid to Molly. "Here you go. One Irresistible," she said curtly.

Killian proved adept at bartending, which shouldn't have been a surprise. They worked side by side, slinging drinks, crushing ice, keeping the party going, the energy high. "Come on, now, you know you've missed me," he said in between serving up a tray of shots for a rowdy group of ladies. "Oh, the silent treatment, is it?" he sighed, when she did not respond. "You can't still be mad at me for what happened the night of your engagement, are you? You are? How boring of you. It's not like you ever came to see me on the boat."

Freya had heard enough. "Killian!"

"Yes, love?"

"Please."

"Please what?"

"Please leave me alone."

"No."

"No?"

Their eyes met, and it was just like the engagement party all over again. There was no denying the powerful attraction she felt toward Killian. It felt just as strong as her love for Bran. As if an invisible force was pushing her toward him. When she thought of Bran, her heart died a little in her chest. She had tried. She had tried so very hard to resist. She had been so very good for so long.

Killian bent his head toward hers, his lips brushing her cheek, but at the last moment she turned away from him and ran to the other side of the bar, her heart pounding in her chest. She turned up the volume on the jukebox. Maybe if she made the music loud enough she could drown out her confused whirl of emotions.

"You don't have to hide from me," he said, finding her a few minutes later in the walk-in pantry where Sal kept the supplies.

"I won't bite, I promise. Hand me that bottle of maraschino cherries."

She shrugged and threw up her hands, as if to give up, and handed it to him. His fingers brushed her skin and she felt the fire between them begin to smolder; she could not look at him without seeing his want and his need all over his beautiful elfin face.

"What are you doing?" she asked, as he put aside the bottle and put his arms around her instead.

"You know what I'm doing." He began to kiss her and push his body against hers, and the heat between them consumed her. . . . What was she doing. . . . Why was she doing it? . . . Why couldn't she stop? Why couldn't she offer even one word of protest?

"Freya," he sighed. His voice was low and musical, playing her like a flute. Then he cupped her face in his hands and they began to kiss. He kissed her all over her face and neck, and they pressed against each other. Their kisses were long and soft, wet and searching; she could feel his excitement growing and she felt as if she were melting underneath his tongue.

This is the beginning of the end, she thought. The first time had been a mistake, a rash, impulsive act by a silly young girl. This time she should know better . . . and yet she had still succumbed. Freya returned his kisses eagerly, and fell headfirst into the abyss.

chapter twenty-two

The Long Road Home

⌒⌒

When it came down to it, one could not meet danger alone, no matter how strong was one's courage. When Joanna returned to the house, she repaired to her bedroom and immediately began to pack. She had no idea where this trip would take her, or how long it would take. Only that she had very little time, and she hoped that after all these years, he would agree to help her. They had a responsibility to this world, after all, those of them who were stuck on this side of the bridge.

Joanna ruminated on their long life here. It hurt her to admit, but the Beauchamps, for all their pride and their history and their magic, had nothing to show for themselves except a broken home, with a son in jail. For all her taste and style and obsession with home improvement and her "good" jewelry (she was especially proud of a pair of small but rare pearl earrings that she wore on special occasions), she was essentially a failure at all the important things. She had failed her son, and she had failed her husband. She could not save her boy back when the world was young, and she had faulted her husband for doing the same when it came to their daughters. It was a sorry business, but at least she was going to do something about it now. She could repair at least one part of it.

"Mom? What are you doing? Are you leaving?" Ingrid blinked

without her glasses. She wore a white peignoir and her blond hair fell to her shoulders. She looked years younger, and Joanna wished she would wear her hair down more often; Ingrid looked so much prettier and softer that way.

"Just for a little while," she replied, folding a sweater and stuffing it into her carpetbag.

"You didn't answer my first question," Ingrid pointed out.

"It's safer for everyone if you don't know where I'm headed," Joanna replied, slipping her ivory wand into the pocket of her trenchcoat. She hoped to spare her girls the pain should she fail in her quest. It was better if they did not know what she was trying to do. She knew how much they missed him and how much they wanted him back. Of course she knew. She knew what she had done to the family, the irreparable line she had drawn; she had broken them in two, but there was no time for self-pity right then. There was no changing the past. "How was the Wagner yesterday?" she asked instead.

"Oh . . ." Ingrid shook her shoulders. Her older daughter, Joanna realized, was desperately, terribly unhappy about something. She wished she knew how to comfort her, but Joanna was not that kind of mother and Ingrid was not that kind of daughter. Their father had been the one who had been good at that sort of thing. The talking and the listening and the emotional support: it was their father they had turned to when their little hearts were broken or when they had happy news to share.

"Well . . . have a safe trip, wherever it is you're going," Ingrid mumbled.

"Take care, dear," Joanna said, giving her daughter a close hug. "Watch out for Tyler, will you?" She couldn't bear to say goodbye to the boy and so she had done the cowardly thing, slipping out in the middle of the night because it would be too painful to have a long and drawn-out farewell. No matter; with luck she would be back soon. She was only leaving to keep the town and everyone in it safe.

DAN JERRODS'S FAMILY ran the only taxi service in town, and he was waiting for her in front of the house with the car, an old Buick with bucket seats that smelled like a cigar store. She climbed in the front seat and placed her battered old valise on her lap and Gilly's case on the floor. "Where to, Miss Joanna?" he asked.

"Train station, please, Dan, and hurry."

"Sure thing."

"How are things?" she asked. She liked Dan, one of the nice young men in town who was always willing to lend a hand with their storm windows every winter. Dan gripped the steering wheel tightly until his knuckles were almost white. "Not too good at the moment, Miss Joanna. Amanda's in the hospital," he said. "Sorry to bend your ear about this. I'm just a little worried about her."

"Not at all. I'm sorry to hear that—what happened? Is there anything I can do to help?"

"It's some kind of virus she hasn't been able to kick," he said. "The doctors said they've seen this sort of thing: it's been going around and she should get better soon, but she's on a respirator right now."

"I'll look in on her when I get back," Joanna promised, giving Dan's arm a sympathetic squeeze. "She's in good hands, Dan. The doctors won't fail her."

North Hampton did not have a stop on the Long Island Rail Road so they drove to the nearest stop in Montauk. The station was deserted since it was close to midnight, and Joanna had to reassure Dan that she would be perfectly fine waiting on the platform alone.

Finally the express from New York arrived. She'd board it on its way back to the city, where she'd switch to Metro-North to get to New Haven. She waited for the crowd to disembark, and noticed a young, good-looking couple among them. They were arguing. The girl was annoyed and the boy was soothing her. No, she was wrong, Joanna realized, from their conversation it was clear they were not a couple, she thought, only friends.

"This is such a waste of time," the girl said. "We should go back to Cairo instead. I doubt I'll even find the town—there's some kind of protection spell around it."

"You said yourself that they might know something. The old ones, to help you. Besides, we've already tried once and failed; there's nothing to do in Egypt if we don't get this information. Plus, I have a feeling we'll get lucky—things are never as hopeless as they seem to be," the boy said.

"What are you looking at?" the girl said suddenly, addressing Joanna.

Joanna recoiled—until now she had not noticed that there was something different about the girl. She had not been in the presence of the Fallen in a long time.

The girl glared at her contemptuously, as if understanding that the old witch knew what she was, and flashed her fangs at her.

Arrogant little brat. Joanna frowned. Of all the things that were an insult to the restriction she lived under, the fact that the Fallen were allowed to use their supernatural abilities stung the hardest. She wondered idly what had brought the vampire girl and her human companion to North Hampton, because of course that was the town they were looking for. They did not look like they were here to celebrate the holiday weekend. The girl was wrong: it wasn't a protection spell; those were too easy to undo. Instead, when they had settled North Hampton all those long years ago, they had chosen to build in one of the few disoriented pockets that resulted from the collapse of the bridge. North Hampton was located in a place in the universe that was neither here nor there, exactly, just slightly outside of time, which was why it was located so close to the seam.

The girl continued to glare at Joanna until the boy grabbed her by the arm and steered her to the street. "Mimi! C'mon," the boy said. "Sorry about my friend, she's not feeling well," he apologized, and they walked away.

JOANNA SIGHED and walked up the steps to board the train. She had wanted to fly but she had to be more careful this time. It would not do to have another UFO sighting in the area. She found a seat in the back, and stored her carpetbag in the overheard. There was no one else in the car and she was glad to be able to spread out on several seats to be more comfortable. She prepared herself for a long train ride in the dark.

After centuries of separation, Joanna Beauchamp was off to see her husband.

chapter twenty-three

Missing

~~~

Monday after the Fourth of July holiday was like waking up from a three-day hangover. Freya opened the bar that afternoon, a bit apprehensive to see what lay in store, how bad the damage had been. She turned the key in the lock and pushed the door open, inhaling the familiar sweet stench of the bar: sweat and cigarettes and spilled alcohol. Friday night had been one of the wildest nights the North Inn had ever experienced, and for many nights and summers after, those who had been there that evening would talk about what happened that night: how the air had cracked with heat and fire; how the music seeped right into your soul, into your limbs; how the drinks were luscious and addictive; how everyone had seemed just a bit out of control. The party had continued to rage, spilling into Saturday and Sunday, with no rest or respite; she had kept the bar open nonstop the entire weekend, the music growing ever louder, the crowd rowdy to the point of obnoxious. It had been a carnival, a circus, and a festival rolled into one.

She was emotionally and physically exhausted, not just from the carousing and the work but from spending the entire three days in the company of Killian Gardiner, neither of them leaving to eat or sleep, catching catnaps in the back while the other tended to the customers. It did not matter that they were soon to be family, that she was to be his brother's wife, that there was a wedding on the horizon—none of it mattered, only heat and desire and *now*. There was no tomorrow. There was only Killian, and Freya was vulnerable to his every wish and command.

He had even offered to help her clean up on Monday morning but she had rebuffed him. She needed a few days to herself. On the way to the North Inn she had called Bran, but his cell did not pick up. She kept dialing it anyway, listening to his message, wanting to hear his voice to bring her back to earth.

She did not know how she felt about anything or anyone. She felt as if she were being pulled in two directions, and if she was so sure once of Bran and their love for each other, she was now equally sure that she could not live without Killian either. What was new? Freya had been the kind of girl who hopped into bed at the slightest invitation; in the past she had many lovers of both sexes, and was constantly in the throes of infatuation. But sex was different, sex was easy—a physical release, a game, a bit of fun—a "shag," as the Brits liked to say. It didn't mean anything. Love was something else, and it was difficult. She was not prepared to feel this way for two men and did not want to think about what it meant. She had been so sure about her feelings for Bran, but now there was Killian, who had become very dear to her in a short period of time.

Thankfully, the bar didn't look too worse for wear. Freya began by picking up all the discarded brassieres from the floor and placing them in the lost and found box. Sal had proposed nailing them all to the wall as trophies, but Freya thought that was just a little tacky and had talked him out of it. The bar backs had swept up most of the grime off the floor and run the dishwasher, taken out the garbage, and swept all the broken glass, so aside from righting a chair here and there, there wasn't too much for her to do. She was grateful. She began her cocktail prep: chopping up mint, squeezing lemons and limes, preparing the sugar water, replenishing the vodka in the freezer. Even on a Monday night the North Inn was sure to draw a crowd.

Freya was thankful to have something to do with her hands; it kept her busy and her mind off Killian. Already he had called several times on her cell but she had declined to answer. She had left him in his bed that morning, slipping out from under the sheets without even a note of explanation. Such a cliché, the morning-after sneak-out of shame.

"We're not open yet, sorry," Freya called, as she heard the bar's front door open and the bell signal the arrival of a customer.

A woman in black walked into the bar. She was tall and striking, with her blond hair pulled up in a tight ponytail. Her face was ageless and serene. "Are you Freya Beauchamp?"

"Yes, I am, who's asking?" she asked.

"I was told I would find Killian Gardiner here," the woman said, without answering her question, which Freya found a tad impolite.

"He's not here right now," Freya said, continuing to wipe the counter.

"Do you know where I might find him?"

Freya hesitated, wondering if she should be truthful, but there was no reason to lie. "He's probably down at his boat. It's docked at Gardiners Island, on the far left side of the house. You can't miss it."

"Thank you."

Freya remembered what Bran had told her of Killian's peripatetic life and how Ingrid heard that he had left a trail of broken hearts behind him. And yet the stern stranger did not look like an aggrieved ex-girlfriend; instead she had the slightly formal air of those involved in law enforcement. Was Killian in some sort of trouble? He didn't seem to be hiding anything. When she asked him about the rumors surrounding his past, he laughed and told her that people liked to tell stories, and that none of them were true.

A few minutes later the front door opened again and a young girl entered. "We're closed, sorry. Come back in an hour or so?" Freya asked, looking up from her chopping board.

"I don't want a drink," the girl said with a frown.

"Good enough, since we're not open yet." Freya smiled. She looked up and took note of the girl's sexual history as it flashed before her eyes: twenty-two-year-old virgin. A few chaste kisses and several unrequited crushes; it reminded Freya a little of her sister's limited experience in that department.

"I'm looking for my roommate."

Freya looked around at the empty bar doubtfully. "And you're looking for her . . . *here*?"

"She said she was going to be here. Friday night," the girl said stubbornly.

"That's three days ago."

"Yeah. I know." The girl sighed. "I mean, she's missing. I'm Pam, by the way."

Pam showed her a photo of a brown-haired girl wearing large glasses. It was the little brown wren, the same girl who had taken the Irresistible potion on Friday night. Freya squinted her eyes at the picture. "I remember her. Molly, right?"

"Yeah. She never came home on the Fourth. She's an adult, so the police told me I had to wait forty-eight hours before they could file a report. They think she just spent the weekend with some guy. But I swear that's not the case. I'm really worried. She's never done anything like this before."

Freya frowned, but past experience told her Pam was jumping to conclusions. With that potion, Molly definitely got lucky on Friday night. She was probably out having brunch with her new love right now. Freya thought of how she herself had spent the weekend—a blur of drinking, working, and Killian. The three days had gone by so fast, and no one knew where *she* was either; it wasn't like she'd left Ingrid or Joanna a message. (Not that either would panic, since Freya came and went as she pleased.)

"She usually calls to let me know where she is," Pam said stubbornly. "I'm worried about her."

Freya remembered Molly that night, dancing on a table, belting the lyrics to "You Shook Me All Night Long," her glasses crushed beneath her feet, her hair wild and loose, swinging her body to the beat of the music, while a group of college boys, red-cheeked and jolly, shouted themselves hoarse in appreciation. Molly had looked as if she were having the time of her life. Later Freya had seen Molly making out in the back with one of the boys, the two of them wrapped around each other so tightly it was hard to see where one ended and the other began.

There was nothing to worry about. Pam might not understand since she had never experienced it: how time sped up and slowed down in a lover's arms, how daily life faded away and everything suddenly revolved around being with one person for as long as possible. Time did not exist where love and lust were concerned. Still, it was always best to be careful.

Freya took the photograph. "I'll ask around. See if anyone knows any of those boys she was with that night. But I'm sure Molly's fine. She'll probably get back this afternoon."

chapter twenty-four

Angel of Death

W hen Ingrid arrived at work on Monday morning, in the stack of interoffice mail she found a memo from the mayor's office informing her that due to limited funds, the city council had cut the library budget again, which meant cutting more hours from the schedule. They were running on fumes as is. The mayor had included a personal note asking for her support of the plan to sell the library during the council meeting at the end of the summer. His smugness and condescension were infuriating. She balled up the letter and threw it across the room.

It was an awful way to begin what was already an awful day; the only redeeming factor was the fact that Caitlin had called in sick, so at least she would not have to hear every excruciating detail about Caitlin and Matt's night of love. While she did not have Freya's gift for affecting her surroundings, her coworkers understood enough to steer clear of her that day. She was not in the mood to perform her usual witchy duties either, and told Hudson to let everyone know to come back tomorrow instead.

Ingrid busied herself with steaming and studying the Gardiner prints and communicating with her source, whom she had sent scans of each page for review. She had gone through the whole set and found dozens of those scroll-like key tags; they were everywhere in the entire plan, and their meaning was still a mystery. Just to be sure, she had consulted one of the architects who frequented the library to make sure it wasn't a design key they had used in the past. He had confirmed that he had never seen anything like it before.

She rolled up the piece of paper and put it aside for now. From the front office, she heard a cold, clear female voice say, "I'm sorry but I insist that she see me."

A few minutes later, when Hudson walked into her office, his face was vacant, his eyes glazed. "You have to make time for her," he said in a flat voice. He left the room and a beautiful blond girl let herself inside, walking with a confidence and a carriage that immediately put Ingrid on the defensive.

Her visitor was about eighteen years old, with hard green eyes and long thick platinum hair that fell down her back. She smelled of power and pampering and the cushion of wealth that surrounded those who were accustomed to the most lavish privilege. Ingrid noticed immediately that there was something more to this girl. She was one of the Fallen. A Blue Blood, an immortal vampire, one of the lost children of the Almighty.

"You're not from here," Ingrid said sharply. "And I don't like my friends to be played with like toys. Your people might have been granted exemption to practice your brand of sorcery but I won't have it in my library, especially if you're looking for help with your cause. It's a hopeless one, if you ask me."

"Relax, *Erda*, I'm not here for redemption," the girl said, taking a seat across from her desk and looking around contemptuously at the shabby surroundings.

"Good, because that's certainly out of our jurisdiction." Ingrid frowned, annoyed that she had been called by her true immortal name. The Beauchamps hardly used their real names anymore; they had gone out of fashion and it would draw too much attention, something the Council had warned them not to do. Of course,

Freya had stubbornly kept her name all these long years, which was just as well since it was pretty, like everything else about her sister.

"And so what can I do for you, Madeleine Force?" Ingrid refused to do the same and addressed the child by the name given the vampire in her heavenly past. They were in North Hampton now, in the early twenty-first century. None of that mattered anymore.

The girl settled back on the chair and crossed her tanned legs. "You know who I am." She looked around with a smug air. "Interesting choice of environment, the armpit of the Hamptons. But this isn't really the Hamptons, is it? Clever use of a disorienting space. Lucky I had a friend who can sniff them out somehow. Took us a while but we found this sad excuse of a town. That honky-tonk bar at our hotel was quite the scene on Friday night. You should tell your sister to cool it down a bit. I don't mind getting spilled on once, but three times in one evening is too much even for my hardworking dry cleaner."

Ingrid bristled. "What do you want, Mimi? That is what you're called these days, isn't it? I read the tabloids."

"I want the same thing you're doling out to the legions of unworthy. Help." Mimi lost her cool façade for a bit, and her face became grave as she tugged the hem of her skirt over her knee.

"What makes you think I would help you? The treaty between our kind doesn't cover that sort of thing, you know that. Plus, I'm bound by our restriction, if you know your history." Ingrid bristled.

"Oh, I don't need your silly magic. Oliver had to talk me into meeting you, even. Apparently he's met your sister before. Not that she remembered him last night, the sad sap. He was so disappointed." She leaned over the desk and drummed her manicured fingernails in expectation.

Ingrid steeled a desire to swat her hand away. "So if you don't need my magic, what are you here for?"

"I need to get a soul out of the Underworld. Trapped below the seventh circle by a *subvertio*. I've already tried and failed once before. I don't mean to let it happen again."

"You know the rules. Once the soul has been bound to Helda beyond the seventh, it is hers forever." Ingrid sniffed. "You're wasting your time; it's impossible. Those are the laws of the universe."

"But there's got to be a way. A barter, an exchange, something," Mimi said, desperation creeping into her voice. "I thought you might know. You guys have been around the longest."

The witch sighed. The Fallen and their problems did not concern her. But Ingrid knew that if she did not get rid of this pesky vampire Mimi was likely to use her powers in the glom to cause disturbance and havoc around town—if she hadn't already. Ingrid had her staff to worry about, not to mention the rest of the community. Sure, the rebel angels had been cast out of Paradise, but they had been practically given mid-world: they ran the whole show down here, while Ingrid's people had been banished to the fringes. Mimi Force had no business toying with the Kingdom of the Dead.

"Please, Erda. I'm begging," Mimi said, tears suddenly springing to her eyes. "I love him. I can't lose Kingsley. If you have anything to share, anything that can help . . . I would be in your debt forever."

Ingrid sighed. "Fine. There is a way to recover a soul beyond the *subvertio*. The Orpheus Amendment. Do you know it?"

"I thought that was just a myth," Mimi scoffed.

"Sweetie, *you're* a myth yourself," Ingrid snapped. "Helda made an exception once, and since then the Orpheus Amendment has stood. Same rules apply. One look back and it's over."

"That's it?"

"That's it."

"I'll take that risk," Mimi said. She stood up and shook Ingrid's hand. "Thank you."

"Oh, and one more thing I forgot to tell you. The Orpheus Amendment demands a sacrifice in payment for the release of a soul," Ingrid said.

"A soul for a soul," Mimi nodded, looking sly. "Don't worry, I was already aware of that part of it. I would never descend into Hell unprepared."

Ingrid hoped she had not made a mistake in helping the young vampire. The Fallen could be a dangerous enemy and she was glad to see her go. In the end Mimi Force had wanted the same thing from Ingrid that her human counterparts did: a way out of an impossible situation. Ingrid could only point in the right direction. The rest was up to them.

chapter twenty-five

Finger-Pointing

‿ᴗ‿

Aside from the recent death of the socialite and Bill Thatcher's bludgeoning, there had been no murders recorded in North Hampton since its settlement. Freya did not watch the news unless someone had the television set to a news channel, nor did she read the newspapers, so she did not know that Molly Lancaster was officially a missing person until Sal happened to mention to her the following week that the boys who were with Molly that night at the bar had been brought in for questioning by the district attorney.

"Wait—you're telling me they think those boys had something to do with Molly's disappearance?"

"Where have you been all week?" Sal scoffed, shaking the paper at her. He was better after his bout with what had turned out to be the flu, but his cheeks were still red and his eyes runny. He also seemed to have lost part of his good humor. When he returned to work he was short-tempered and easily annoyed.

Freya didn't answer and continued to mix coltsfoot and columbine together for a new concoction. Bran was still away; they had been able to speak to each other briefly the other evening, but the connection had been bad and all she heard was gurgling and hissing from the wire. He felt farther and farther away from her every day. She had tried hard to avoid seeing Killian again, although he appeared in her dreams every night. If only she could see Bran again, but he would not return for a few more weeks.

She read the headline story: Derek Adam, Miles Ashleigh, Jock Pemberton, and Hollis Arthur had been brought in for questioning. Witnesses who were at the North Inn the night before the Fourth of July told the police that Molly acted out of character that evening, dancing wildly and "flirting with every boy in the place." She had left the bar with Derek in Jock's car with Miles and Hollis in the backseat. Through his lawyer, Derek declared that he and Molly had gone down to the beach to make out, but that he had left her there because she told him she had to meet someone else at the beach, a story that no one, including the reporter who intimated that the boys were lying to save their skins, was likely to believe. The boys ranged in age from nineteen to twenty-three years old, rich college kids whose families had deep North Hampton roots. The lead police investigator on the case, Matthew Noble, would not make any comment.

"Those poor boys," Freya murmured.

"Boys?" Sal huffed. "They're gonna fry. Who's going to believe they just left that girl down at that beach? Please, you know they killed her and hid the body. They're guilty."

Freya looked up. She hadn't realized she had spoken out loud and wondered why she felt sympathy for the suspects. Then she realized: she believed them. Molly had taken an Irresistible potion, a concoction that could never bring about any harm or violence to its taker. Freya had seen to that when she made it; it came built in with a powerful protection spell to make sure this sort of thing never happened. Whatever happened to Molly that evening had nothing to do with the love potion, which meant it had nothing to do with the boys she met at the bar.

She was certain the boys were telling the truth, that they didn't kill Molly. But how could she prove it?

She tried to recall whom she had seen at the bar that evening, if she had picked up anything, any sign of distress or intent, but she wasn't Ingrid, a seer, someone who could peer into a person's future, into their lifeline. If Ingrid had been there, would she have seen what type of darkness would soon claim Molly? But who knew if Molly was even in danger? She was an adult; what if she just decided to disappear on her own? It was possible. Could everyone just be jumping to conclusions?

"I think we better put these away for now," Sal said, picking up the laminated potions menu. He read the newspaper over her shoulder and pointed to the damning sentence in the middle of the paragraph, reading it aloud. "'The girls said that there must have been something in Molly's drink that made her so wild. Some kind of crazy potion.' Hear that, Freya? Some kind of crazy cocktail from the North Inn made her act slutty, they're saying. They'll come after us for sure."

"No, they won't." Freya shook her head, aghast. How could anyone believe that? Besides, how could anyone think a cocktail could lead to her disappearance? It was ridiculous. Wasn't it? She tried to remember what happened that night—she could picture every moment clearly, saw Killian enter the bar, snuggling with her a little too close behind the counter; she saw herself making the potion, Killian by her side. Could it be possible that she had put in too much vetiver root? And if she did, what of it? It wasn't a harmful herb; it was only there to enhance the drinker's desirability. It seemed highly unlikely that it could cause any harm. Of course, magic was unpredictable, and there was a possibility that something might have gone wrong. But she had seen nothing in the boys' spirits that night except for raucous enthusiasm for the evening's delights and the usual schoolboy excitement caused by the presence of pretty girls. If one of them was a killer she would have seen it. She *always* did. Except for Bill

Thatcher. No one had solved that particular murder yet and the police seemed to be as clueless as they had been when it happened. There was no hope for his wife, either. Maura's family was talking about pulling the plug.

All right. She had to try harder to remember. Who else had been at the bar on Friday night? It was all a blur; there was a blank haze over her memory, perhaps a side effect of the guilt she felt for cheating on Bran. She felt sick, like she wasn't herself. She should have paid attention. Maybe if she wasn't so busy making out with Killian all weekend she would have noticed something. Now Molly had disappeared and boys whom she had joked with and liked were under suspicion.

"You'll see. We should keep our heads low. Only a matter of time."

Freya felt a darkness settling into the room. "You think my cocktail killed her, Sal?"

"Course not," Sal sniffed. "I don't know what you put in those drinks, but they are potent. Lots of people been talking, mostly about how good they make them feel, how they've met the love of their lives in our little bar. But I think people here are going to want an answer. And those are rich boys. Their parents are going to find every scapegoat they can. You be careful, maybe take a few days off."

chapter twenty-six

The Worm Turns

～❧～

A week after Freya was encouraged to take an unwanted leave of absence, Ingrid was contemplating quitting her job altogether. And without it, what would she have? For Ingrid, if work was unbearable there was no reason to live. She never had much of a home life in the first place and she missed her sister's sparkling company. Before Freya met Bran, Ingrid could count on her sister for movie nights, the occasional dinner or two. But ever since the engagement Freya was hardly home, even with Bran away in the city or on trips so much. Ingrid wondered about that; she thought Freya would miss him more, but she had the same red cheeks, dreamy expression, and late nights whether he was in town or not. Maybe they were having a lot of . . . what did they call it? Phone sex? Ingrid shuddered. Lately Freya had seemed out of sorts and agitated, however, so maybe the separation was beginning to take a toll.

As for where Joanna had gone, Ingrid could not even hazard a guess. Her mother was somewhere her cell phone service did not reach apparently, since calls to Joanna went straight to voice mail. Ingrid could always use the underlayer to probe for her location, or maybe send Oscar to look for her, but Ingrid had a feeling her mother wanted her privacy.

Ingrid never felt lonely, not when she had so many books to

read and such good friends at the library, a job that she had looked forward to every morning for the past seven years. She knew that her mother believed that she was wasting her time, her skills, her intellect, her everything, working in some pokey small-town library, and that Freya thought it was all so incredibly boring. But to Ingrid, her library was her home; yet for the last several weeks she had been going to work with a heavy heart, and she wondered if maybe her mother and sister were right. If maybe it was time to quit. Practicing magic again had returned excitement and purpose to her life, but she did not have to do it in the library. She could set up her own clinic, a proper one, with an office, a schedule, and a receptionist. There were so many things she could do with her magic other than cure nightmares and help women conceive.

On a lighter note, since the Fourth of July, however, Ingrid had noticed there was less of that gray darkness in people's spirits. Maybe it was dissipating from the town; even that weird toxic sludge in the middle of the ocean had stopped moving, and the latest reports said it looked as if it were finally shrinking. Although the latest news reports said that a similar mass recently reappeared near the Alaskan coastline.

She parked her bike and chained it to her usual post. Hudson's bike was already in its place. The door was open, the lights were on, and everything was bright and orderly. "Good morning," she said, trying for cheerfulness as she walked to her desk.

"Morning." Hudson yawned.

"Hi, Ingrid." Tabitha smiled. She was only in her second month and enjoying every minute of it, even the wretched morning sickness and the inability to eat anything but tea and crackers and still look puffy.

There was nothing from Caitlin but stony silence. Ingrid ignored it, as she didn't much care what the latest drama was in that particular romance novel. For the past week Ingrid had had to endure Caitlin's prattle about how she and Matt were going away for a romantic weekend later that month, to a bed-and-breakfast in Martha's Vineyard. Caitlin had regaled Hudson and Tabitha with the details of her trousseau—lingerie, champagne, the works. Hudson had fun modeling the nipple covers, while Tabitha gave too-earnest pointers on the advantages of lubricant and other erotic accoutrements including a much-too-detailed description of various handcuffs, metal rings, and electronic devices. It was right about then that Ingrid had begun to question her commitment to the job. Either she would have to fire Caitlin or quit herself. But she could not take one more day of the entire office sending the girl off to romance nirvana with condom banners flying.

When Caitlin left the room, Ingrid texted Hudson.

<<what's wrong with her?>>

He swiveled around, a wicked grin on his face. He motioned to Tabitha to shut the door. "You haven't heard?" he whispered.

"Haven't heard what?" Ingrid asked.

"Romance weekend on Martha's Vineyard is off!"

"Pardon?"

"You left too early yesterday."

"Obviously."

Tabitha looked over her shoulder and filled her in. "Matt came by yesterday afternoon as usual. I saw them fighting outside. Then he drove off without her. I asked her what happened and she said it was over. He'd canceled the whole weekend because he had to work on that missing girl case, you know, Molly Lancaster. He said it wasn't working, anyway. He wasn't feeling it. He was sorry."

"Oh, dear!" Ingrid said.

"I know!"

"Poor Caitlin," Ingrid said, feeling a little sorry for the girl. Just a little. She knew it was difficult when someone you liked stopped liking you.

"Anyway, Caitlin thinks he's a liar. That there's someone else. You remember how the night of the concert was supposed to be his lucky night? Well, that's when he told her he wanted to wait until it was special. That's when he asked her to go to the Vineyard with him, but now that's off, too," Tabitha said.

"So . . . they haven't . . . ?" Ingrid craned forward.

"No!" Hudson interjected, looking disappointed. "Looks like the only one getting lucky in this office is me, since Tab is afraid of 'hurting the baby.' But now my Scott is withholding since I told him I didn't think he could quite pull off the male Capri pant."

"If you ask me, they were an odd match, anyway," Tabitha said, rubbing her belly, which was showing the tiniest little bump.

"Shhh—she's back!" Hudson warned. Ingrid pretended to be busy with a drawing and the other two went back to their computers.

SUDDENLY the day seemed so much brighter. The women who came to visit Ingrid at lunch were treated to a host of charms and spells that not only took care of their aches and pains but were sprinkled with a lightness, a joy, a little something extra that had been missing from her magic before. Her money-bag charms smelled like honeysuckle, her spells seemed to emit a golden sparkle, and even her knots were beautiful and perfect, each a work of art.

"Well, if you aren't little Mary Sunshine," Hudson teased. "This morning you looked like you were ready to drink hemlock."

"Shush," Ingrid said. "I have no idea what you're talking about." She tried to maintain a straight face as she returned to her desk. Her computer screen signaled the arrival of an instant message.

<<i think i know what these blueprints are showing & what the keys mean>>

<<?>>

<<but first i need u to do something for me>>

<<?>>

<<can you get to fair haven? inside the house?>>

Ingrid hesitated before typing in an answer. After thinking about it for a few minutes, she wrote, *yes*.

chapter twenty-seven

Heart Sick

୬୧

North Hampton was still reeling from the news of Molly Lancaster's disappearance when the mayor's office announced that he had failed to show up to work that Monday and could not be located. He had left his home in the middle of the night with no word to his wife or his staff. After the disaster of the oceanic earthquake and Molly's mysterious absence, an ill feeling began to grow around town; some began to whisper that North Hampton was cursed, that it was no longer the bucolic little town it once had been.

At home, watching the whole sad story play out in the news, Freya turned off the television and sat pensively for a few minutes. She had to pick up Tyler from preschool soon. She put on her coat and looked for her keys. First Molly Lancaster, now Mayor Hutchinson. What was going on? Things like this never happened in North Hampton before, unless you counted what happened to the Thatchers. Freya tried to recall the last time she had seen the mayor; he used to stop by the bar every once in a while but hadn't come by in a few weeks, most likely due to that fidelity knot that tied him to his home—not that Todd was the type to flirt with any of the girls at the North Inn. He was too concerned about his career to do something that stupid.

Freya was tired of moping about the house, and the news of

the mayor's disappearance depressed her. She had forgotten how boring life could be without the bar to attend to, without something to do, people to see, drinks to make. At least Ingrid seemed to have cheered up from whatever was making her grumpy for the past few weeks, which was good since Oscar could be irritable whenever his mistress was feeling out of sorts, and Freya didn't much like getting nipped by his sharp beak just because Ingrid had forgotten to buy his stash of Cheetos. The griffin liked them so much his beak was bound to turn orange one day.

The house was emptier than usual, as Joanna had yet to return from her trip. Her mother had left in something of a rush right after the holiday weekend. Ingrid had seen her off but explained that Joanna had not told her where she was going, only that they were allowed their wands again; although Freya had not found much use for hers. It was nice to have it back, however; she had forgotten how smooth it felt, how much more powerful she was with it in hand.

She drove to the school, and walked to the small cottage that housed the pre-K class. Tyler was playing with blocks and looked up balefully when he saw her. "Where's Lala?" he demanded, arms crossed.

"Come on, Ty, you know she's not back yet." The little boy felt Joanna's absence keenly. Yesterday he had thrown his arms around in a massive tantrum when she picked him up.

"Don't wanna go with you. Want Lala!"

"Oh, sweetie, come on," she said, trying not to lose her patience with the child. She was bored and frustrated as well, but she did not want to take it out on him. They walked to the gate and she put Tyler in his car seat, clicking the straps tightly around his chest.

"What can you do?" he asked suspiciously.

"What do you mean?"

"Lala can make my airplanes fly. For real," he said in an accusatory tone.

Freya knew Joanna was showing off her magic to the little boy, but it was still shocking to hear it mentioned so casually. Her mother didn't seem to follow any boundaries when it came to indulging him. Freya remembered her childhood well, and it did not include a plethora of baked goods and innumerable talking stuffed animals. Mostly she remembered her mother grousing about how difficult it was to raise children.

She looked around to make sure no one was looking their way. "Well, I can do this," she said, turning into a black cat. Then, in a blink, she was Freya again.

Tyler giggled, then he coughed. There was a dime-size dollop of phlegm in his hand, and Freya noticed the green tinge. When they arrived home, she asked Gracella if she noticed Tyler was coughing again. The housekeeper nodded. "The doctors are giving him another round of antibiotics. They said it should clear up in a week or two."

"He does seem all right, there's just that odd cough . . . ," Freya said, feeling the first whisper of fear. Joanna wasn't the only one in the household who loved the boy. "He'll be all right," she told Gracella, and she wondered whom she was trying to convince more, the boy's mother or herself.

BRAN CALLED later that evening. He apologized for being hard to get ahold of; he was traveling all over the place and time zone changes made communication difficult. "How's my girl?"

"Missing you," she said, feeling a tightness constrict in her chest. "When are you coming home?" *When will you return to me?*

"Soon, I promise." Where was he now? What town? What country? She couldn't keep track anymore. He was simply just "away." There was a long silence at the end of the line and Freya began to worry. "Bran, are you there?"

"Yes, sorry, I had to return a text. Madame wants to know if you have any thoughts about the wedding plans she sent over the other week," Bran said.

Freya had barely given the event a second thought, and it surprised her to realize it was happening; she had almost forgotten. Of course they would have the proper ceremony, a white dress, five hundred guests, an orchestra, the works. "Tell her she can do whatever she wants. The flowers, the food, the guests. As long as they invite my family and Sal and Kristy, of course. Whatever she wants."

"You don't care?" he asked. "That's a new one. For a bride, I mean."

She was going to be a bride. The word struck like a knife in her chest and twisted brutally. For a moment she could not speak.

"Hey, sweetheart, what's wrong? Are you crying?"

"No . . ." She shook her head even though he could not see. "No. It's nothing."

"Tell me . . . you can tell me anything, you know."

She shook her head and didn't speak. Tears began quietly streaming down her face now.

"You know I love you, no matter what," Bran said, his voice tight and nervous. "Whatever happens, I'll always love you, Freya. Always."

"I know," she whispered. "I love you, too."

She hung up the phone, her heart beating in her chest. Would Bran still love her, truly, if he knew what she was doing? What she had done? Would he love her the way she was? Could she ever be true to him? Monogamy was not in her nature, and she wondered why she had even agreed to this wedding, to this marriage.

The phone rang again and she picked it up, thinking it was Bran again to reassure her of his love.

"Freya." Killian's voice was husky and low. They had not spoken since their wild weekend together. "Did I do something wrong? You never return my calls. I miss you." Hearing his voice was like a balm to her broken heart. Maybe she was meant to be with Killian, but she would never know unless she did something about it. The thing was, she missed him, too.

Freya wiped her tears. "All right. I'll be right over."

She was tired of feeling guilty. Bran was far away. She knew he had work to do but she couldn't help holding it against him. Maybe things happened for a reason. Maybe they were already broken, even before Killian came onto the scene.

Because like everything that took place this summer with Bran and Killian, she felt as if she were part of a larger story, and the curious, reckless part of Freya—the one who drank too much and played with matches and broke a million hearts before breakfast—wanted to see how it would all play out in the end.

chapter twenty-eight

The Hidden Door

⌒⌒

Ingrid looked around the empty ballroom at Fair Haven and shook out her legs. Flying always gave her cramps, especially when she took Oscar's form. Like Freya with Siegfried, and Joanna with Gilly, Oscar was part of her, and she could turn into his shape at will. She did not do it often, only on occasions that demanded it. During Freya's engagement party she had noticed that the top windows to the ballroom were always left open. Now Ingrid had flown in through one of them before dawn, when everyone in the household was sure to be asleep. She could have taken a broom, but since Joanna had been spotted the other day Ingrid thought it would be more prudent if she assumed an animal-like shape. There were many ways for witches to travel, and like her brethren Ingrid preferred the more natural one: lifting into the air and rising to the heavens as her magic lessened gravity's hold on her core. They used the brooms to ground and center themselves, an anchor to the earth that no longer held them when they were flying.

She texted to her source.

<<i'm inside>>

<<good. you have the blueprints with you?>>

<<yes.>>

<<excellent, go to the ballroom. center tag. something's different about it.>>

He was right. There was something a little off about the center tag in the ballroom floor plan; the little diamond that pointed toward the walls in the room she was standing in was surrounded by that strange calligraphy of symbols. And one of the points on the diamond was just a little askew. It may have been the careless hand of the draftsman, but the whole tag seemed to cant slightly toward the right-hand corner of the room. The tip of the diamond on that corner was just a bit longer than the others', as if it were reaching toward that far corner, pulling the eye toward that part of the room. She scanned the room and found that corner. It was an exhilarating feeling, understanding an abstract drawing of a space and its relationship to the real world.

<<ok i've found the wall,>> she texted.

<<knock on it, what does it sound like?>>

As directed, she knocked on the wall, making a dull heavy thud.

<<heavy, like there's something behind it>> Ingrid knew that a standard wall would have a hollow sound, sharp and round.

<<what do you want me to do?>>

<<see what's underneath.>>

Ingrid left the room and returned a few minutes later with a crowbar that she had found in the garage. She took the sharp end and dug it into the corner of the wall. The blade slid forward, splitting the paint as it bit into the wall. Ingrid decided she would just have to try one of Joanna's restoration spells to fix it after she found out what was behind it. No time to think of the damage she was doing now. She was on to something here.

She pushed the blade deeper into the wall, but it stopped after half an inch. She wedged the end of the crowbar sideways and a chunk of the wall the size of a baseball fell off and landed on the floor. She picked up the piece of plaster and examined it. A renovated house like Fair Haven should have walls made from cement plaster spread in layers on a wire mesh. The cement would be coarse and sandlike, but Ingrid was holding a chunk of Sheetrock that was much older. She tossed it back to the floor and knelt below the hole she had made. Along the break she saw the paint chipped by the blade of the crowbar. The outer paint layer was a thick, glossy emulsion. It had the dark, rich sheen of lead-based paints. But underneath the paint, where the crowbar had cracked the finish, there was something else. She kept chipping at it until all the new paint was gone and she could see what was behind it.

It was a door. It did not have hinges or knobs but Ingrid recognized the shape right away. The cracked wood gave off a faint scent of pine. As she inhaled its bright, clean smell, she was transported into her deep past.

She thought of a place long forgotten, which had become more myth and legend than any truth, a dream. She remembered what she had told that young vampire. *You're a myth yourself.* They all were, they who lived and breathed and walked in mid-world like and unlike the humans surrounding them.

She touched the pine gently and turned back to the drawing of the wall she had broken. It showed a wood door stretching from floor to ceiling, an elaborate design sketched on the surface. They were instructions for the artisan, who no doubt would have to spend years carving the elaborate panels. The designs, she saw now, were the same as the small decorative scrolls around each of the key tags.

She took several pictures with her cell phone and zapped them over to her source.

<<do you see what i see?>>

<<yes. just as i suspected>>

<<what is it?>>

<<not now. will tell u later. get out of there first.>>

Ingrid waved her wand and muttered an incantation that restored the wall to its former state. It was a shoddy spell; she wasn't as good as her mother at restoration, but having the wand helped. She was almost done when she heard footsteps in the great hall, coming closer. Ingrid quickly took Oscar's form and flew out the window, just as Killian Gardiner walked into the empty ballroom.

"Is anyone here?" he called. "I heard someone in the house. Show yourself!"

Ingrid flew away, her heart thudding in her chest. That was a close one. What was that door and where did it lead? She left the island, thinking of the sentence her family had endured for millennia. The broken bridge, her lost younger brother. What was behind that door? Her source knew. She would find out soon enough.

chapter twenty-nine

Husbands and Wives

❧

The last time Joanna had been at the sprawling university in western Connecticut, only a few hours away from North Hampton, was at Ingrid's college graduation. The school had looked particularly fine that day, with its blue banners flying and the apple-cheeked graduates milling among the alumni in shiny black top hats and greatcoats, swinging mahogany canes bedecked with ribbons in the school colors. Oh, she had been so proud that day! Joanna had been nervous, of course, that she would run into her husband, but thankfully he had kept his distance even then. If Ingrid ever discovered that her father had taught at the same university she had attended she was certain to hate her mother for keeping it a secret. Joanna had forced the good professor to take a leave of absence for four years while his daughter was enrolled.

Joanna walked about the tree-lined paths, past the Gothic buildings. It looked the same as it always had, the limestone and the ivy. "Excuse me," she asked the nearest young person. "Could you help me find Professor Beauchamp?"

Just because she had not spoken to her husband for the better part of the century did not mean she had no idea what had happened to him. Far from it. She had kept tabs on him since their separation. It wasn't too difficult. She knew he had spent most of his time along the coast; but when the work dried up along the shore, he had left the fishing business and settled into the quiet life of a university professor. He had been teaching for many years now; it was a miracle no one noticed how old he was, but then he was probably just using the same spell she used to be able to live in North Hampton for as long as she had.

She visited his office, but his teaching assistant said he hadn't been keeping office hours all week. Joanna was able to procure his home address, which turned out to be not too far from campus. In a few minutes she found the small, well-kept building. The superintendent let her inside the front door when she told him she was the professor's wife. His apartment was on the ground floor.

"Hello? Anyone home? It's Jo." She rapped on the door before entering and found it was ajar. She slipped inside. It was a small studio apartment, and Joanna was not prepared for what she found. A tiny room, spare and monastic. There was one small futon, with folded blankets, a refrigerator the size of a small cabinet, one writing desk with nothing on its surface except for a few photographs. There was a picture of Ingrid taken during graduation at the university—he had probably snuck that one while no one was looking—and one of Freya from when she had been on the cover of a magazine, when she used to live in New York. She felt a pang of sorrow and regret.

They had been happy once, as happy in a marriage as anyone could be, imperfect and struggling against each other as all couples did. There had been fights and rages and tempers. He was not a patient man and she was as stubborn as he had been. If not for the trials, perhaps they would still be together. If only he had done as she had asked maybe things would have turned out differently for them. . . . What was she thinking? There was nothing he could have done, nothing any of them could do to stop the trials from happening. That was made clear the moment the bridge was destroyed and they were trapped in mid-world. To remain here, they would have to follow the laws of its original inhabitants; they had no jurisdiction and could not interfere in the human realm.

Joanna removed her coat and sat on the futon, with Gilly perched on her shoulder. She was going to wait for as long as it took for her husband to come home.

After a few hours, she had dozed off, when the door opened slowly.

"Norman?" she called. "Is that you?"

chapter thirty

The First Stone

ᴖᴖ

The next day, Ingrid was still thinking of the hidden door she had discovered in Fair Haven. The minute she arrived at work she sent an instant message to the address she knew by heart. There had been no communication the night before, which she found a bit strange, and she was eager to find out what her source had discovered. He usually responded within minutes, if not seconds, but after an hour there was still nothing.

<<hey how r u? what did u figure out?>>

She hit Send and waited. The screen remained unchanged. She went back to work, deciding to tackle the rest of the Gardiner prints and ready them for the framer. The other day she had picked out a nice balsa frame, cheaper than the ones they were accustomed to in years past, but now that every little penny counted she had to cut corners somewhere. Strange, the drawer where she usually kept them was empty. She distinctly remembered putting the main floor plan back in its storage container with the rest of the drawing set when she returned to the library yesterday afternoon. Maybe someone had moved them to the conference table? No. There was nothing there.

Ingrid's heart began to pound. She walked quickly back to her computer and sent another message to the same address.

<<hey, are you back yet?>>

<<hello??>>

<<if you're there pls answer>>

She saw her messages piling up on the screen with no response. Finally, she wrote:

<<something's wrong. i can't find the blueprints.>>

"Did you move my prints?" she asked Hudson after hitting Send. "You know, the Gardiner blueprints of Fair Haven for the show?"

Hudson looked up from his work and removed his noise-canceling headphones. He cleared his throat. "No. I haven't touched them. Maybe Tabitha knows?"

Tabitha did not know anything about the blueprints and neither did Caitlin, who was back to work after a bout with the flu. Hudson had locked up the night before, activating the alarm as usual. There was nothing amiss: the alarm hadn't gone off, and aside from the blueprints, there was nothing else missing. Not that there was anything particularly valuable in the library in the first place.

Ingrid tracked down the janitorial services they used, but they reported seeing nothing out of the ordinary the night before. She went back to the storage room and opened the drawer again. Empty. She checked her computer. No reply yet. The blueprints were gone and her source was unreachable. She picked up her phone and dialed Killian Gardiner.

"Hello," he answered sleepily.

"Killian—hi. It's Ingrid Beauchamp."

"Hi, Ingrid," he said sleepily. "What can I do for you?"

"Killian, did I wake you? I'm sorry but it is half past noon," she couldn't help but add.

"And your point is?" he asked amiably.

"I apologize, that was rude of me. It's been a long day. I was just calling about those blueprints of Fair Haven. Did you by any chance come by to take them back?"

"Why would I take them back?" he asked, sounding more alert this time. "I gave them to you. Why do you ask? Did something happen to them?"

"No, no . . . no." Ingrid shook her head vigorously even if Killian could not see her. It would not do to panic anyone else. "I think the staff moved them to the other closet. Sorry to bother you."

"No worries," Killian said.

She hung up the phone, her heart beating wildly. The scans. She had scanned all the prints, she thought, executing a search on her computer. She had scanned all the sheets that contained the strange tags and elaborate symbols. But just as she suspected, every single file connected to the blueprints was gone.

Ingrid tried not to panic. Who would steal the blueprints? And erase all the records on her computer? And why? Then Hudson burst into the room. His tie had come unknotted and he looked uncharacteristically frazzled. "I think you better come out to the front—it looks as if Corky Hutchinson has lost her mind."

INGRID FOLLOWED HUDSON to the main area to find the news anchor standing by the returns desk, looking hysterical and crazed in a pajama top and baggy sweatpants. When she saw Ingrid she pointed a red-manicured finger in her direction. "It's all her fault!" she screamed.

"Excuse me?" Ingrid asked. The library was full of mothers with toddlers, teenagers at the computers, and the regular patrons at the magazine racks. Matt Noble was returning a few paperbacks and rushed to her side.

"What's going on?" he asked, looking from Corky to Ingrid.

"She was the one! She did it!" Corky screeched. "She made me give Todd this . . . this knot under his pillow! He couldn't sleep . . . he's been acting so strangely—she did something to him!"

"Corky, calm down, what are you talking about?" Matt came around to restrain Corky by the shoulders since it looked as if she might take a swipe at Ingrid.

"She's a witch! She did it! She made this happen! With her black magic and those stupid knots!" Corky screamed.

"I'm so sorry . . . but it doesn't work that way," Ingrid said, backing away and shaking her head. Every part of her body was shaking as well, but she tried to project a sense of calm.

Matt looked questioningly at Ingrid. "Hold on . . . what do you mean? What's all this about magic?"

"He hung himself! With a knot! It looks just like this one!" the woman hissed, holding up the little brown knot that Ingrid had given her a month ago.

"What's going on?" Ingrid looked to Hudson for help. People were beginning to stare and congregate, looking at Ingrid with curiosity and fear. Ingrid had a flash back to her past, when the crowd had first gathered around her at the square that fine morning. They had circled her, just as the patrons of the library were doing now.

"As if you didn't know! They found his body this morning! Todd hung himself! At some skeezy motel on Route 27!" Corky cried.

Ingrid gasped. "Is that true?" she asked Matt.

The detective nodded. "We answered a 911 call from the motel this morning. The police are still there. Corky, calm down. Let's get you to the station." He gave Ingrid a long, searching look and led the newswoman out the door.

"Christ . . . what a crazy bitch!" Hudson said, walking out of the office. Ingrid noticed that everyone in the library was looking at her skeptically, some with outright hostility. "Are you okay?"

Ingrid nodded even though she wasn't. First the blueprints went missing, and she had stopped receiving texts or instant messages from her source, and now she was being accused of what . . . she wasn't even sure . . . but she couldn't shake off Corky's hateful words and accusations.

Tabitha gave Ingrid a pat on the back. "Don't worry, no one will listen to her. You had nothing to do with this," she said stoutly. "She's lost her husband and she doesn't know what she's talking about."

There were only a handful of women waiting to consult with her that day, which made Ingrid feel even worse. She tried not to think too much of it, but she couldn't help but think it had something to do with those terrible things Corky had said that morning. What was it that awful woman had said? Black magic? That she was a witch—a hag—a false medicine woman?

Ingrid thought of what Freya was going through: Sal had told her to stop making potions and had, effectively, fired her. From now on, the town would keep its eyes on them. Ingrid felt a chill up her spine. She had lived through this once before; she knew how the story ended.

Once upon a time in Massachusetts, Ingrid had a thriving practice, a clinic just like this one, but then the whispers had begun, and the accusations had started to fly. But this was not back then, Ingrid tried to tell herself. Maybe no one needed her help because everything was peachy-keen. Right. And if Ingrid believed that, she had a bridge she could sell to herself. Gallows Hill might be gone, but its shadow lingered, and Ingrid was not foolish enough to think that what happened once could never happen again.

And the day was still not over. Before the library closed, she received another visitor. Emily Foster walked in, pale and trembling. "Ingrid. Do you have a second? I need to talk to you."

chapter thirty-one

Marooned

❧

Freya watched Killian put the phone gently back in its cradle, admiring his profile and the arc of muscles on his broad back. She placed the palm of her hand on his skin; she could never stop touching him. They had spent the entire evening pleasuring each other, trying new and exciting variations of the same dance, and for a moment there she had been worried he would never tire, he had been that insatiable. . . . She had never met a man who could keep up with her, but she had found her match in him. They would finish only to start again a few minutes later, an innocent hand on a leg, or a brush against a cheek leading back to where they began, and Freya discovered she was getting turned on just thinking about all the things he had made her feel last night. His skin was smooth to the touch and, like everything about him, physically perfect, no nubby ridges or dryness or scars, evenly bronzed all over.

They were in his cabin on the *Dragon,* and through the portholes she could see it was daylight, probably just after noon since the sun was casting no shadows. What day was it? She wasn't sure. Where did time go when she was with him? She never noticed, it was an elusive quality, and she could never remember what they did—when they weren't in bed, that is—and it seemed as if they were always in bed whenever they were together. There should have been a hermetic, somewhat stale quality to the room, since they had not left it in a few days, and Freya had made all their meals on the small galley stove with whatever she found in the fridge. But instead of smelling like sex and sweat and cooking oil, the room was bright and clean, and when she closed her eyes she inhaled the fresh scent of pine and flowers. She wondered why he preferred to live on the boat rather than in Fair Haven, which definitely had enough bedrooms, but ever since the beginning Killian had made the fishing boat his home.

"Who was that on the phone?" she asked, releasing her hold.

"Your sister," he said, lying back down on the pillow and folding his arms behind his head, a thoughtful look on his face. His dark bangs covered one eye and he brushed them off impatiently.

"Ingrid? What did she want?" Freya propped herself on an elbow.

"I lent her some blueprints of the house a while back for her art show. It sounds like they're missing," Killian explained. "She didn't say so, but I could sort of tell."

"What is it about those blueprints? Bran asked about them the other day," Freya said, picking at the lint on the sheets. "Ingrid told him she found something cool in the design keys in those blueprints. There's some kind of code that she's almost figured out, which has some historical significance." She was babbling and trying to change the subject, as she was talking about Bran in Killian's bed.

Killian raised his eyebrows. "You spoke to Bran?"

"Yesterday." She leaned back and pulled the covers over her face.

"Hey," he said, gently drawing down the covers.

"I don't know what I'm doing here." She shook her head and couldn't look at him.

"Yes, you do."

"Listen, I gotta go," Freya said, pulling away so that she could put her clothes back on.

"Don't go." He began to kiss her neck, soft butterfly kisses that electrified every sense in her body. "You just got here."

Freya had a déjà vu feeling—hadn't she been in this same situation with Bran not too long ago? And now she was in a different bed, with a different brother. "Killian, come on. I got here four days ago." She pushed his arms away gently.

"I love you," he whispered. He was leaning forward so that his head rested on her shoulder and his hands cupped her breasts gently, making her feel warm all over.

"You're not allowed to say that," she said. "I told you. Nothing's going to change. I'm still going to marry Bran in September." She bit her lip.

"Don't do this to us," Killian warned, gripping her shoulder tightly.

"There is no us, Killian. There never was."

"Don't say that," he said desperately.

"Stop it, you're hurting me," she said. Her heart was breaking, as well as his. She loved him so much. It was love she felt for him, deep and abiding and entrenched, a fierce white fire, and yet it was wrong. She knew it was wrong, that being with him was wrong. If only she had met him first. If only . . . But it was too late now. She and Bran had found each other and she had promised Bran she would marry him, and marry him she would. It was the right thing to do, it was what she was meant to do. She couldn't change her destiny.

Killian stood and began to pace the room, running his hands on his face, looking lost and confused and anxious. "Freya, please" was all he said.

"This is . . . this is just a mistake," she told him, zipping up her jeans and putting on her shirt. She jammed her feet back into her sneakers. "I'm so sorry, Killian. I really am. But I told you from the beginning that this wasn't a good idea."

AFTER LEAVING THE BOAT, Freya had to walk for a while to clear her head. She didn't want to keep thinking about Killian and wandered aimlessly for a few hours. With a start she realized she was practically in the middle of town, near the police station, a small building near city hall. Since she was there, she thought she would ask about the progress they had made in their investigation of Molly Lancaster's disappearance, maybe ask if she could talk to some of those boys, see if she could sense anything from them. While she was still mostly confident that there was no way her potion could have been part of what happened to Molly, she was beginning to entertain the possibility that perhaps something in her magic could have gone awry, and she wanted to see if she could do anything to help. While she still did not believe the boys had anything to do with Molly's disappearance, she knew she was in the minority. Many people in town were already grumbling that the boys had received preferential treatment from the district attorney.

The police station was its usual shabby chaos. "Hey, Freya." Jim Lewis, one of the patrolmen, greeted her with a smile. "What's up?"

"Just thought I'd drop by, see what was going on with the Lancaster case?"

"Yeah, I can't really talk about that right now," he said, shaking his head.

"You can't or you won't, Jim? Come on, it's me. Remember how I helped you catch that bicycle thief?" Freya wheedled.

"I know, girl. But this is different."

"What's going on?" she asked, as she noticed all the detectives crowded around Matt Noble's cubicle. "Is that Corky Hutchinson? Did something happen with Todd?"

"Can't say. Can't say." Jim drummed his fingers on the reception desk. "But I will tell you about the Lancaster thing. One of those college boys looks like he's going to crack. There'll be an arrest soon, you can count on it."

WHEN SHE GOT BACK to the house, Gracella practically pounced on her the minute she walked through the door. "So sorry to bother, Miss Freya, but it is Tyler."

"Of course, not a bother at all. What's going on?"

The housekeeper twisted the chamois she was holding. "His fever is very high. Since last night. I think maybe I take him to hospital but I am scared. Hector is away and . . ."

Freya followed the anxious mother to the cottage. Tyler's room was on the second landing, a cheerful place filled with cartoon imagery on the wallpapers and whose bookshelves were stocked with toys of every shape and size. The toy soldiers were heaped in a pile, the puppets lay still on the footlocker. The train set was silent and waiting. In a bed shaped like a racecar, Tyler was wrapped up in a comforter, like a small turtle. She was shocked to find him so changed from just a few days ago. He had lost a lot of weight, and he had no color in his cheeks.

"Hey, kid," she said gently, putting a hand on his forehead. It was burning. "Yes, let's take him to the hospital now. There's no point in waiting," she said to Gracella. "I can drive."

They bundled the boy in the backseat. "He'll be okay; I'll call Joanna as soon as I drop him off," Freya said, as she drove mother and son through the empty streets of North Hampton to the small county hospital. "I promise," she said, even though she knew she had no right to promise anything. Freya knew as well as her sister the limit to their mother's powers, especially when it came to those she loved.

chapter thirty-two

Thief in the Night

L ater that same evening, Ingrid had a dream. It began when she realized she was not alone in bed. There was a heavy weight on her body, and now there was a tug at her pajama bottoms. She stirred and attempted to pull them back up but she found she could not, and now her top was being unbuttoned, the air cold on her skin, and she was not sure what was happening—where was her blanket? Then there was a hand on her mouth and she was jolted awake but she could not scream. She could not even open her eyes.

There was a man on top of her; his hands were warm and soft and his body lay heavy upon hers, his hands on her chest, and she was naked underneath him; she struggled against his weight but there was nothing she could do, she was immobile and helpless and then he began to push himself into her, and now he was inside and moving so slowly and she wanted to scream but she could not, because he was kissing her so sweetly and her body was responding to his touch and she could not stop herself. She was wet and he was hard and it felt good. It felt so good to be underneath a man, to be taken and loved, although this was not love.

Suddenly, her eyes flew open and she could see him.

The beautiful, elfin face, coal-black hair and blue-green eyes.

And he was stronger now. . . . His hands were around her throat, and he was choking her, digging deep into her neck, causing her to gasp as he pushed relentlessly to a climax. . . . This was *really* happening. . . . Killian was trying to kill her. . . . She could feel her spirit begin to waver and flicker in the glom. . . . She would die—no!—she would not . . . she would not let this happen. . . . With all of her strength Ingrid folded her knee and pushed it against his chest; it was enough to unbalance her intruder, and he released his hold on her neck.

Ingrid opened her mouth to scream . . .

And woke up.

This time she was truly awake.

It was just a dream, after all. Ingrid sat up in her bed, gasping and shaking; she was fully clothed and alone, but the back of her shirt was covered in sweat. Still, it was only a dream. A nightmare. She had dreamed that Killian Gardiner had raped her and tried to kill her, and it had felt so real, she felt sick—aroused and confused and violated at the same time. She had thought she was going to die.

What just happened?

A vision? A sending?

Then she understood.

It all made sense now. Freya's strange, jittery anxiety at her engagement party, the burned flowers, the tousled hair, her long silences and absences with no explanation, her red cheeks and flushed countenance. She thought of the way her sister had acted the entire summer—daydreaming, distracted, confused, and then snappy and curt. That was not like Freya. Something had happened, more specifically *someone* had happened to her. Just like before. Of course, it all made sense now.

Ingrid got out of bed and put on her robe. She looked at the clock. It was only half past midnight. Freya was still out for the evening, but Ingrid thought she knew just where to find her. The sisters had seen each other briefly when Freya had returned from the hospital. Ingrid was worried about the boy, too, and hoped his flu would not get any worse. She could not imagine otherwise. Even though Freya was not allowed to work at the North Inn anymore, she could not keep away and was now one of their best customers. Ingrid was not a regular patron of the North Inn, but she had nothing against bars and understood the pleasures they provided: convivial company, the comfort of a well-made drink, and the aural excitement of a good jukebox. Once in a while she and the library crew headed there on Friday nights, but since Tabitha had gotten pregnant and Hudson was trying the latest detox diet, they hadn't visited the watering hole in a while. She walked into the crowded hall and nodded to a few familiar faces.

"Can I get you anything, love?" Kristy asked. The gangly bartender threw a rag over her shoulder and waited for Ingrid to order.

"Nothing tonight, thanks. I was just looking for my—"

There was a huge whoop from the other end of the counter and Kristy shrugged. "She's in fine form tonight. I told her if she didn't settle down I was going to cut her off in a bit," she said, making a slashing motion in front of her throat. "She won't tell me what's wrong but she's been hitting the tequila pretty hard."

Ingrid nodded. Tequila was Freya's answer to any emotional upheaval. She looked to where the commotion was and found her sister downing shots and calling out the answers to trivia questions in between sucking lime halves.

"Freya!"

"Inge! What are you doing here?" Freya asked, looking surprised but happy to see her. She grabbed Ingrid in a bear hug, and Ingrid smelled the alcohol on her breath.

Ingrid wasted no time. She leaned close to her sister's ear and whispered angrily, "Are you having an affair with Killian Gardiner?"

Freya sobered up quickly after that.

"DON'T DENY IT," Ingrid warned, as she drove her sister home. Freya had pleaded to be able to finish her drinks but Ingrid was not having it. Now the sisters were sitting in the car, Freya staring pensively out the window, while Ingrid fumed at the steering wheel.

"I'm not," Freya said a tad petulantly. Of course Ingrid was bound to find out about her and Killian. She had been waiting for this to happen; the only surprising thing about this development was how long it took for Ingrid to come to this conclusion. Her sister usually knew all her secrets even before she knew them herself.

Ingrid looked at her sideways. "I felt it."

"Ew! Don't tell me how! You had one of your creepy dreams?"

"Creepy doesn't cut it." Ingrid shuddered, remembering the cold hands around her neck and the way his body had felt on hers. She shook her head. "What are you doing? I thought you were in love with Bran, that you thought he was 'the one.'"

"I know. I told Killian things were over between us this afternoon. I ended it." Freya sighed.

"Good." Ingrid looked at her sister from the corner of her eye, so she could still keep an eye out for oncoming traffic. "It's for the best, Freya. Remember what happened last time you got married."

Freya did not answer and they drove in silence for a while, along the dark and deserted highway. "I'm scared," Ingrid said finally. "I had a horrible day. Someone called me a witch this afternoon, in front of everyone at work."

Freya flinched. "Yikes."

"Corky Hutchinson. I knew I shouldn't have given her that stupid knot. She wasn't going to keep him home. Damnit!" Ingrid never cursed but she was unnerved and upset. "Pardon."

"It's not your fault," Freya soothed. "We all know your magic doesn't work that way. Your knot didn't kill Todd. He killed himself, Ingrid. Who knows why."

"I don't know . . ." Ingrid chewed her bottom lip. "I want to think that I couldn't have done anything, but I was so upset. He's going to tear down the library. . . . What if I didn't mean to do it but it still happened? It's been so long since I've practiced magic, I might be rusty. I could have inadvertently twisted it the wrong way." Ingrid felt a cold dread sinking in her stomach. What if, even if she had not meant to practice black magic, she had done so anyway? There weren't any rules when it came to this sort of thing. Anything could happen. She could have killed Todd. Maybe she did.

"You're being paranoid," Freya soothed. "You can't even hex a fly. There's no way you are to blame for what happened to him."

"But I was so angry . . . and Corky, she screamed it, in front of everyone. She called me a witch! Almost everyone in town has been to see me, Freya. They believe I practice magic. They've seen it work for them."

"So?" Freya shrugged.

"So? Don't you remember what happened last time we practiced magic openly?"

Freya began to doodle on the condensation on the window from the air-conditioning. "Seriously? That's what you're worried about? This is North Hampton! And last I checked, the calendar said we were in the twenty-first century. They might think that you've cured their aches and pains and made some difficult problems go away, but deep down? Do you think they *really* believe in magic? No freaking way. *No one* believes in us anymore. We're safe," Freya stressed. "Look around, this is a world of science and technology, of computers and gadgetry. They have iPads and GPS and microwaves. They don't even worry about death, because according to them, you can beat cancer by just eating tofu! This isn't like before."

"I hope you're right."

Freya rolled down her window to feel the ocean breeze. "I'm sure I am."

Ingrid stopped the car with a screech and Freya's head bumped the dashboard. "Oops, sorry about that," Ingrid said. "There's something else I've been meaning to tell you. You know that guy Mom saved from death? Lionel Horning?"

"Yeah? What about him?"

"Well, he's missing," Ingrid said. She couldn't believe she had forgotten to mention it until now, but she had been so rattled by Corky Hutchinson's actions that afternoon and that terrible dream she had that evening that it had completely slipped her mind.

"What do you mean he's missing?"

"Emily came by, said he's been acting weird, talking about a path in the mountains and how he didn't belong around here, and how he was taking a few people with him."

"What?"

"I know. It sounds like he might be going zombie." Ingrid sighed. Like Freya, she knew that when a human soul had spent a considerable amount of time in the glom, there was the risk that the physical body would not accept its resurrection if the soul and the body had grown too detached from the other. It rarely happened, Joanna was too good at her job, but it wasn't unheard of for the dead to come back to life only to succumb to a bad case of zombititis.

Freya gasped. "You don't think he had anything to do with Molly . . . ?" she said.

"I don't know—I mean, Lionel isn't violent. I mean, unless Helda put more of herself in him before Mom got him out of Deadville."

"Since when has he been missing?"

"Since the Fourth of July weekend." The same night Molly Lancaster had disappeared.

"Oh, good lord!"

"There's another thing," Ingrid said, twiddling her thumbs. She pushed up her glasses on her nose. In her haste to find her sister, she had forgotten to put in her contacts. Her black-rimmed spectacles made her look older than she was; Ingrid hated wearing them, as she looked too much like the classic small-town librarian already.

Freya turned to her sister. "There's something else other than a possible zombie on the loose in North Hampton?"

Ingrid tried not to look too sheepish. "Right after the holiday weekend . . ."

"Yeah?"

"Someone came to visit me. One of the Fallen."

Freya glared at her. "A vampire came to visit you and you didn't tell me? Why not?"

"I didn't think it was important." Ingrid sighed. "I don't know. I was embarrassed. I couldn't make her go away so I helped her. I know the rules, we're not supposed to have anything to do with them. But she asked for help and I gave it."

"When was this?"

"I told you, right after the Fourth. She said she'd been in town all weekend, mentioned seeing you at the North Inn that Friday night."

Freya tried to remember. Wouldn't she have noticed a vampire at her bar? The last time she had come in contact with the Fallen was through the boy she had cured in New York last fall, right before she moved back to North Hampton, and with a start she realized she might have caught a glimpse of him somewhere lately—was it at the North Inn? What was his name again—Oliver? And wasn't he with some icy blonde? Was that his new vampire? It was all so hazy. But then, that was the evening when things began to happen with Killian. No wonder she hadn't paid attention. "Who was she? The blonde?" she asked.

"Azrael."

"Interesting. So, the freaking Angel of Death blows into town just as a girl goes missing and our mayor turns up dead!"

"By why would she care about them?" Ingrid argued. "You know the Fallen are bound to that Code of theirs. They're not supposed to bring harm to humans, and there hasn't been a human death attributed to them in centuries. It just doesn't make sense . . ." Then her face went pale. "Wait a minute . . . I told her about the Orpheus Amendment . . . that she would need a soul to sacrifice to Helda for the one she wants returned, and she said she already knew about that part, that she was prepared for it." Ingrid looked horrified. "You don't think Azrael could have taken Molly, do you? Or Todd?"

"Anything could happen," Freya said. "Especially with zombies and vampires around. Next thing you'll tell me Dad's back."

"Actually . . ." Ingrid bit her lip. "Never mind." Freya didn't seem to catch it so Ingrid soldiered on. "Anyway, what do you think we should do?" In times like these, she looked to her younger sister for action and leadership. At heart, Ingrid was a seer, someone who studied and analyzed situations; she liked to lay the facts on the table and let someone else make the hard decisions.

"First we'll pay Azrael a visit," Freya said. "Then we look for Lionel."

chapter thirty-three

Safe House

ᴖ

"I thought Mom had all the tunnels destroyed," Ingrid said. They were standing in front of the door to Freya's closet. They had driven back home instead of driving to the city, at Freya's behest. "There's really one still here?"

Freya put her hands on her hips and smirked. "She kept the wands, Ingrid. Don't you think she might have kept a few other things?" She threw open the doors, tapped her wand, and a light emanated from the end, guiding the way. "Anyway, it's so ridiculous. Why would I have to live in some dingy walk-up in New York when we had this all along?"

Every witch abode automatically sprouted magical pathways, which the witches could use to travel long distances that would otherwise be tiresome by broom. But when the house in North Hampton was built, the Council had ordered them destroyed as part of the restriction. Freya always suspected that Joanna had kept one as a safety precaution and, a few decades ago, discovered she had been correct in her assumption. She led the way inside, past the racks of coats and furs and the sign she'd made that read, "Looking for Narnia? You're in the wrong universe," until they found themselves in Freya's old apartment in the city.

Since it was connected to North Hampton, like the town it

existed just slightly outside of time; so that while in the physical world it was only several hundred square feet, it was also a huge mansion with a fireplace, a beautiful kitchen, and plush English country furniture. "Nice, right?" Freya smiled. "You can't get this on the market these days for what I paid."

"So while we were living in drudgery and couldn't even use magic to clean the dishes, you were living *here* all these years? No wonder you never came home."

"Hey, I found the tunnel that led to this safe house. Mother must have kept it around in case we ever needed to get out of North Hampton. Useful, right?" Freya smiled. "God, I've missed this place. I used one of her old spells to redecorate. I figured the restriction only applied to new magic."

"All right, then. How do we go about finding a vampire in this city?" Ingrid asked, nodding approvingly at the plush surroundings. "It's not like they're listed in the phone book."

"Actually, they are," Freya said, firing up her computer and taking a seat at her desk. "The Fallen kind of run New York. Let's see what we can find." She typed Mimi's name into a search engine.

Since Mimi Force was the beautiful and fashionable daughter of one of the wealthiest men in the city, if not the world, there were many entries concerning her frenetic social life, including numerous mentions in the tabloids and gossip columns. There were articles documenting her beauty routine, her eating habits, what nightclubs she currently frequented. However, the Internet did not reveal any private details. Like many of the rich and famous who lived within a cocoon of privacy rare to ordinary folk, the Force holdings and estates were mostly hidden through a network of trusts and attorneys.

"If you want to know what she wore last week to some party, I can tell you, but I don't think we'll find an address," Freya said, tapping the keyboard in frustration.

Ingrid perched on the armrest of Freya's chair and peered at the screen. "Well, then, if we're not going to find her that way, then the best bet is to try and ambush her at one of these parties."

"You're a genius; I know that's why we're related." Freya smiled, pulling up a site that listed the social events scheduled for that week. "Here we go. The Blood Bank Committee has some kind of party tomorrow night, which is technically tonight since it's already tomorrow. All the Blue Bloods are sure to be there, Mimi included. It's their little pet charity to keep the blood supply clean." She yawned. Ingrid had fetched her at the bar around midnight and it was already the wee hours of the morning. "Let's get some sleep so we'll be ready for the ambush. If Azrael did take Molly, she's not going to give her up easily."

FREYA SLEPT FITFULLY, tossing and turning in her bed. She could hear Ingrid snoring from the guest room, but it wasn't the reason for her insomnia. She couldn't stop thinking about Ingrid's strange dream about Killian—her sister would not divulge any more details, but she got the gist of it, and it bothered her. Why would Ingrid dream that Killian wanted to kill her? Killian liked Ingrid, as far as Freya could tell; she couldn't see how he could wish her harm . . . except . . . but that had happened so long ago now, he couldn't possibly still hold it against her?

When she wasn't worrying about that she could not stop agonizing about the way she had ended it with him earlier. Was it really over between them? She could not imagine never seeing him again, even if it was probably for the best. Bran would be home soon; he promised that after his big summer project was wrapped up he would leave the traveling part of his work to others. She could not keep up the façade and the lying anymore. Being in love with two men at the same time was not what she had signed up for when she had launched this affair. She had to stop acting and start thinking; for too long she just rushed into things without worrying about the consequences. Like agreeing to marry Bran after only a month, or having sex with his brother after meeting him for the first time at a party. She had to get her life in order and commit to the direction she had chosen, which meant marrying Bran in September. Things were great until she met Killian. She was happy, she was in love, and then he came into the picture. But she had allowed him in, she reminded herself.

She finally drifted off to sleep just as morning broke, and when she woke up it was the afternoon. She could hear Ingrid puttering around in her dressing room, searching through the racks of clothing. "What time is it?" she asked her sister.

"Five o'clock. You slept the whole day. Come on, get up, the party starts at six. I want to be there early."

Freya rubbed her eyes and moved slowly out of bed. She walked to the kitchen and helped herself to a cup of coffee from a pot Ingrid had made.

"Is there anything you own that isn't see-through, thigh-high, or backless?" Ingrid asked, looking around vainly for something that she could wear. Many of Freya's dresses boasted all three qualities. "You do realize you dress like a . . ."

"Hooker?" Freya offered cheerfully, sipping the coffee and instantly feeling awake. She joined Ingrid in the walk-in closet and began rifling through her things. "No, you won't find something in there that doesn't reveal some part of your body, and no, I never get any complaints about my wardrobe. Jeez, you're worse than Mother," Freya said, removing her bathrobe and slipping into a tiny black dress.

Ingrid gave a scandalized groan. "Don't say 'hooker'; it's common."

"Lady of the night, then?" Freya laughed, leaving her sister to fret about a dress alone. She sat at her vanity table and began to apply her makeup.

"How's this?" Ingrid asked, coming out to show her what she had found. She was wearing a simple dark dress with long sleeves and a longer hemline. "I feel lucky I even found it. I didn't think you owned anything that covered your arms."

"You look like a nun," Freya said as she brushed her cheeks with rouge. "I bought that for a costume party. This is New York, Ingrid, and the party is at the rooftop of the Standard Hotel. You can't look like you've come straight from the sticks. Also, it's August. You're going to boil."

"I just feel more comfortable in this."

"Nun."

Ingrid regarded Freya's plunging neckline with a skeptical eye. "Are you sure you don't have that dress on backward?"

"You're funny. Let's go," she said, blotting her lipstick with a tissue. "Try not to embarrass me."

chapter thirty-four

The Vampires of Manhattan

~~

The Standard Hotel was located in the far west side of town, by the Hudson River. Ingrid was never one for trendy events, and so the sight of hulking gorilla bouncers and a barracuda in a black cocktail dress wielding a clipboard at the entrance made her a bit nervous. "Do you think we'll get in? We don't exactly have invitations," Ingrid whispered. "And that one looks like Fafnir in a skirt," she said, meaning the legendary dragon that jealously guarded a treasure trove of gold.

"Relax, that's only the doorgirl; they come with the territory. She doesn't have any power over us," Freya said. She walked confidently up to the velvet rope. "Freya and Ingrid Beauchamp, we're here for the Blood Bank party. You don't need to check the list."

"See?" Freya said, as the velvet rope was unhitched and they made their way to the elevators that would take them to the rooftop. The party was already in full swing, and the indoor Jacuzzi was bubbling. Ingrid tried not to stare at the human girls in the tub, some of whom seemed to have lost their bikini tops; it was hard to tell with the bubbling water. This was quite a different scene from the usual staid North Hampton affair; the vampires were breathlessly chic in white linen, with bored, blank faces, and Ingrid did feel a bit out of place in her long-sleeved dress.

"Let's get a drink," Freya suggested, heading toward the long black bar and quickly procuring two full martini glasses.

Ingrid took a sip. "What's with all the salty foam?" she asked, wiping her lips with a napkin.

"Just drink it," Freya said, gazing at the crowd, keeping an eye out for the vampire princess. "Do you see her anywhere?"

Ingrid shook her head. "Tons of Blue Bloods and their familiars but no Azrael."

"She's got to be here somewhere," Freya said. "She's supposed to be *hosting* this party." Although from living in the city she knew that just because boldfaced names were on the invitation it did not necessarily mean they would be expected to actually attend the party—it was one of those unwritten social agreements.

All around the rooftop, small groups were gathered on massive orange lilypads that were on the synthetic grass covering the floor. A few people were playing with telescopes that were installed by the edge. The view of the city was breathtaking, but Freya was more riveted by the sight of a familiar face that stopped her in her stilettos.

"Where are you going?" Ingrid asked.

"Back in a sec," she told her sister, walking to the dark-haired man talking intently to a tall brunette at one of the cocktail tables. The woman had a cold, commanding beauty, and Freya thought she looked a bit familiar, but couldn't place her.

"Bran?"

When he heard his name, he looked up, and his confusion soon melted into a smile. He was wearing a blue blazer with frayed seams and a faded gingham shirt. "Freya! What are you doing here?" He excused himself from his companion and stood up, taking Freya to the side.

"I could ask the same of you." She did not want to feel jealous and yet jealousy was seeping in every part of her body. Who was that woman he was with? Why was Bran talking to her so intensely? They had looked as if they were arguing, and that woman had a possessive air around Bran that Freya did not like very much. "You're in New York? I thought you were in Asia."

"We just got back; one of the board members couldn't make it so we decided to fly here and do the meeting at the Rockefeller Center offices. It's great to see you," he said, smiling. "What made you decide to come?"

"Ingrid had some business here, and I thought I'd tag along," she said. It would be too much to explain, and she felt shy around him for once. After missing him for so long, it was strange to be in his presence again, as if he wasn't quite real. She wanted to kiss him, or touch his cheek, but she could not. She could not bear him to know what she had been doing in his long absence. Sleeping with his brother, betraying every promise she had made to him from the beginning.

"We're supposed to go back to Jakarta tomorrow for the presentation, but I'll tell them they can go without me," he said, as if he could read her mind.

"No, no . . . don't do that. I'm only here for a night and I don't want to keep you from your work." She forced herself to stop acting aloof and kissed him soundly. He was sweating and nervous, dear sweet boy. "Go on, really. You'll be back in town next week. I'll see you then. I gotta go anyway."

"Are you sure?" Bran looked confused and hurt. "Can you wait a moment? I have to speak to Julia about the project—she's one of our analysts—but I want to spend more time with you." The woman he was with looked at the two of them impatiently and began to walk toward them. He looked over his shoulder and raised a finger.

"Yes, don't worry about me . . . I'll see you when you get back, okay?" Freya said, relieved that there was nothing to be jealous about after all. Bran was just caught up in his work as usual. She gave him one last kiss and walked away to look for Ingrid.

She found her talking to a group of Blue Blood vampires. "Bran's here," she whispered. "But it's okay, he's with his charity muckamucks. I told him I'd see him back home."

"You're looking for my daughter? Excuse me interrupting." The Blue Blood socialite who addressed them was regal and elegant, with a stately way of speaking. "I'm Trinity Burden Force." She looked at the two of them keenly. "Freya and Ingrid Beauchamp. The witches of East End. To what do we owe the pleasure?"

"Mimi visited our town and met with my sister. We need to ask her something," Freya said. "Do you know where we can find her?"

"You'll have to travel to Cairo to do so. She left the city the other day with her human conduit. She said she had something to finish back in Egypt that was more important than graduating from high school. No, I don't know when she's coming back; my daughter operates on her own schedule without informing me of any changes." Trinity smiled thinly. "As your own mother can attest, I am the last to know."

"Great," Freya said, when Trinity took her leave. "If Mimi took Molly, they're halfway around the world by now, and she could have given her to Helda already in exchange for whoever she wanted out of there. How long do you think it will take us to get to Cairo?"

Ingrid shook her head. "We don't have time for that right now. We'll deal with that later. Right now we need to find Lionel. Emily just texted me. She thinks she might have spotted him out on the farm."

"That's a relief," Freya said.

"No, you don't understand—all the animals on their farm are dead, and she thinks Lionel might have killed them."

chapter thirty-five

The Covenant of the Dead

᠋ᴗᴗ

Lionel Horning and Emily Foster lived in an old farmhouse on land that had once been part of his grandparents' dairy farm, and the two artists had a small menagerie, with chickens, goats, and a milking cow. Lionel had converted the house to a loftlike space where they lived and worked. When the sisters arrived, Emily was waiting for them with tea and biscuits. "Thanks for coming so quickly—how did you get back here so fast? I thought Ingrid said you were in the city?" she asked as she poured them each a cup of tea.

"We were on our way back when you called," Freya said smoothly. There was no need to explain how the closet in her room made traveling from North Hampton to New York as easy as walking down the hallway.

"When did you discover the animals?" Ingrid asked.

"This afternoon. When I went to refill the water for the chickens." Emily's hands shook so badly that her teacup rattled in its saucer. "I was going to call animal services but I thought you might want to take a look."

"There's no time like the present. Let's go," Freya said a tad impatiently, standing up. It was so North Hampton of Emily Foster to offer them tea and make polite chitchat when they were there to figure out if her husband had turned into a bloodthirsty zombie. Emily led them out through the back door toward the barn.

"Hold on. . . . What is that? Can you hear it?" Freya asked. "Like rushing water underground." She knelt down to touch the ground; the earth felt damp and the rumble grew louder.

"It sounds like waves," Ingrid agreed.

"It's the underground river that runs directly underneath the barn," Emily said. "In the 1850s a well was built on this site. I can't believe you can hear the water. I've never heard it myself. Lionel claimed he could feel it surging when he painted, but then again Lionel said a lot of things," she said, walking up to the barn door. She wrapped her fingers around a brightly galvanized handle and pulled. The big door heaved and began to move sideways on a metal track. It rolled for a moment and then stopped. Emily grimaced. "You might want to hold your breath. The smell is disgusting. Anyway, if you just slip in and move along the wall for a few paces there should be a light switch on your right-hand side. Just be prepared. I would come with you, but I just can't go in there again." She turned and quickly backed away from the door, wiping her hands on her jacket twice and then shaking them in the air as she walked away. Freya saw her heave a sigh of relief as she exited the barn.

Ingrid's face puckered. A sickly sweet smell drifted out from inside the barn, acrid and rotten. "You first," she told her sister.

Freya smirked as she slipped slowly through the opening. It was dark inside. In the dim light she could see there was some kind of mound on the floor, but it was too dark to make anything more out of it. She felt something brush her left shoulder and shivered, but it was just Ingrid inching into the room next to her.

"The switch," Ingrid whispered. Freya was already reaching sideways with her right hand, feeling up and down the wall in broad arcs. Her fingers scraped the wall as she *she led* ...

little toggle.

"What *is* that?" Ingrid asked. The mound at the ...

room was clearly moving, its surface undulating, b...

was a trick of the light. "Can you just get the damn ligh...

on!" Ingrid begged, wishing they had thought to brin... ...heir

wands.

Freya's finger finally hit the trim plate. The switch clicked, and there was a pause as the ballast in the old fluorescent light buzzed and cracked before kicking on. The light blinked and finally the room was awash in a pale bluish glow.

The mound at the far end of the room turned out to be a pile of torn and bloody animal carcasses, fur and feathers mixed with blood and entrails in a chunky soup of rotting flesh. Blood splattered the walls and floor and tiny maggots crawled over everything. Freya tried not to vomit and Ingrid blanched at the sight.

"That's enough," Ingrid said, looking sick. "Let's get out of here."

Emily was waiting for them outside and rolled the barn door closed. "Sorry you had to see that."

"So what makes you think Lionel did that?" Ingrid asked, as Emily led them to a second, smaller barn that housed the artists' studios.

"This morning I was by the window, washing dishes, when I thought I saw a man outside. It looked like Lionel from behind, so I called out to him. He didn't turn around, but he'd been acting so strange since he got back from the hospital so I let him be."

"How long has Lionel been missing now?"

Emily looked embarrassed. "A few weeks. Almost the entire month. Since right before the Fourth of July he said he hasn't been feeling well. Then that Friday I came home from the market and found everything in disarray." Pulling the door open,

...hem inside the cozy farmhouse to the back where Lionel ...pt his studio. "I'm sorry I didn't say anything earlier but he does this once in a while."

Tacked on the far wall were several large-scale canvases showing a silver gate, the mountain high above the hill, trails that led to unknown paths, eerily specific to the Kingdom of the Dead. One of the canvases was torn, and there was paint splattered over the canvas in a haphazard motion, in contrast to the almost photographic quality of the painting underneath.

"But you didn't come see me until the next week," Ingrid pointed out. "Why not?"

Emily shrugged and righted a chair. "He's a bit absentminded and we give each other a lot of freedom. We don't need to check in with each other. I thought maybe he'd gone to the city—he sometimes stays at the Chelsea Hotel—but I called over there and he wasn't registered and no one at his gallery has seen him either. That's when I started to worry. There's been no activity in his accounts, and it's not like him to be gone this long. I was sure he'd be home by now. Then this morning, I thought he was back and wanted to check on the animals. I sort of forgot about it. . . . I've been working, so I'm a bit distracted as well. . . . Then this afternoon when I saw what was back there. . . . I'm kind of freaked out."

"Is there somewhere you can go? I think it's best if you don't stay here," Ingrid said.

"I could go to my sister's, I guess. Ann's in Wainscott; it's not too far. Why? You don't think he would come after me, do you? I'm not even sure it was Lionel, it might have been someone else." She shook her head. "You think this might have had something to do with what your mom did to Lionel?"

"Emily . . ."

Emily balled up her fists. "It's all my fault. I asked for the help." She seemed to have an internal struggle with herself. "I'll go to Ann's." She looked at the sisters plaintively. "You'll try to find him? Maybe help him? Don't hurt him, okay?"

They tried to assure her that all would be well as they bade good-bye. When they were alone in the car, Ingrid exchanged a look with her sister. The heads of all the animals were torn off, their entrails severed. "If something went wrong with his resurrection, it's possible that he's now trapped between life and death," she said. "He's alive, but his body is decomposing and he'll need to . . ."

"Feed, I know. Those animals looked half-eaten." Freya was silent for a moment as she tried to think. "It's been so long since Mother has done something like this, it's possible something went wrong."

Ingrid hit the gas and they peeled away down the farmhouse driveway. They could still see Emily in the living-room window, watching them. "Zombies," Ingrid muttered. "What do we know about them?"

"Other than that they're uncoordinated, they don't know what they're doing, and they're basically walking corpses with a taste for brains?" Freya asked.

"So Lionel Horning went zombie, killed Molly Lancaster, hid her body, and then came back to the farmhouse and slaughtered his animals?" Ingrid suggested. "Seems like a lot for one zombie to do, if you ask me. They can't even walk properly."

"Unless . . ."

"Unless what?"

"Remember the Fontanier case?" Freya asked. "When we were living in France in the twelfth century?"

"Remind me?" Ingrid asked.

"Jean Fontanier was a farmer; he got killed accidentally when his horse spooked and threw him. His widow came to Mother but she refused to bring him back as he'd been dead for more than twenty-four hours. So his widow went to Lambert de Fois."

Ingrid nodded. It was starting to return to her. Lambert de Fois was the head of their coven then. "Right."

"The stupid warlock raised him from the dead, but it didn't take. We all thought Fontanier had gone zombie, but it turned out that wasn't the problem."

Ingrid sighed. She remembered all too well now. By resurrecting the farmer after his body had been cold for a day, Lambert de Fois had broken the Covenant of the Dead, and Helda had not been pleased. "No. That wasn't the problem at all."

"Jean Fontanier wasn't a zombie. Helda made sure he returned to life as something else. A demon."

chapter thirty-six

Family Secrets

～๑ ๑～

One of life's greatest pleasures was returning home after a long trip, Joanna thought, as she put her carpetbag down in the hallway and hung her hat back on the hook. Gilly flew to her usual perch on the ceiling cove as Joanna turned on the lights. She was surprised to find the living room a mess, pillows on the floor, water bottles and wineglasses on the coffee table. The kitchen was worse, with its usual pile of dirty dishes and used pots on the stove. Joanna had gotten used to having the Alvarezes taking care of everything, and Gracella kept a very neat house. She rang the cottage but there was no answer. It was too late to say hello to Tyler anyway, she decided. She heard a car pull up and her daughters' voices carry up from the driveway. Oh, good, they were home, she had quite a lot to tell them.

"Girls!" she said, throwing open the door.

"Mom!" Freya said, feeling guilty at the sight of her mother, even though nothing that had happened was technically her fault and at least one was certainly Joanna's doing. Still, she did not relish telling her mother that in her absence, Ingrid had helped a vampire who had visited their town and that the nice guy Joanna had raised from the dead was now a zombie or, more likely, possessed by a demon.

"Where have you been?" Ingrid wanted to know.

Joanna ushered them inside and closed the door. "I've been looking for your father," she said, wringing her hands. "I need his help. Listen, girls, there's something you need to know about him—"

"I know where he is," Ingrid interrupted.

"What do you mean, you know where Dad is?" Freya asked, staring at her sister. "And you didn't say anything? How could you?"

"I'm sorry. He wrote me a few months ago. He wanted to get in touch with all of us, but he thought he'd try me first. He thought Mother would be too mad and that Freya would just burn his letters."

Freya crossed her arms and flopped down on the nearest couch. "He was right about that. He left us, Ingrid. He abandoned our family! Don't you get that?"

"I'm sorry, Mother. Freya. I didn't want to tell you . . . I knew you would be angry, but I miss him so much. And he misses us, too. He just wants us to be a family again."

"Yes, about your father," Joanna said, her forehead creasing. "I need to tell you girls something. It's very hard for me to say and I hope you will find it in your hearts to forgive me."

"Why? What are you talking about?" Freya asked.

Joanna looked them both straight in the eye, with her head held high, as if steeling herself for the gallows. "Your father did not leave you. I tossed him out. I told him he had to leave us alone and that if he tried to get in touch with either of you I would make sure he regretted it forever."

For a moment neither of the girls spoke and a heavy silence fell, fraught with centuries of loss and heartache and resentment. Ingrid thought about all they had missed: years of her father's sage advice, his protection, his love. Freya could not even speak. The betrayal was so cruel she felt a compression in the pit of her stomach, as if she were going to vomit. "Why, Mother?" she finally whispered.

"I'm so very sorry, my darlings. I could not stop myself, I was so angry about what happened during the trials. I wanted him to do something about it—break you both out of jail, use his power to sway the judge—but he would not. Because of the laws of mid-world of course. But I wasn't thinking rationally."

Freya blinked back tears. "You lied to us. You told us he left us, that he was ashamed of us. That he didn't want anything more to do with our family."

"It doesn't matter now," Ingrid said, sitting on the couch and putting her arms around her sister. "We can't get those years back. But there's something else you need to know. Dad was helping me with something important. And I think something might have happened to him. He hasn't returned any of my messages for several days."

"Something has happened to him," Joanna said. She took another deep breath. Freya wondered if she could stand to hear another revelation.

"He's gone to see the White Council," their mother told them. "I went to his apartment and waited for him. A messenger from the Council came by, with a letter granting him permission to speak, but obviously he decided not to wait for it. He's left to consult with the oracle. He's probably there already."

Freya gasped. "But why would he do that?"

"I don't know. Unless word about our actions here have gotten back to him somehow; maybe he was reporting our violations of the restriction." Joanna crossed her arms.

"Dad wouldn't do that," Ingrid said loyally. "If he went to the oracle there has to be a good reason for it."

"What was he helping you with, anyway?" Freya asked.

"The Fair Haven blueprints. I found something—these odd

little design keys. Dad was decoding it for me. He said he'd figured out what they were, but then he disappeared."

"So maybe he wanted to talk to them about that?" Freya suggested.

Joanna whipped around to address Ingrid. "Fair Haven? You and Dad were doing something with Fair Haven?"

Ingrid described the key tags with the decorative scrolls. "I guess I should have asked you first, Mother, since you might know if there's something unusual about Fair Haven that we should know about."

Joanna shook her head. "Only that the Council told us when we settled here in North Hampton that the seam was there, the boundary where the living and the twilight worlds meet. But I think there might be something more to it. Before I left, I went out to Fair Haven, where the gray darkness in the water seems to have concentrated."

"It's not just here; it's in the South Pacific, and near Alaska as well," Ingrid said. "And I saw on TV the other day they think they might have found one near Reykjavík."

Joanna inhaled sharply at the news. "Whatever is in the oceans is not of this earth, I'm quite sure of that. I went to look for your father because I was hoping he could help me figure out what it was and where it came from so we could stop it. That spell I put on it won't last. I'm going to need both of you to help hold it up."

"We'll start immediately." Freya nodded.

"Good. With the three of us I think we can hold it back a while longer until we figure out how to get rid of it entirely." Joanna looked at her girls. "One more thing. What happened to the house? Has Gracella not been by to clean it? And how's my Tyler doing?"

"Tyler's in the hospital," Freya said. "Don't worry, I checked on him. He has a fever and an infection but the doctors say they have it under control."

Joanna tried to keep calm. If Tyler was sick, the hospital was the safest place for him to be. "First things first: Gardiners Island and then the hospital."

They were preparing to leave when there was a sharp knock on the door, and the three women jumped and looked at each other fearfully.

"The Council!" Ingrid yelped.

"The oracle doesn't knock," Freya scoffed. She peeked out the window and saw several police cars parked in the driveway, their lights flashing. "What on earth?"

"Open the door," Joanna instructed.

Ingrid moved toward the front door and flung it wide. "Matt!" she cried, her hands flying to her glasses. In all the ways she had imagined Matthew Noble visiting her home, this certainly was not one of them. The detective looked apologetic as he stepped inside the doorway with two policemen behind him.

"Hey, Ingrid, I'm really sorry to bother you, but I'm hoping your family has some time this afternoon to come down to the station and answer a few questions," he said, looking tired and anxious.

"Why?"

"Can we talk about it when we get there?"

"Do we have to?" Freya demanded. "Don't you need a warrant— or something?"

"No, we just want to ask some questions," he said sternly. "It's standard procedure."

"Matt—what's going on?" Ingrid asked fearfully.

"Why do you need to talk to the girls?" Joanna asked, her manner and tone imperious, as if the police detective were an underling daring to address the queen.

Freya snorted. "We're being arrested, aren't we?"

"Not at all, not at all. Look, we just want to ask you a few questions," Matt repeated for the third time, shaking his head slightly at Ingrid, as if to say he couldn't speak freely at the moment.

"Fine," Freya said. "Ingrid, let's go. See what they want to talk about." They motioned toward the door, but the detective stopped and looked apologetically back at their mother.

"I'm sorry, ma'am, but we'd like to talk to you as well," he said.

"Me? Why?" Joanna's forehead crinkled in worry.

"We'll get into it down at the station. Ladies?" Matt asked, leading them to the patrol cars parked in their driveway. One by one, the Beauchamp women were placed in the backseat, and the police car sped away, sirens on and lights flashing. They might not have been arrested, Freya thought, but it sure felt like they were in trouble.

the gods must be crazy

chapter thirty-seven

The Salem Trials

こ

Freya made a face at her sister, who sat stoically next to her in the backseat of the squad car. Her mother was on the other side, and none of them had said a word since they were taken into custody. When they arrived at the station, the three of them were separated, and Freya was left to ponder her fate and that of her family alone in a small room. The patrolmen who were her friends did not look her in the eye when she was led in, a bad sign. She wondered what was going to happen when the door opened, but it was only Ingrid who walked in, her face ashen.

"What's going on? Did you talk to Matt? What's happening?"

Ingrid shook her head. "No. They wanted to talk to Mother first. They had to use the room to interrogate someone else, so they moved me here. I have no idea what's happening."

"Some friend you got there," Freya muttered. She leaned back in her chair and looked around the small room with the one-way mirror. She wondered who was watching them. "Well, this brings back memories."

Her sister closed her eyes and bit the top of her thumb. "I know."

Freya sighed. In 1690 they had settled in the pretty little town of Salem in Massachusetts. Their lives had brought them to the New World as healers. Their mother had been one of the most sought-after midwives, had delivered healthy babies in a time when so many women died in childbirth and so many newborns died of fevers and pox. Ingrid worked in the community the same way she did now, doling out household charms and spells. Their father was a fisherman, due to his ability to maneuver the waters and bring in plentiful harvests.

Then something terrible happened. Bridget Bishop, who helped Joanna with the washing, came to her for help during her pregnancy and died in childbirth. Bridget was very dear to the family, and Joanna had not been able to help her. Then the rumors started: Freya was said to be conducting an affair with a boy who had pledged to marry Ann Putnam, who would become the ringleader of accusers. Ann and her friend Mercy Lewis testified that they had seen Freya and Ingrid "flying in the air through the winter mist." The trials were a farce, but effective. The community turned on them, branding Freya a slut, Ingrid a bitch, and Joanna a monster. Norman and Joanna had been spared but they were given a more terrible punishment. They had to watch as their daughters were hanged at Gallows Hill in 1692.

Freya shuddered. She could still remember the feeling of the noose around her neck, the scratchy rope that made her skin itch. The way the crowd had spat and thrown rotten food at their cart, the hatred and the fear and the hysteria.

"Don't," Ingrid said, as she knew exactly what Freya was thinking. "It doesn't help."

The Salem trials were the beginning of the end of practicing magic in mid-world. When the girls were reborn, they found a new world and new rules awaiting them. The family had resettled in North Hampton, and Joanna explained that the White Council had paid them a visit right after the burial. The Council told them that in order for any of them to continue to live in mid-world, every one of the *Waelcyrgean* would now have to adhere to a new condition: The Restriction of Magical Powers. In effect, it meant that they could no longer practice the art of magic and witchcraft without punishment and recrimination from the Council. They were to live as humans, with lives that were as ordinary as possible. There could be no more undue attention that would jeopardize knowledge of their existence. To continue to survive in mid-world they had to agree to live in the shadows. Those who did not comply would be in breach of Council laws and would be severely punished.

Their mother also told them that Norman had left the family for good, and they never saw their father again.

Back in Salem, as in North Hampton today, Freya understood that they would not be allowed to use their magic to save themselves. That had been made clear from the very beginning, when they found themselves stuck on the other side of the bridge, right in the dawn of the world. Sometimes Freya wondered how it was that she was so old and yet so young at the same time that she found herself in the same place as she had centuries before. Would she never learn? Maybe the Council was right, maybe magic had no place in mid-world. Every time they practiced it in the open, this happened: an anxious mob, a swift rush to judgment; and the result was always the same—witches hanging from the gallows, or burned at the stake, their ashes scattered to the four winds.

They sat in the room for what felt like an eternity but in reality was only a few hours. The policemen were kind and polite, especially those who had worked with Freya before, bringing deli sandwiches and drinks from the vending machine. But they were not allowed to leave. Matt Noble checked in on them from time to time, but Freya had been able to understand from his tight-lipped anxiety and Ingrid's mournful gazes that while he was not happy about what was happening, he had no power to stop it, either.

Finally, the door opened and their mother was allowed inside the room.

"What's going on?" Freya asked, helping Joanna to the nearest chair.

"It's the most absurd thing," Joanna said. She looked at her daughters, completely mystified by the situation in which they had found themselves. Here there were, afraid of the Council's recriminations, worrying about thunderbolts from the sky, and they had forgotten that the human realm was historically the area that had brought them the most pain.

"Okay, what is it? What did they want to talk to you about?"

Joanna looked at her girls with an expression of disbelief. "Maura Thatcher woke up from her coma."

"That's good, isn't it?" Ingrid asked.

"Well, yes. Except she told the detectives I was the one who attacked them the night that Bill died, that she saw me hit him on the back of the head with a rock. Then I did the same to her. Can you imagine? According to her, I killed him. "

chapter thirty-eight

A Good Offense
Is a Good Defense

~~

B efore the girls could react, the door opened again. Matt Noble entered the room and addressed the three women grouped around the table. "I'm so sorry. It's quite late and we're going to have to continue this another day." He looked plaintively at Ingrid but she refused to acknowledge him.

"So we're free to go now?" Freya asked.

"Even me?" Joanna asked tentatively.

"Yes, even you, Mrs. Beauchamp." Matt nodded. "Again, I apologize for the inconvenience. We're hoping you can come back tomorrow and answer our questions then."

Freya nodded curtly. "Come on, Ingrid, Mother," she said, leading her sister and mother out of the room. Ingrid looked as if she had gone catatonic, and Joanna appeared exhausted beyond reason.

"We're not coming back tomorrow," Ingrid said, finding her voice and looking straight at the detective. "Not without our lawyer."

O NE GOOD THING about lawyers, Ingrid thought, was that they were always punctual. Attorneys and their bills always arrived right on time. Antonio Forseti was a defense lawyer with a sterling reputation. He was also a warlock and an old friend of the family. Like the Beauchamps, he had been unable to practice magic since the restriction had been imposed on all of their kind. Instead he had used his natural talents at negotiating, striking balances, and using mediation to build one of the largest and most successful legal firms in New York City. He arrived the next afternoon armed with news.

"So I talked to the DA down here," he said, taking a seat at the head of the formal dining room. Forseti was a large man with a powerful barrel chest and a full head of dark hair, and his handshake had left Ingrid feeling a bit bruised.

"What did he say?" Joanna asked, her voice rising a few octaves. "Am I to be arrested?"

The girls had spent the evening calming down their mother, who had been on the verge of hysterics all night. Joanna had argued for leaving town as soon as possible, and only when Ingrid reminded her that leaving forever meant never seeing Tyler did she stop pressing them to run away.

"Not yet. Right now, it's just Maura Thatcher's word against yours, and she just got out of a coma. They don't have anything to prove it's true, nothing that'll hold up in court at least. Not yet."

"What about us? What do they want to ask us about?" Freya wanted to know.

Forseti gazed at them intently. "They want to ask about your potions and Ingrid about her knots." He took a long sip from his coffee cup. "They found Molly Lancaster's body buried a few miles away from the beach. She was beaten to death. The Adams boy's confessed, said it was him, that he killed her that evening."

Freya put her hands to her mouth, horrified to think of the terrible fate that had befallen the girl. Until Forseti spoke she had been hoping that Molly had somehow skipped town on her own, had merely run away.

"So, Derek confessed. But what about Freya? What does it have to do with her?" Ingrid demanded.

"His lawyer is arguing that Derek was a victim. That he had no control of his actions, they were a reaction to Molly taking one of Freya's magical potions," he said. "If they prove he was a victim of your witchcraft, then his charge gets bumped down to third degree. No intent, just misdemeanor; with a first-time offender, he might do a year."

"What about me? Is that what they think, too? That I killed the mayor?" Ingrid asked.

The bulky lawyer nodded. "Yes, they think they can prove your charm drove the mayor to take his own life."

"This whole thing is preposterous!" Freya laughed. "Dark magic? Are they insane? They're going to argue that in a court of law? What century are we living in?"

He sighed and held up his hands to signal that he wasn't finished. "Corky Hutchinson's father is a retired judge with some pull with the DA's office, and the Adams boy's parents have hired a real expensive sleazebag, bringing up case law that hasn't been invoked in centuries. But just because it hasn't been used doesn't mean it doesn't stand. There're a lot of antiquated laws on the books. And don't forget, in Salem, they hanged nineteen of us without cause."

That took the fight out of Freya for a moment, while Joanna began to sniff and Ingrid clasped her hands together. It was just as it was before. The only difference was that Forseti was wearing a more expensive suit. This was Salem all over again. A small town in hysterics. Accusations from high-ranking families in a tight-knit community. Witches on trial. Magic the root of all evil. What humans did not understand they were always afraid of. The Beauchamps had believed that the people of North Hampton might be different; they were wrong.

"What's the worst they can do?"

"If they prove their case, which I'm not saying they'll be able to, you'll both be convicted of being accessories to murder, which is a felony, and, depending on what they can prove, could carry a sentence of life in prison."

"What about Mother? Is Maura's testimony going to hold up?"

"Possibly, if they can find more evidence to build their case. Right now we could argue that she's confused, that she's not a reliable witness. According to Mrs. Thatcher, they bumped into Joanna that evening, and when they turned around to walk away Joanna attacked them. On a good note, they're not accusing you of being a witch, so your case is pretty straightforward. If Maura Thatcher's all they've got, it's not much; so for now, I'm not too worried."

"But I wasn't even anywhere near the shore that night! It was January. I was in bed by then! And why would I possibly hurt them?" Joanna asked, fanning herself.

"Can you prove it?"

"I'm not sure. I'll have to check my calendar, see where the girls were that night and what they remember."

Freya frowned. "I'm pretty sure I was working that night."

"And I would have been asleep." Ingrid sighed. "This is hopeless."

"All right, fine. So they think Mom's a murderess who goes around knocking old folks on the head, and that Ingrid and I are big bad witches. What do we do now?" Freya asked.

Forseti took a big gulp of his coffee. "You want my advice? And I know you do, otherwise Joanna here wouldn't have called my office at two in the morning. It's an easy out. You ready?"

The girls nodded.

"You answer their questions, you tell them what you know but you hammer home the point. Magic. Does. Not. Exist. What,

226

are they crazy? Your potions were just cute little cocktails and Ingrid's a kook, you know, one of those ladies from the library who've read too much Zoroastrianism." Forseti shrugged. "This isn't Salem. It's a different time. A secular time."

"That sounds reasonable enough." Joanna nodded. "What do you girls think?"

Freya shrugged. "I guess. I mean, I'm with you, Mr. Forseti, I don't see how their accusations could get very far in court, but . . ."

"But?"

"I'm worried."

"Of course you're worried, sweetheart. Being questioned by the police is not a laughing matter. I'm not laughing. But trust me, I've got this one in the bag."

Ingrid frowned. Forseti certainly looked different from the last time they had seen him, but otherwise everything else, including his absurd confidence in the legal system's ability to give them a fair trial, was exactly the same. "With all due respect, Mr. Forseti, the last time you advised us, you also argued that magic was not real and we were hanged anyway," Ingrid said.

"So, what are you saying?" the lawyer asked, looking offended.

Ingrid looked at her family. Her mother had aged a hundred years in one night, and Freya looked as if she were about to faint. "We tell the truth this time. Our magic *is* real. We *are* witches. But we had nothing to do with this. We don't practice black magic and we didn't cause Molly's murder or the mayor's suicide."

Freya nodded slowly and the color returned to her cheeks.

Mr. Forseti shook his head. "Dicey, dicey, dicey."

"Are you sure, Ingrid?" Joanna asked. "I hope you know what you're doing."

"I'm sure." Ingrid nodded. She remembered Salem all too well, sitting in that small prison cell for eight months, subsisting on stale bread and water. She had watched her fellow witches carted off down the hill never to return. She had sat in the courtroom and listened as a succession of her dearest friends had called her names, had blamed her for every disease and run of bad luck they experienced, had turned her helpful advice into a twisted tale of black magic and devilish sorcery. Every day she had waited for the sound of the carriages that would take her to her death. She had not been afraid of death, but she had been deathly afraid of pain. A round of questioning was only the beginning; soon there would be an arrest, a trial, a conviction if they were not careful. The hanging trees were gone now, but one could still live out the rest of this lifetime in a prison cell. Life imprisonment meant something else for the immortal.

Maybe her mother was right: their only chance was to run, to hide in the shadows and disappear. But this was her home. She thought of her friends, and of Matt, who had whispered in her ear as she was led away: "I believe you."

She looked at her family. "It's time to own up to the truth. When they ask us what we did, we'll tell them. We'll admit to who and what we are. Freya?"

Her sister nodded. "I don't see any other way. And Ingrid's right. I don't want to live a lie anymore. What can we lose?"

Everything, Ingrid thought. But she was willing to take that chance.

chapter thirty-nine

The Brief Wonderful Life of Tyler Alvarez

~ex~

S ince Forseti was still negotiating with the police department
for a time that would be more convenient for the women to
meet and answer questions, Joanna took the opportunity to
visit Tyler at the hospital the next day. The children's wing was
painted a cheerful blue and pink, but Joanna thought she had
never entered a more depressing place. So much false hope and
promise, when, really, all around was the scepter of death at the
doorstep, snatching away the most precious of lives. Children
should not be allowed to get sick or die; it should be a rule,
Joanna raged. One should not leave mid-world until one had had
a full life . . . at least until eighteen? Thirty? Sixty? Time did not
mean anything to those who had too much of it, but it was even
more precious once it was limited.

She had promised herself she would never love another child.
After what happened to her boy she knew she would not survive if she lost another. How could she let this happen? And the
girls—she could not even think about the ongoing investigation
and the girls' upcoming interrogation. She hoped they knew what
they were doing, but she was worried they were far too optimistic about their chances. The world did not change; she had
been around long enough to understand that much. Children
died. Either on the gallows or in a hospital.

Joanna looked at the small, shriveled form in the large bed, connected to a maze of wires and drips. She stood at the far side of the bed, while his parents kept vigil on either side, his mother holding his hand. Tyler had been moved to the ICU a few days ago. After Freya and Gracella had brought him in he had recovered only to get sick again, this time with a worse infection. The doctors could not explain it: there was no bacterial infection, and he did not respond to viral treatment, either. But Tyler was not the only one: there were two other children on the ward with the same symptoms; and in the main hospital, there were adults with the same phlegmy, forceful cough, the same ragged breathing. Like Tyler, the victims had displayed milder symptoms in the beginning that could be attributed to allergies or the flu; but one by one they took a turn for the worse, with complications that affected lung and brain functions. Freya was visiting her boss, Sal McLaughlin, who was down the hall, and Joanna bumped into Dan Jerrods, whose wife, Amanda, was now on life support.

She watched Tyler's chest rise and fall, heard his difficult breathing. The attending doctor entered. "Tell me the truth . . . how bad is it?" she asked.

The young resident looked at his feet, his voice strained. "There is nothing we can do for him now but make him comfortable. I am so sorry."

The Alvarezes turned to her to translate. What did the doctor say? What did he mean? Joanna shook her head and began to cry softly, and that was when Gracella began to scream. Hector tried to calm his wife, and the nurses surrounded them. They were taken to another room, where Gracella was given a sedative.

Joanna stood, rooted at the spot, still trying to process the doctor's words. *Make him comfortable. Nothing we can do.* Was this truly the end? Was there nothing anyone could do for him? She clenched her fists and cursed the gods who could not hear her. This was just like before. She could still remember the voice that had doomed her son to eternity, how her boy had been enveloped by smoke that rose from the ground and then taken down to limbo, to nowhere, to serve his sentence.

The door opened and Ingrid appeared, holding a fruit basket. "It's from Tabitha and Hudson. They heard. How is he?"

"The same. No, actually, that's not right. He's worse."

"I'm so sorry, Mother." Ingrid squeezed her shoulder, but she was crying herself.

"I know, my darling." Joanna patted her daughter's hand and held back a sob.

"And there's nothing . . . I mean, I know there's nothing you can do . . . but . . . ?"

Joanna shook her head. She cursed the magic within her. Her useless, useless magic. This was the greatest tragedy of her gift: Joanna could bring anyone back to life, could cure any sickness, could bring health and happiness to the person dying in the next room. She had saved Lionel Horning from the Kingdom of the Dead.

But her magic was immune to those that she loved. She remembered that girl in Salem, Bridget Bishop, whom she loved as she loved her daughters. Bridget had died in a river of her own blood, while Joanna remained shocked and helpless, unable to do anything to save her.

Over the next several days, the Beauchamps brought Christmas in August to the children's ward, especially Tyler's room. While the attorneys negotiated, Freya made beautiful feasts, huge cakes dripping in cream frosting, fat éclairs swathed in chocolate sauce, the most succulent pastries and the largest chocolate chip cookies. Ingrid made spells to keep Tyler's pillows plump and fluffy, charms that allowed his sheets to stay dry even through the night sweats. Joanna brought the dancing puppets, the warring soldiers.

One evening, Tyler opened his eyes. He saw Joanna and smiled.

"What do you want, my darling? My sweet? My dearest love?" she asked as she smoothed his hair.

"Want to fly," he said, looking longingly out the window. "Outside. Like you."

So that evening, Joanna conjured up a broomstick—she did not need it but it would be easier for Tyler to have something to hold on to.

They flew out of the hospital bed and to the stars, the boy's laughter carrying over the treetops.

chapter forty

Twenty Questions

❧

Since Freya had nothing appropriate to wear to a meeting with the police, it was her turn to borrow something from Ingrid's closet.

"There," Ingrid said. "Now you look innocent."

"We *are* innocent." Freya rolled her eyes. She glanced at herself in the mirror. She was wearing a cashmere twinset, a plaid skirt that hit her knee, and low-heeled shoes. "Everyone thinks so." She glanced at the cards that had arrived once the news had spread that the police were interested in talking to the Beauchamp women about their so-called magic.

Ingrid nodded. Many of their friends in town had sent notes of encouragement and love. There was a sweet note from Tabitha, a funny one from Hudson, and even though Sal was still in the hospital, Kristy had left a message on the machine earlier saying that if there was going to be a witch hunt, the Beauchamps were welcome to hide in her house until it blew over. They had nothing to fear; the town was behind them, unlike Salem, where they had been friendless and alone. It gave them courage to face the day ahead.

Forseti was waiting for them with his car. "Where's Joanna?" he asked, when he saw it was only Ingrid and Freya.

"It's better if she doesn't come with us," Freya said. She and

Ingrid had decided last night that it would be better if they faced the questioning on their own. Joanna was too excitable and they did not want to upset their mother further; she was already inconsolable about Tyler's sickness.

At the police station, they were ushered into the same small interrogation room where they had waited before.

"Where's Matt?" Ingrid asked the detective who followed them into the room. "I thought we were here to talk to him."

"Detective Noble is out on another job," the detective replied with a smirk. "Shall we begin?"

Ingrid paled as she took her seat. Freya felt her stomach sink. The detective was a humorless type with a bad combover. He dismissed Forseti's handshake and did not look either of the girls in the eye. Freya recognized him from the bar. (His secret sexual perversion: watching high-heeled women crush the life out of small animals. Sick.)

Freya was up first.

"Miss Beauchamp, I have here a cocktail menu from the North Inn bar. Is this the one that you made?" he asked, sliding over the laminated menu.

Freya looked at Forseti, who nodded. They had gone over the routine several times now and she was prepared. "Yes," she answered. *Admit to witchcraft, but emphasize theirs was a harmless magic.*

"Allow me to read from this menu. '*Irresistible*: Vodka, pureed cherries, powdered cattail, and lime juice. Not for the shy. Prepare to lose your inhibitions.' Can you tell us what this means?"

"It's a love potion," she said slowly.

"Obviously." The detective sneered. "And it's supposed to render the drinker—irresistible? How exactly?"

"The herbal remedies in it create a glow around a person; it heightens their pheromones—their attractiveness quotient, let's say."

"By magic."

"Yes, if magic is the word that means making the impossible possible. I bring out the magic that is inside a person and make it visible. The potion lets everyone see the best parts of the person, and therefore makes them more attractive," she said, using the carefully rehearsed words her lawyer had approved.

"So it works."

"Yes."

"Are there any dangers that could arise from being so attractive? For instance, could a person find someone so attractive it could lead to a loss of control on their end?" the detective mused.

Forseti coughed. "My client is not going to answer speculative inquiries like that one."

"Excuse me. Let me rephrase it. . . . How do you quantify its power? How can you be sure that it had no adverse effects on the unsuspecting public? Could this potion, for instance . . . drive a man to do something he might not do otherwise?"

The defense attorney glared at the detective and turned to Freya. "You don't have to answer that, either."

"I know," Freya said. "But I will. No, it could never harm the person who had taken it. I'm quite sure."

"You can't explain it, but you're absolutely certain it could not lead to violence?" he barked.

"It doesn't work that way."

"How does it work, then?"

"I told you, I don't know. It's just . . ." Freya sighed. "Magic."

The detective nodded, scribbling his notes. "Exactly. Thank you, Miss Beauchamp."

INGRID WAS NEXT. The unsmiling detective asked her to turn to the computer that had been set up on the desk. On the screen there were two photographs. One was the fidelity knot she had given Corky Hutchinson, magnified so that everyone could see each whorl clearly. On the other side was the noose that Todd Hutchinson used to hang himself. The knot on the noose was an exact replica of the one next to it.

"Tell me about your magic," he said.

"Mostly I work with little charms, talismans, spells. A lot of the magic I work with is in knots. It's how sailors used to divine the winds."

"You gave this knot to the mayor's wife, did you not?" he asked, pointing to the first knot.

"Yes."

"For what purpose?"

"She suspected her husband of cheating on her. I made her a knot and told her to put it underneath his pillow. It would keep him from straying; it would keep him home. But only if she was there as well."

"Do you admit the knot on the noose looks a whole lot like the knot you made?"

"Yes, but . . . the knots don't work that way," Ingrid protested. "They would never drive anyone to suicide. At best, they would unravel—"

"So you're saying that this little talisman, as you called it, did nothing to lead to the mayor's death. That it was just a coincidence that it looks just like the one he hung himself with."

"Yes."

"That the knot you made did not drive him sleepless, or change his personality, or cause him to be estranged from his wife. So what does it do, then?"

"I don't know, but I know it keeps people together if they want to be together. It makes something more visible that isn't there."

"And there is no possible way it can go wrong?"

"Well, I didn't say that—"

"So there is!"

"I don't know," Ingrid said, slumped on the chair. "This has never happened before. We practice white magic. We don't—"

"White magic!" The detective sneered. He slammed his notebook on the table. "I think we're done here."

As they walked out of the police station, Ingrid turned to Forseti, who was wiping his brow with a handkerchief. "I can't believe Matt wasn't even there to help us. Do you think we did the right thing in admitting that we're witches?" she asked.

Freya sighed. Her sister was so obtuse sometimes. "If it wasn't, it's too late now to change things."

"You really think we'll be arrested?" Ingrid asked, horrified, since their lawyer had gone mute.

Freya's shoulders slumped. "What do you think?"

Ingrid had to admit that perhaps they had miscalculated their strategy.

chapter forty-one

The Poisoned Tree

ᴒᴄ

The end of August arrived, humid and sticky, but no arrests were made. Joanna, Freya, and Ingrid each retreated to their own corners to deal with their anxiety and frustration in private. Freya went back to the bar, surreptitiously helping out with the bartending, while Joanna spent most of her time visiting Tyler in the hospital, and Ingrid worked at the library.

It was after hours and the library was ghostly quiet and deserted, but Ingrid took comfort in the familiar and well-loved surroundings. She sat at her desk and went through everything that had happened in North Hampton that summer. The silvery tumors she'd found in the women; the rash of unexplainable diseases affecting the townspeople; the dead animals in Lionel Horning's barn; the underwater explosion that had released a poisonous toxin, one that was similar to others found around the world—was it possible they were all linked? There was something here she was missing, something that would allow her to pull it all together.

It all tied back to Fair Haven and the missing blueprints, she was sure of it. Mother said that Fair Haven held the seam, but there had to be something more. There was something there that someone did not want her to see, did not want her to find out—and with a flash, Ingrid remembered the image she had taken on her phone earlier in the summer. She'd taken not only a photo of the door but of the ballroom floor plan as well and sent both to her father. She turned on her desk lamp to a brighter setting and removed her phone from her purse. Her fingers quickly tapped and swept the touch screen until the tiny image of the blueprint appeared. Yes! She sent it to a computer terminal and a few minutes later the page from the missing architectural plans was rolling out of the library's decade-old printer.

Ingrid examined the paper. The printer had automatically sized the tiny photo to fit a letter-size sheet, and the image was grainy, as it had been enlarged many times its actual size. She found the scrollwork in the tiny architectural drawing key, a swirl of dark lines and cryptic characters. As she examined the curving arabesques she caught sight of another faint image, lines and text running at an odd angle across the image. These characters were smaller and lighter than the rest of the text, and some of the characters looked different from those on the key.

She brought the drawing over to the old copier, laid it on the glass, and set the enlargement to two hundred percent and the brightness to the lowest setting. A large blackened image rolled out the far end of the machine, and when she looked at it closely she noticed that the second set of text was actually written backwards, as if seen through a mirror. Ingrid puzzled over it for a moment until she realized that the bright little flash on her new phone must have shone though the thin paper, revealing the lines that had been written on the back of the sheet. She tried to think if she had ever examined the backsides of blueprints and could not remember ever doing so. Blueprints were several feet long and wide and a person reading them tended to just open the page halfway to stare at some portion of the drawing. To flip the pages completely over would have required a desk eight feet wide.

Ingrid grabbed the sheet of paper and ran into the bathroom, excited by her new idea. She held it to the mirror and snapped another photo with a real camera, one with a much higher resolution. Using the mirror would invert the text so that it could be read. She took the camera back to her desk and printed the new photo.

Now she understood. The text was separated into two bands; the top was written in Norse, the language she had learned as a child from her father. The second line contained the same lettering that surrounded the design tags, in a language she could not understand. The characters corresponded to one another, like a Rosetta stone. Since she understood the first language, that was all she needed to decipher the keys.

Ingrid worked on translating quickly. The letters were faint and there were spots where words and characters dropped out, but she could still glean a basic understanding. The first sentence, a title of sorts, read: "Yggdrasil."

Yggdrasil.

Ingrid leapt from her desk and dashed to the back of the library, where they kept the reserved books no one was allowed to borrow. There was a book there, one she had inherited from her father many years ago, that she had donated to the library when she first started. A book that contained their history. The front cover was nearly torn from the book when she pulled it from the shelf, although it appeared to have spent the better part of the last few decades entirely undisturbed.

Yggdrasil.

The word resonated with power. Ingrid sat on the floor in front of the bookshelf resting the heavy book on her folded legs. She flipped through the pages, turning them back and forth until she found the section she was looking for.

Yggdrasil: The Tree of Life that held the Nine Worlds of the Known Universe.

There was a picture of a mighty tree growing in the void of space. Free of the earth, its shape formed a perfect hourglass, with a circle of branches at one end and a ball of roots at the other. The tree floated, its densely woven branches forming a spiraling shape that reminded her of the Fair Haven blueprint. She compared the image in the book with the image on the architect's drawing and suddenly, everything made sense.

Fair Haven was somehow a part of this great and ancient tree; it housed an entryway into the skeleton of the universe. She began to translate the design tags, finding their corresponding meaning in Norse. Ingrid studied the terms one by one, jotting down the translations as she worked diligently for the better part of an hour. Her head hurt a little and her eyes felt dry from straining at the faint symbols. Ingrid penned the last character and then pulled back, her spine aching from having sat bent in one position too long, but she had found what she set out to discover.

She read the translation again, and her mind whirled, recalling that clandestine trip to Fair Haven when she had discovered the hidden door. At the time, she had guessed that the house had been built to create the mystical doorway. But now she understood from reading the symbols that the house was not an entryway to the tree but had been created as a fortress to protect it. The house was a barrier, not a door.

Ingrid gasped. It was all so clear now. She knew now what was causing all the problems—the silvery darkness, the underground explosion, the barren women, the dead animals, the toxin in the water and in the air. It all pointed in the same direction, to the man who had handed her the plans to the site from the beginning.

Killian Gardiner. He was a Guardian, an immortal who was, historically, meant to protect Fair Haven and the tree. But what if instead of protecting the tree, he had endangered it somehow?

He had come back to Fair Haven after traveling the world. He had worked off the coast of Australia and on an Alaskan freighter—places where the toxin had also been found. She did not know if he had been near Reykjavík, but she would bet on it. He had traveled the globe, spreading the toxin.

As she read the words again she found she could barely breathe. *"The time of* Ragnarok *is at hand, when the earth is submerged in poisoned water. Thus will begin the age of the wolf, when brother will turn against brother, and the world will be no more. Lest the poison of the Nine disperse, the living should not pass the way of* Yggdrasil.*"*

chapter forty-two

Götterdämmerung

⌒ꝰꝰ

For millennia, back when the earth was new, Asgard and Midgard were connected by the Bofrir bridge, made from the bones of the dragons who came before. One terrible day the bridge was destroyed. The damage to the bridge was permanent, and the cause of its destruction came as a surprise to all, for the culprits were revealed to be Fryr of the Vanir and his great friend Loki of the Aesir, two daring young gods whose childish prank brought a terrible consequence. The bridge was the root of the gods' power, and Loki and Fryr were accused of trying to take the power for themselves.

As punishment for their actions Loki was banished to the frozen depths for five thousand years, while Fryr was consigned to limbo for an indefinite period since his crime had been the greater one. It was his trident that had sent the bridge to the abyss.

With the bridge destroyed, the gods were separated. The Vanir, the gods and goddesses of hearth and earth, were trapped in Midgard; while of the Aesir, the warrior gods of sky and light, only mighty Odin and his wife, Frigg, remained in Asgard, both of their sons lost to them for thousands of years. Their *sons*: Balder and Loki. Branford and Killian Gardiner.

Killian Gardiner. Loki. Killian. Loki.

Her lover. Freya knew what she had to do once Ingrid told her about the breach of *Yggdrasil*. The toxin was the sap from the poisoned tree, and there was only one man in the whole universe who would find it amusing to destroy the very foundation of their world and bring about *Ragnarok*. The end of times. The doom of the gods. Freya realized that the sand giants were Loki's Snow Giants, his guards. They had come back and circled the house at Fair Haven, to be close to their master. She raced as fast as she could to Fair Haven and found Killian in his usual place, aboard his beloved boat.

She climbed on board and faced him. "I know, you know," she said. "I know who you are and what you've been doing." The realization had been slowly dawning. She'd denied it, never dared to admit it to herself, even privately, but now there was no way to ignore it.

Killian took her hand in his. "I'm so glad. I've been waiting so long . . . five thousand years, with just the memory of your kiss to sustain me . . ." He gathered her in his arms and kissed her forehead. "I missed you so much. More than you will ever know," he said.

Even if she burned with hatred, she allowed him to kiss her and to lead her to the cabin below. She had to keep him there until Ingrid could figure out how to fix what he had broken; she had to keep him distracted and keep him company. There was the same urgency in his kisses that had been there the night of the woods, the same passionate intensity.

And then Freya noticed they were not alone.

"Madame said I would find you here, but I did not believe it at first." Bran Gardiner stood in the doorway of the cabin holding a gun. His brown eyes shone with a deep despair. "So, you have what you wanted after all, brother." Freya had forgotten: she was supposed to meet him at the North Inn an hour ago, and of course he had gone looking for her. This was supposed to be their big joyful reunion.

Bran Gardiner. Balder. The God of Joy and Peace, of Beauty and Light, who personified everything that was good and true in the world. The best of them all. Her kind and gentle mate. They were made to be together. His mother, the goddess Frigg, had decreed that nothing on earth could hurt him. Yet she had forgotten to shield him from the most dangerous thing of all. The mistletoe. Her kiss. Her love.

Once upon a time in Asgard, the goddess Freya had two suitors, two handsome brothers to claim her hand. She had chosen Balder as her immortal mate. Enraged and jealous, Loki vowed revenge; and on the eve of their wedding, his poison-tipped arrow met its mark. The arrow pierced Balder's heart and sent him to the Kingdom of the Dead.

Freya lost herself to grief and madness until her sister, Erda (Ingrid), who could see the future, gave her a ray of hope. She comforted Freya, telling her that in her lifeline, she saw that one day, in a different universe, in a different time and place, she and Balder would find each other again.

Thousands of years later, she met Bran Gardiner and she knew he was the one she was waiting for. Her own dear Balder. They had found each other, only to be destroyed by Loki once again. This time, she had let the snake into her bed.

Freya stood up from the bed and started to speak, but Bran shook his head. "Don't," he said to Freya. "I can't even look at you."

"Bran, put down that gun, it's over," Killian said hoarsely, as he moved slowly away from the bed and toward his brother. The two men sized each other up, and Killian appeared larger than he had been just moments ago, looming over Bran with an unexpected strength.

Bran wavered, and the gun tilted from his hand. Killian took the opportunity and knocked the gun from his brother's grip. The weapon twisted violently around, and Killian's fingers wrapped the trigger and squeezed. The sound was thunderous, like a crack from the heavens. This was no ordinary gun. Freya screamed. The bullet flew just over Bran's shoulder, nipping the edge of his neck and drawing blood. Thick red blood seeped from the cut, spreading outward in a crimson circle that quickly enveloped his shoulder.

Freya heard a snap then, like bones cracking, as the two men were pressed chest to chest; four hands wrapped the gun, both men pawing wildly at the weapon as they tried simultaneously to control the gun's trigger and to point the barrel at the other. Killian yelled in pain and pushed back hard, heaving forward with both legs. The force of his blow sent both of them tumbling to the ground with Killian on top.

The weapon fired twice more and both shots cut through the drapes and burst the windowpane. She couldn't tell whose finger had triggered the shot, as their bodies concealed the gun. Anyone could be in control. Bran freed his left hand from the weapon; drawing backward quickly, he caught Killian hard in the jaw with a punch. Without stopping he drew back twice more, delivering two hard punches to Killian's face. Two more shots fired. A stream of plaster drifted down from the cabin ceiling.

Who had fired the gun? Freya wondered. Who was winning? She dove toward the men, her hands scrambling for the weapon, but she was too late. The barrel contained six bullets. The last shot rang out, but this time there were no broken windows or cratered ceiling. The bullet had found a home in one of the brothers.

With ferocious strength, Freya ripped Killian off Bran, who lay motionless on the ground, and Killian tumbled away, his leg covered in blood. A hole was torn through his pant leg and blood poured from the open wound. Without thinking, she pressed her hand to the wound, stopping the flow for a moment.

Killian groaned, and all the color drained from his face; but he would live, Freya thought contemptuously. She got up to tend to Bran, but with a shock, she saw that he had disappeared.

There was no one else in the room.

chapter forty-three

The Curse of
Freya and Balder

ฝ๛

L oki! What did you do! Where is he?!" she screamed. Where
was her beloved? Had he left her forever?

Killian blinked his eyes open and looked at Freya. "Loki? He
escaped? You have to catch him . . . follow him . . ." He coughed.
"Before he . . ."

"Stop it! Stop lying. What do you mean Loki has escaped?"
she said, feeling as if she were about to lose her mind, just when
everything had begun to make sense.

Killian shook his head, and he looked so wounded that it was
as if a light began to catch fire in her mind. Everything that had
been hazy and confused and twisted before began to dissipate
into the cold, clear light of the truth. When she said his name, it
was as if she were waking up from the deepest sleep. "Balder, is
it really you?"

"Yes. Yes, of course." Killian's face, bloodied and weary,
broke into a beautiful smile. The smile of the boy who had won
her heart in Asgard. The smile of her beloved. He looked the way
he did when she had first seen him, a beautiful boy playing his
lyre at the edge of the forest. With those gorgeous blue-green eyes,
merry and playful and light.

Then Freya realized—she *had* recognized him, from the very
beginning, at the engagement party. It was why she was drawn

to him from the start, the minute she saw him, why her love for Bran had been conflicted and confusing, saddled with guilt and sadness. Now she understood why she had been so agitated that evening.

Bran Gardiner was Loki. The God of Mischief and Chaos. Trickster. Shapeshifter. The Sly One. Con man. Liar. Thief. Loki had spun a web of lies from the very beginning, had tricked her into falling in love, had woven a spell around her heart, a powerful glamour that had bound her to him. That first night when she had met him, when her dress had slipped, she realized now, was his doing, so that he had an excuse to touch her. Then those nights at the bar, seven in all, where he had stared at her; all the while he was hypnotizing her to make sure she was the one who made the first move, to complete the spell.

"There are no words . . ." Freya bowed her head in grief.

"I did not wait five thousand years for an apology," he said softly.

"I am not worthy of you."

"You do not understand. We belong together. Always," Killian said. "I could not say anything. I was bound by the prophecy and could not reveal myself until you had recognized me for who I was. I could only hope, although I did try to warn you all about the danger in my own way."

"The dead birds on the beach that Joanna found in the beginning of the summer. That was you, wasn't it?"

Killian nodded.

"How did you know I was here? How did you find me?"

"Bran tracked me down and sent me an invitation to the engagement party. I think he could not help himself. He wanted me to see that he had won, that he had found you first. So that I would know that he had what I wanted more than anything in the world. He always blamed me for his imprisonment in Helheim."

Freya realized that Bran's plan would have worked if he had not been so sure of his victory. But his pride became his undoing; by tempting fate and inviting Killian to witness his triumph, the spell he had cast over her heart had begun to fade the moment she had seen Killian. She had even tried to wed him that night in the forest. She had known who he was, truly; part of her had always known.

"When I arrived he told me his sentence had ended, that he'd been freed by Helda. But I began to be suspicious. Here, open the closet door, there's a bag on the floor."

Freya did as told and brought out a brown paper bag. Inside was a wool hat, flecked and crusted with blood. "This is Bill Thatcher's," she said.

"I found it in the basement when I first arrived and I hid it away until I could find out whose it was and where it was from."

"He was the one who killed Bill. Bill and Maura always walked that ridge, across from Fair Haven."

Killian nodded. "Bran came to Fair Haven in the middle of January, on the eve of the full moon. He must have worried that they had seen him in his true form when he first came to the house, so he attacked them."

Now she understood why she could not see who had murdered Bill; Loki's magic had prevented her from doing so. "He disguised himself as my mother." Freya told Killian what had happened— that Maura Thatcher had woken from her coma and fingered Joanna as Bill's murderer.

"I stayed so that I could figure out what he was planning, and because I could not keep away from you, of course. I suspected he was lying, that he had not been released and instead had broken out of his prison, and in so doing let darkness into this world. I still do not know how he did it—he must have a powerful weapon at his disposal, something that has allowed him to travel between the realms."

"His ring. He carries a ring on him," Freya said. *It is my fa-ther's*, Bran had told her. *It is dear to me; it is all I have left of him.* "Odin's ring." Made of dragon bone, it could take its bearer through the Nine Worlds, she told Killian.

"So that is how he broke out of his confinement. I thought it might have something to do with Fair Haven, where he was liv-ing, and on a hunch I sent Ingrid the plans, thinking she might be able to unlock the code."

"She did. She knows what's in Fair Haven. It holds a branch of *Yggdrasil*."

"So that was his secret," Killian said. "He had used the path through the tree to arrive in Fair Haven, for he knew the legend of the Guardians, and as one of us the house would accept him."

"I told him that you had given the plans to Ingrid and that she was close to figuring it out—he must have stolen them back, and that was why he attacked her, using your form. Oh, Killian, I've been so—"

"Stop. He has always played us false. It is his way. He knew what he was doing when he breached the tree and released the poisoned sap into Midgard."

"Then we are lost," Freya whispered. Her happiness at find-ing her true love was tempered by knowledge of the darkness that Loki had unleashed upon the world.

Ingrid appeared at the door. "I'm sorry to interrupt. But, Freya . . ."

"What's wrong?" Her sister looked fraught.

"It's Tyler. He passed away a few minutes ago."

chapter forty-four

The Labyrinth

～

T hen we don't have much time," Killian said. "It's the poison. It's stronger now. The children are the most vulnerable, but there will be more victims, more deaths, if we do not stop this."

"Ingrid . . . Killian is—"

"I know," Ingrid said with a brief nod. "I figured it out as well. Remember what I told you about *Ragnarok*? First the oceans will die? And how the toxin that's in North Hampton is similar to ones found near Sydney, Greenland, and Reykjavík? They just found one near Vietnam. Bran has been spreading it around the world since he arrived in Fair Haven in January." She explained how at first she had attempted to trace it to Killian's travels, but she could not find the Alaskan freighter where he was supposed to have served, nor the Sydney resort where he was supposed to have worked as a scuba instructor. As far as she could see, Killian had never been to any of those places, and with a start she'd realized that the person who had told them that Killian had traveled the world was Bran.

She began to investigate Bran's background and travels, and she realized her mistake in identifying the brothers as soon as she put together the news clippings about the toxin's locations with a copy of Bran's itinerary from the Gardiner Foundation, which was published on their Web site. The dates and places matched exactly. Under the cover of charity work, Bran had traveled to each and every place on the map that the toxin had been found. The explosion in the middle of the summer meant the tree was beginning to collapse inwardly. Her suspicions confirmed, she had done a little more digging on the foundation and discovered that in contrast to all the hype, there was very little good it was actually doing; most of its work seemed to be tied up in endless bureaucratic meetings; the foundation had hardly given any money to any of the causes it supported. It was a tax front, a fraud, a way to hide the Gardiner fortune.

She told all this to Freya and Killian. Now she understood that Bran was Loki all along. Like her sister and mother, she had been fooled; due to the restriction, they had been rusty and blinded and lost without their magic, and had failed to sense his use of a powerful spell. She blushed to think of her dream of Killian the other night. Another of Loki's tricks, of course, to throw them off his trail.

"I know where he's headed," Ingrid said. "Through the secret door in Fair Haven. In the ballroom. Come on."

"Go," Killian said to Freya. "He has Odin's ring; he could be anywhere in the universe by now."

"I can't leave you here," Freya said.

"My leg's shattered, but I can control the bleeding; don't worry about me. I'll only slow you down."

Freya kissed Killian once more and then joined her sister. "Let's go. It's time to end this."

INGRID LED THE WAY to the ballroom. She cast a spell that shattered the plaster and revealed the ghost door she had found underneath.

"Okay, so how do you open it?" Freya asked.

"Watch." Ingrid had read about the tree in her father's book. The language she had been unable to decipher, she now understood, was the language of the dragons and the giants who had come before the gods. She placed her hands on the door and murmured a few words.

The door creaked open to reveal nothing but darkness. Ingrid took Freya's hand and together they slipped through the portal. As her eyes slowly adjusted to the dark, she saw that a pale blue glow lit the coarse thicket that surrounded them. The space, if it could be called that, smelled of damp earth and wood. There was a path that led forward, deeper into the thicket.

However, before they could walk any farther, they came upon Lionel Horning. He was covered in blood, and they could see that he was rotting from inside out; half of his face was missing and he leered at them with his one good eye. "Stop," he said in a hoarse voice, raising a hand that was missing two fingers. "You may not enter." Their friend had been turned into a guard dog, an obstacle to block their way.

"Oh, Lionel . . ." Ingrid sighed. "The toxin. It must have been in his blood, in his system, when he swallowed all that ocean water, which is why the resurrection didn't take."

"So I was wrong. He's not a demon," Freya said.

"No, definitely zombie," Ingrid said. "The river underneath their farm . . . it leads to the ocean. The toxin must have been strong there. He's been breathing it. He swallowed the water and then he was living in a poisoned space. No wonder."

"Lionel, I'm so sorry but I have to do this," Ingrid said, raising her wand. White rope appeared from the end of her wand and wrapped tightly around Lionel, creating a straightjacket. "That will hold him. I don't think we can bring him back, his body is too decayed. But if we stop Loki it will restore Lionel's spirit and send him to Helda as he was."

There was a cry from beyond, on the other side of the path that led away from the tree. "It's Tyler. Ingrid—you get the boy. We've got twenty-four hours before the Dead claim him forever."

"What about you?" Ingrid asked, already turning to the sound of the boy's cries.

"I'll take care of Loki," Freya said, pushing farther into the darkness.

chapter forty-five

Trickster's Queen

ೋೋ

Freya ran her hand over what appeared at first to be a dense cage of vines, but as the darkness slowly gave way to starlight she saw that she was standing in the midst of a vast labyrinth, hollowed from the roots of a tree that seemed larger than the sky itself. The massive roots stretched as far as she could see, in all directions. Above her was a blanket of stars. The small blue lights did not flicker; their light was strong and constant.

Freya glanced at the unfamiliar stars. She was not in Midgard anymore, or even the world of the glom, of that she was sure. She was somewhere else, somewhere beyond the universe itself.

She found a dark line that cut across the sky like a blackened version of the Milky Way, and knew it had to be the trunk of the tree. As she made her way toward the center, the knotted field of roots would open up and allow her to surge ahead—only to lead her to a dead end, where she had to push her way through to the other side. The wood was hard and tore at her skin; her arms were caked with dirt as she hacked her way forward.

In the distance she heard a faint voice casting a spell, and a passage opened in front of her. Free for a moment from the thicket, she ran forward through the darkness. A booming voice emanated from the end of the passage.

"Freya, my love, come to join me?" Bran emerged from the darkness, his eyes shining with malice. The glow of kindness around him, Freya now saw, was part of the glamour he had cast. His awkwardness and nerves were a sign of how difficult it had been for him to keep the spell intact.

"Not at all," Freya said, holding her wand aloft. The ivory bone shone in the light.

"Your magic is wasted on me." He sneered. The man she knew as Bran Gardiner was gone. Every time she looked at him she understood something new. Madame Grobadan was the giantess Angrboda, Loki's eternal mistress. No wonder she did not care for Freya.

"Not at all; I think you have been away for so long you have forgotten who *I* am," Freya said, drawing herself to her full height. As her lover he was subservient to her forever; that was the power she held over men, the way she had been made from the beginning. "Give me the ring, Bran," she said quietly. "You cannot deny me."

Bran stood in front of her in his true form as Loki, his features oddly elongated, almost grotesque. He moved toward the shadow to conceal himself as he spoke. "You may take the ring but there is no point in having a life with your dear Balder if the world in which you live is poisoned. Let me keep it and I will be able to staunch the bleeding." He looked at Freya, but her gaze was unyielding.

"Give me the ring." It was a command from a goddess.

Bran could not resist. Freya felt a warm, putrid air embrace her, and when it dissipated Odin's ring lay in the palm of her hand. She saw that it was not made of gold at all; its surface was dull white and porous, a bone ring carved from the last shreds of the bridge. A final token of a power older than the gods themselves, it had been lost by Odin during the last battle of Asgard.

It did not belong in this world or any other. Its time was past. She held it between her fingers and began to crush the frail shape. Tiny splinters showered from her hand. The ring was so soft, as if carved from a feather, it could be ground into dust at the slightest touch.

"Do not harm it. Return it to me and I shall give you what you desire," Loki whispered. "If those who placed me in the abyss find me here, I'll not be sent back this time, I will simply be wiped from existence. And I hope you would have some bit of love left for me still."

His every word is a lie, she thought: he will do nothing to help you. Freya looked at him once more, but she saw nothing of the Bran she knew. She held the tiny ring between her fingers and slowly ground it into dust. "I'll not be a fool for you any longer, Loki."

"Idiot!" he screamed, diving forward to catch what ashes he could as they drifted to the ground. Loki gathered himself from the wet earth and faced her. "Then you shall spend the rest of your existence in a dying world."

"No, Loki, I will not. You will exit as you entered Midgard, through the hole you made in the trunk, and your leaving will close it behind you. The Tree of Life will be whole once more." This was Ingrid's idea, and she hoped her sister was right—that once he crossed *Yggdrasil* once more, the wound would close and the toxin would disappear.

Loki hesitated.

"It's your only way out of here now that the ring is gone," Freya said. "Without the ring, it is the only path that remains open to you. You have only one place to go. I don't think you want to wait around to see what will happen once Balder gets ahold of you." The God of Light and Fury would be a fearsome enemy now that he was restored to his full strength and no longer bound by the limits of the curse.

Loki didn't respond for a while. He simply stood still, his mind whirling, and then he smiled. "You are more like me than you think, dear Freya." With that he spun around and faced the great trunk of the tree. He uttered garbled words in a language Freya did not catch.

The stars above dimmed as the paths through the great thicket of roots seemed to shift and change in the darkness, revealing a scarred black tear in the face of the tree. The opening looked more like a wound, a mighty rip, and a powerful force emanated from it, blowing a noxious hurricane wind from the shaft. Loki put one hand on the torn bark, for a moment he paused as if to turn and bid farewell, but he did not. Instead he bit his lip and cast himself into the void. The black fury billowed once more from the hole, as if consuming the dark god of mischief only increased its power.

Freya was thrown to the ground as the earth heaved. The heavens went dark and the blackness spread all around her. "Loki!" she called. There was no answer. She closed her eyes and rode out the storm as the fury enveloped her like a tornado, swirling in all directions. Finally the hurricane stopped, and when she opened her eyes the tree was whole once more.

She picked herself up and dusted off her knees. "Ingrid! Are you and Tyler okay?"

"We're here!"

Freya ran toward the sound of their voices.

Ingrid was out of breath. "I found him on the path. But he hadn't gone beyond the first gate yet. Hurry, it's almost daylight. The Covenant!"

"What about Lionel?" Freya asked.

"I couldn't find him. But if Loki is gone from here then Lionel should be on his way to Helda as he used to be. And without the corruption in his soul."

"Are we going home now?" Tyler asked.

"Yes. Hold my hand and don't let go."

The little boy looked frightened, and Freya remembered that he did not like to be touched; but after an internal struggle he took Freya's hand and, in the other, held Ingrid's.

They walked like that, with the child between them, until they were back in the house.

chapter forty-six

The Judgment of
the Council

J oanna saw them emerge from the front door of Fair Haven. She ran to Tyler, enveloping him in a bear hug. "You did it," she said to her girls in awe. She had forgotten how strong they were, had forgotten in the years of living quietly that her children were formidable and ferocious. "You did it."

"Yes," Freya said, walking over to Killian and taking his hand. His leg was still wrapped in the tourniquet she had made. "But who knows where Loki will end up next."

"It's all right, he won't be free for very long," a new voice said.

Ingrid looked up. "Dad?"

A man stood quietly in the shadows. He was tall, gray-haired, and handsome, but his face was weary and his beard a tad unkempt. He was wearing a worn cardigan and gray slacks, the academic's uniform. Freya hugged herself tightly but in the end she ran to him as Ingrid had done.

"My girls." It was all Norman Beauchamp could say at the moment as he embraced them and even Joanna had to blink back tears.

"*Skaði*, you're crying," Norman teased.

"Oh, *Norðj*, stop." She sighed.

The god of the seas released his daughters and looked at them seriously. "Your mother told me you had gone after Loki on your own. I was worried, but you have both accomplished more than I hoped. Midgard is whole once again."

"Where did you go, Dad? Did you really get an audience with the White Council?"

"Yes. I went to the oracle and spoke to Odin himself. Once I deciphered the code on those plans Erda sent me and saw that the roots of the tree were in Fair Haven, and when I saw those reports of oceanic disturbance, I began to think that perhaps the toxin of *Ragnarok* had been found in our world, which could only mean one thing. Loki had escaped from his chains and had come to unleash his vengeance upon us."

"Great minds think alike," Freya said, nudging Ingrid.

Norman sighed. "I bring other news as well. The Council has been aware of your flagrant and repeated violations of the magical restriction that has been in place since the Salem trials."

"Oh, great."

"What are they going to do?" Ingrid asked fearfully.

"It's very simple, really," Norman said. "To live in this world, you must continue to abide by its rules and the laws of its citizens, just as we have always done. If no charges are brought against you, the restriction will be lifted and you may continue to practice magic as long as you do not draw any more attention to your supernatural abilities. This will apply to all of our kind who are still on this side of the Bofrir bridge."

Freya exchanged a smile with Ingrid and Joanna. They could practice magic again! Before they could celebrate, Norman raised a hand. "But if you are arrested, tried, and proven guilty in a court of law, you will be found in breach of the restriction and you will both be sent to the Kingdom of the Dead for ten thousand years in service to Helda."

"So if nothing happens, we're free. We can be witches again, all of us." Freya smiled, thinking of everything that had been denied them for hundreds of years. She would have to get her broom out of storage and find a decent cauldron that could stand up to the potions she was eager to create.

Her father nodded. "Yes."

Ingrid shook her head. "But if they bring charges against us and we're convicted, we go to Helda as slaves."

"Correct."

"But what about Loki? He's still out there."

"The Valkyrie will find him."

Freya thought of the woman who had visited the bar looking for Killian right after the holiday, and realized she was from the same tribe as the woman whom she had seen in New York talking to Bran. She remembered how nervous Bran had been that evening, how eager to get away from the Valkyrie. She did not feel as bad now that she knew Loki had been able to fool the fierce warrior maidens as well.

Killian squeezed her hand, but she wasn't thinking of him or their love right then. Nothing was decided yet. Their fate, once again, was in the hands of the human realm.

chapter forty-seven

Law and Order

ᴖ

The annual library fund-raiser was held at the back garden of the main building, in front of the view that had almost doomed the library's existence. However, there was no more threat of that happening, as the new mayor was more interested in preserving North Hampton as it was than creating new development. Blake Aland was now building his new condominiums on the far side of town.

Ingrid walked through the party, smiling at her guests, feeling pleased and happy. The exhibit had been praised by art and architectural historians as a significant survey of architectural work. Every major house and project was represented, in prints that were elegantly framed and set on the walls. Freya had talked her into wearing a bright-colored dress with a low neckline, and she wore her hair down for once. She felt light-headed without her strict bun and was surprised to find how long her hair had gotten.

She waved to her sister across the room. Freya was in a liplock with Killian; the two of them were planning a wedding sometime next summer. They should really get a room. Libraries were not hotels.

Her parents were standing politely next to each other by the punch bowl. At least they were being civil. Ingrid wondered how old she would be before she stopped wishing they would get back together.

Her friends were all there: Hudson was roaming the party offering champagne, while Tabitha manned the dessert table with a beaming smile.

"Ingrid?" Matt Noble looked crisp and handsome in a khaki-colored suit, much sharper than his usual rumpled wear. "I almost didn't recognize you."

She did not blush and took his hand instead. "It's so good to see you."

"Likewise."

"I just wanted to say—"

"Don't, please," he said. "You don't have to keep thanking me every time you see me. I didn't do anything really."

Hardly. A few weeks ago the murders had been solved. First, Maura Thatcher had fully recovered and retracted her statement. She had no idea why she had said Joanna Beauchamp had attacked them. Killian had turned in the bloody cap worn by Bill Thatcher, as well as a bloody pile of clothing that he had found in the basement near the incinerator in Fair Haven. The jacket and pants were unmistakably Bran's, and they were splattered by blood that matched Bill's and Maura's.

Molly Lancaster had been sexually assaulted and beaten, just as Derek had confessed. However, intrepid detectives discovered that cell phone records showed that the last number Molly dialed was to an account owned by Todd Hutchinson. And when the DNA tests came back, it was his DNA that was found on her body, not Derek's. The poor boy had broken down and provided a false confession as part of his attorney's plan to pin the blame on Freya.

It all came out then: Molly Lancaster and Todd Hutchinson were having an affair. When Freya had seen the mayor masturbating to online porn, he was actually watching Molly on the screen. After sexually harassing her all summer, he had carried on a sexually abusive relationship with the young intern. Files retrieved from his computer confirmed it, as well as e-mails from Molly that said she had broken up with him right before the July Fourth holiday. Her diary, which she kept in a secret code online, documented the entire sordid affair. She had written that she was going to the North Inn that evening to meet someone new, someone her own age.

Her phone showed a series of texts from the mayor demanding her whereabouts and ordering her to wait for him on the beach. When he got there, he killed her out of jealousy, as he had seen her kissing someone else.

Freya had not been able to read the mayor's desires; they had been blocked by Ingrid's fidelity knot: the sisters' magic had canceled each other's out. A week later he ran away and went into hiding. He told his wife to meet him at the motel. When Corky arrived she found him hanging from the ceiling, with a note confessing to the whole sordid mess. When she cut him down, she fashioned a knot around his neck similar to the one she had received from the witch. No one knows why Corky Hutchinson wanted to pin her husband's death on Ingrid, but her lawyer was pleading insanity due to shock and sorrow.

Molly's murder and the mayor's suicide had nothing to do with magic. Or a vampire. Or a zombie. If Azrael had taken a human hostage, it was not one from North Hampton, and out of their jurisdiction. But Ingrid was sad about Emily and Lionel. Lionel's body turned up in a meadow and they had buried him with a small ceremony at the local cemetery. Emily was moving out of town, after the death of her animals and her partner; North Hampton was not the same for her. Ingrid would miss her, but there was nothing she could do now. She tried to find comfort in the fact that Lionel was now resting in peace, embarking on a new journey of his own and not damned for eternity.

Only after everything was over did Ingrid find out that far from leaving them to their fate, it was Matt who had pressed the police to look for more evidence and drop the interrogation. He had been working all along to help them. Now he was standing before her holding a glass of wine and smiling.

"Matt!" Caitlin came between them. She looked ravishing in a red dress and high heels. "There you are. I want to . . ."

Ingrid felt her heart beat a little faster, but she kept the smile on her face. So they had gotten back together after all. Perhaps Romance Weekend on Martha's Vineyard would happen again soon. She excused herself and walked away.

A few minutes later Matt appeared by her side again. "Hey."

"Oh, hey."

"Listen . . . Caitlin and I—"

"You don't have to say anything, really. I'm happy that you and Caitlin got back together."

"Really? Because I kind of wish you weren't," he said with a frown.

"Excuse me?"

"If you'd let me finish a sentence once in a while," he said, gazing into her eyes, "you'd know."

"Know what?"

"Caitlin and I aren't together. She wants to, but . . ." Matt shrugged.

Ingrid could feel a ray of hope begin to bloom in her heart. "But?"

"But I don't," Matt said, putting down his drink and shoving his hands into his coat pockets like a little boy. "Look, you remember that time . . . when I asked you . . . if you could help me ask someone out?"

Of course she did.

"I don't know what came over me, but you looked so angry and put out that I just said the first name that came to mind. And then you didn't seem bothered that I was dating Caitlin, but . . ."

"But?"

"I should have just been honest from the beginning. About who I really wanted to go out with. It's just . . . you never seemed to like me. For a while there I thought I really annoyed you."

Ingrid was embarrassed at her actions. She had been mean to Matt, and for no reason other than she liked him; and because she had never felt this way about someone, it unnerved her.

"But then, Hudson said . . ."

"What did Hudson say?" Ingrid asked eagerly.

"He said you were really happy to hear that Caitlin and I broke up, so I thought that I might have reason to, you know, hope again."

"Uh-huh."

"We're awful, aren't we?" Matt put his hand below her chin and Ingrid could feel her entire body tremble from his touch. He had helped her. He had pressed the police to find something—had argued for concrete evidence. He believed her, he believed in her. "I mean . . . I've liked you a long time, Ingrid. I've read all those awful books you keep making me read. Don't you think that maybe . . ."

Then it was Ingrid's turn, and she put her hand on his face. And in the middle of the party, in front of everyone at the gala, she kissed him.

Matt grinned.

Ingrid blushed. "I don't know what came over me," she said.

He grabbed her hand and held it. "I don't know what you are, Ingrid Beauchamp, if you're a witch or not, but I'm hoping that you'll go out with me sometime."

Then he kissed her, and in the middle of their kisses, she murmured, "Yes."

Ingrid did not know what the future would bring. She had never been in love before, and with a human no less. But for once she did not want to find out. She would just let it happen, as Freya liked to say, and enjoy the ride.

Epilogue

H er shift ended at midnight, and Freya walked out to the parking lot. Just as she reached into her handbag for her keys, a hand came out of the shadows and clutched her wrist. She wanted to scream, but when she saw who was holding her she could not speak. She could not believe it.

The boy in the shadow put a hand on his lips. He was golden-haired and beautiful as the sun. Looking at him was not unlike looking in a mirror.

"Fryr?" she whispered. "Is that really you?" Her twin brother. "You're back! Mother will be ecstatic!" She reached to embrace him but something in his drawn face told her it was not a good idea.

"No!" he warned. "No one can know I'm here. Otherwise I won't be able to have my revenge."

"Revenge? What are you talking about?"

"I was set up. That day the bridge fell, when I went there, it was already broken. Someone else had taken its power." His face darkened. "Freya, if you love me you'll help me find the one who is to blame for everything. The one who destroyed the Bofrir and who left me to rot in limbo for eternity."

"If you mean Loki, he is gone and the Valkyrie will find him."

"No, Loki is nothing but a fool. I have no quarrel with him. I am looking for Balder. In this world he is known as Killian Gardiner. He was the one who took the power of the Bofrir for himself and set me up to take the fall. Help me kill him, Freya. If you love me, you will help me destroy him."

Acknowledgments

Thank you to my husband and collaborator, Mike Johnston, without whom my books would simply not exist. Thank you to Mattie, for being so patient when Mommy is "on deadline" and who wants to grow up to be a "bookstore writer." Thank you to my family and friends, who put up with not seeing me for weeks and months while I am writing. Thank you for being there when the writing is done.

Thank you to the fabulous team at Hyperion: Ellen Archer, who believed in the book from the first moment; Barbara Jones, Kristin Kiser, Marie Coolman, Bryan Christian, Sarah Rucker, Maha Khalil, Katherine Tasheff, and Mindy Stockfield. Special thanks to my editors: Jill Schwartzman, Elisabeth Dyssegaard, and Brenda Copeland. Thank you to Richard Abate, agent, friend, and advocate.

Melissa de la Cruz is the author of many best-selling novels, including the Blue Bloods series; the Au Pairs series; the Ashleys series; and Angels on Sunset Boulevard. She is also a frequent contributor to *Glamour*, *Marie Claire*, *Teen Vogue*, and *Cosmopolitan*. She lives in Los Angeles with her husband and daughter. Find out more at www.melissa-delacruz.com